NECESSITY

By Brian Garfield:

FICTION

Necessity
Checkpoint Charlie
The Paladin
Wild Times
Recoil
Death Sentence
Hopscotch
The Romanov Succession
Kolchak's Gold
The Threepersons Hunt
Gangway! (with Donald
 E. Westlake)

Tripwire
Death Wish
Line of Succession
Deep Cover
Relentless
The Last Hard Men
Sweeny's Honor
Sliphammer
Bugle and Spur
Arizona
The Vanquished

NONFICTION

Western Films: A Complete Guide
The Thousand-Mile War: World War II in Alaska & the
 Aleutians
I, Witness: True Personal Encounters with Crime (ed.)

NECESSITY

BRIAN GARFIELD

ST. MARTIN'S/MAREK
NEW YORK

Library of Congress Cataloging in Publication Data

Garfield, Brian, 1939–
    Necessity.

    I. Title.
PS3557.A715N4   1985   813'.54   83-24490
ISBN 0-312-56258-6

First Edition
10 9 8 7 6 5 4 3 2 1

This book is dedicated with love to Bina.

Acknowledgment

For friendship and for many things, including the details of skip-tracing techniques related in this book, my warm thanks to Joe and Dori Gores.

NECESSITY

1 It is the sixth day after the theft. She pulls off the Interstate in Tucson, a city she has never seen before. According to the atlas it is a county seat and the second largest city in Arizona—population half a million people.

It seems as good a place as any for a beginning.

The coppery taste on her tongue is a symptom of fear: a familiar companion but unwelcome all the same.

While a fat man with a bandit's mustache fills the tank she puts a quarter into a newspaper vending machine and leafs through the *Arizona Daily Star* until she finds the address of its editorial offices.

She pays cash for the gasoline and asks directions and tries to ignore the lechery that leers from the fat man's eyes when he thinks she's not watching.

He has been neither articulate nor accurate; she has to stop twice to ask directions. These guide her along wide boulevards debased by plastic and neon, then into scrub desert beaten raw by the sun. Mountains loom all around in a moderate brown smog. The six-lane traffic is incongruously heavy: it seems out of kilter, out of time on this primitive ground.

She has turned the air conditioner all the way up but still the steering wheel is nearly too hot to hold. The car is four years old, 67,000 miles on the clock, not in the best of working order—she bought it for cash in a dying town near Scranton from an unemployed miner who'd taken an ad in one of the supermarket throwaways. In terms of probabilities she doubtless is lucky it's still running at all.

The miner hated to part with the car but he needed the $1,500—he has mouths to feed—and she doubts he'll get around to recording the transfer of title until he receives next year's reregistration bill from the motor vehicle people. Long before then she'll be rid of the car and in the meantime it is as anonymous a pale blue midsize as can be found and there's a good chance no one will ever trace it to her.

The wig makes her scalp itch. She feels clammy, uncomfortable with sweat: partly fear, partly the end-of-June heat. Even behind the reflecting lenses of her sunglasses she has to keep her eyes squeezed into a painful squint.

This climate can make one listless—or careless. It won't do to drop one's guard; it won't do to disregard even for a moment the fact that they're after her.

Pennants hang listlessly above a lot that offers enormous mobile homes for sale. Little stucco houses have weeds, cactus, old cars and broken-down pickup trucks for yard ornaments. And there's not a pedestrian in sight. Not even a dog.

Arizona Daily Star. The modern structure is as wide and low as a trucking warehouse. She finds a space in the parking lot and walks inside and the cool is as sudden and free as what you feel when you emerge from a sauna.

"I wonder if I could see the obituaries for the first three months of 1953."

She is steeled to answer questions with inventions but the girl behind the Information counter is incurious. "That's in the microfilm section." The girl directs her back into the maze.

She carries the bulky shoulder bag tight against her

side as she explores the corridors. Really it's too big for a handbag but she hasn't let it out of reach in the three days since she bought it.

Half the money is inside it; the other half, with the diamonds, is in the suitcase locked in the trunk of the car.

An old man with sad bassett eyes brings out his film containers and shows her how to use the viewing machine. "Pretty soon they'll have all this stuff in the computers and it'll be real easy to find. But the computer don't go back that far just yet, thank God, so they still need me."

She thanks him and sits before the screen of the microfilm reader, turning the crank, searching each day's issue for the obituary page.

She finds a possibility—January 13, 1953: she rereads it several times but decides against it, partly because the date unnerves her (ludicrous superstition!) and partly because she doesn't like the name of the deceased, Agnes Leonora Dapp. Surely there'll be something more mellifluous than that . . .

The town was much smaller thirty-one years ago. A tenth of its present population. An overgrown cowtown, really; she rolls past February headline stories about rodeo parades and an El Conquistador Horse Show. Not many babies were born, let alone died, that season. She prowls on.

March 27, 1953. She leans toward the screen.

DIED: Hartman, Jennifer Corfu, aged 17 days, of cardiac deficiency. Infant daughter of Samuel P. G. Hartman and Jennifer Corfu Williams Hartman, 2675 No. Eastbourne Dr., Tucson. Private services will be conducted March 29th at Gower Funeral Home. Parents request that donations in lieu of flowers be sent to the Tucson chapter of the Nat'l Heart Ass'n.

She writes it all down and, on her way out, consults a current local telephone directory. No Samuel or Jennifer Hartman.

That's good: they've moved away or died.

She stops again at the Information counter. A pulse lurches at the back of her throat; she endeavors to smile. "How do I get to the county courthouse?"

2 "Jennifer Corfu Hartman." She prints the words clearly, then fills out the rest of the form. Date of birth March 10, 1953. In the block under Purpose of Request she writes, "Lost the original. Am applying for passport."

Her hand trembles when she turns it in but the grey-haired Chicano clerk has a friendly smile. "Likely take a couple hours. You might want to get lunch."

"Thank you."

3 She puts the certified copy of Jennifer's birth certificate in her bag in the same compartment with the birth certificate she obtained two days ago in Albuquerque for Dorothy (NMI) Holder, who died in 1955 at the age of 22 months. The traffic accident killed the little girl's parents as well. The Albuquerque newspaper gave up a grisly photo of the wreck and the information that the father was studying agricultural science on the GI Bill: poor bastard survived two years in the Korean war only to be wiped out by an oil-slippery road surface.

She parks in a shopping mall, zips up the compartment in her handbag and goes from one big department store to another, buying clothes off the rack. Jeans, blouses, two skirts, shoes, toiletries and cosmetics—even underwear: she wants nothing on her person that can be traced back more than five days.

In a cheap cluttered surplus store she buys an inexpensive suitcase. She carries it out in her left hand, the shoulder bag snug in her right.

She won't be remembered. She's paid cash for everything and she stays hidden behind the big sunglasses and the dark wig she bought three days ago in Denver.

The plan seemed to take shape overnight and the details have dropped into place with a speed that still bewilders her because she wasn't aware she was capable of such cunning.

Now an instinct for thoroughness keeps nagging her to remember every item of the scheme.

In a dusty hot alley behind a restaurant she finds a garbage bin higher than her eye-line. She transfers the cash and the diamonds to the new bag and then searches through her old suitcase, trying to force herself to be dispassionate but when she comes to the photograph of Ellen it is not possible to disregard the lump that fixes itself high in her chest. It won't go up and it won't go down.

With dread reluctance she puts the snapshot back where she found it, closes the suitcase and boosts it onto the lip of the garbage bin until it tips over and drops out of sight inside. She hears it dislodge glass bottles as it falls.

Probably it will be crushed in the mechanism of a garbage truck—buried under half a ton of waste in a county dump where nobody will ever find it.

Even if someone does, most likely this will be as far as they'll be able to trace her.

5

She drives away, seeking the Interstate. Her tears, she thinks at first, are for Ellen—for the photograph. But eventually she realizes it is more than that.

The suitcase contained the last of her belongings from home. Everything personal: everything but a ring of keys and a driver's license and a valise full of diamonds and cash.

On your own now, Jennifer Corfu Hartman A/K/A Dorothy Holder. Starting newborn. Might as well be stark naked.

4 She breaks the 500-mile trip to Los Angeles with what promises to be a sleeplessly hot night in a nondescript motel on the California border.

She eats in a diner and fends off the awkward advance of a middle-aged drunk who seems not so much offensive as simply lonely; he drives away in a car with Indiana plates, after which she goes for a short walk while there is still a dusky light on the desert.

Rather to her surprise the Colorado River turns out to be a muddy trickle at the bottom of a wide dry weedy riverbed spanned by bridges that seem ludicrously too huge for the tiny flow underneath. For a moment she suspects her own elaborate scheme must be equally disproportionate—but then she thinks: there's no such thing as too careful.

She's reasoning with herself:

"If you don't do this right they will find you and kill you."

Startled by the sound of her own voice she looks all around to see if anyone has overheard her. This is just terrific.

Turning into one of those crazy bag ladies who crawl the city streets like slugs, incessantly talking to themselves in loud voices.

Try to relax. Gentle down.

Oh God. Oh dear God.

On the way back to the motel she catches her reflection in a shop's glass door. The dark wig still has the capacity to startle her. It's the third wig she has employed. First there was the long straight brown one—it gave her the appearance of the sort of graduate student who's deep into health foods and Zen—and then in Pennsylvania just before buying the blue car she changed to a frizzy Afro-style dark red wig and wore it as far as Denver. She remembers leaving it in a trash bin in a roadside rest area.

In the room she considers switching the television on but she doesn't really want that sort of company; she sits in the plastic armchair listening to the walls shudder when the big trucks rumble past. They set up a rhythm in her mind: a music to which she fixes images of a dancing couple in tights and ballet slippers gliding across a long diagonal of light. For a moment she is caught up in her visualization of the formal pas de deux—the sensuous nobility of its gesturings—and then she remembers that she must no longer admit to an interest in dance.

The trucks rattle on.

She thinks of Ellen and weeps again.

Later in a half-waking dream she pictures big faceless men coming in the door, hauling her to her feet, manhandling her outside into a car—all this without ever speaking, for she visualizes them as sinister menacing hulks who prefer wordlessly to rend her nerves and provoke her broken babblings, the sort of damaging confidences that she might blurt out merely to fill the dreadful silence. . . .

Can the scheme work? Is there any chance at all? How many things can go wrong? How many things has she failed to take into account?

And what of Ellen?

Ellen, poor thing. So betrayed . . .

It is past midnight before she gets into bed; another hour and a half, drifting between innocence and evil, before she finds sleep.

In the morning it is easier: daylight pushes the panic back. She is relieved to get on the road.

5 At an exit just past Blythe marked Gas—Food—Fuel she aims the car into the first filling station she sees. Under the alluring sign sixty feet high it turns out to be an unappetizing dump but she's too numbed by road weariness to seek another.

A punk-haired teen-age hoodlum slams the nozzle into the filler pipe and leaves the pump ticking while he checks the oil and smears bugs across the windshield with inadequate swipes of a long-handled squeegee. She stands in the shade waiting; the kid darts his furtive eyes toward her and she wishes she were wearing something that had more practical armor than this thin cotton print.

She pays in cash and drives around the side to park in the shade while she visits the Ladies'; it's not until the tires crunch that she notices where the filthy pavement is strewn with the glittering remains of broken beer bottles.

It's a choice between broken glass and the hot sun: she chooses the shade, steps out with care, and picks a path away from the car, tiptoeing through shards.

The stifling bathroom is repulsive visually and olfactorily. She departs in record time. Nevertheless the upholstery is so hot she can't relax her spine against it. She sits bolt upright when she backs the car out.

Watching her, the young hoodlum stands beside a gas pump with a bottle of beer in his hand. His very lack of expression seems malevolent.

The desert has been carved into farms here, kept alive by the trickle of water at the bottom of tapered concrete canals; past the irrigated area there's nothing but scrub and sand and the heat against which the air conditioner struggles.

She has gone only a few miles and she's doing about seventy when the wheel begins to pull to the left and she hears the rapid flubbing tattoo of the collapsing tire. With more stoical resignation than anger she takes her foot off the gas and fights the wheel, hauling it to the right. Thank God for power steering. Prompted by a fragment of memory from her teen-age years she forces herself not to touch the brake pedal.

The car chitters all over the road. It feels as if it's ploughing through thick mud but in fact the speed is still high—fifty miles an hour now and only dropping slowly. She thinks: emergency brake? Does that operate on the back wheels or the front ones? But she's not sure; she knows only that if she does the wrong thing it may flip over, as her mother and father found out.

She lets it coast, weaving from lane to lane. She's very lucky there's no traffic.

Finally the momentum comes off the charging automobile and she is able to horse it onto the shoulder.

She steps out into the blast of heat and examines the damage.

The car droops over its flat tire.

She's no mechanic but she knows this much: drive any farther on it and the wheel rim will be destroyed.

All right then. What are the choices?

You're supposed to wait for help. She knows the procedure. Open the trunk and the hood; tie a scarf on the door handle and lock yourself inside the car.

In this sun with the engine idling and the air conditioner blasting—how long will it be before the old car overheats and dies?

And who wants to sit here for six hours expiring of dehydration before the next highway patrol cop drives by?

And do you really want to take the chance that a cop won't ask to see some identification?

Change the damn tire, then.

There must be tools in the trunk. She opens it and sees the spare and realizes she's never paid any attention to it before. Suppose it's flat?

Leaning in under the useless shade of the upraised trunk lid she unscrews the butterfly nut that secures the spare. Just this little effort drenches her in sweat. Now to lift the thing out and see if there are tools under it.

She hoists it over the bumper and lets it bounce when it hits the ground. What do they make these things out of—solid lead?

At least it bounces. Maybe it actually has air in it.

She sees a cluster of cars approaching as if afloat on watery mirages that hover above the highway. She pretends to busy herself in the trunk and does not look at the cars as they whoosh past. The last one seems to slow down and she glances that way as it goes by—an open convertible, young driver in a cowboy hat. He seems to be looking at her in his mirror but she doesn't try to flag him down and finally he guns it and the old Cadillac fishtails away with a loud pneumatic hiss of noise.

I wonder what he thinks he's proving?

She recognizes the jack and the tire iron with its socket-wrench end and its pry-bar end. These two—are they all the tools you need?

You changed a tire once, remember? Four o'clock in

the morning after the homecoming game and the fraternity beer bust. Can't remember that boy's name. He was so stoned on grass he just lay back and laughed: "Far *out!*" And you changed the tire while he waved the flashlight around so that your work was illuminated as fitfully as a battlefield under artillery attack.

But I got it done, didn't I, and drove the worthless kid home and left him asleep in his car and walked half a mile to the bus stop.

She's thinking: how come you were so much smarter when you were eighteen?

Hard to breathe now: this air feels like sawblades in the throat.

Naturally it has to be the left front tire and this shoulder of sandy hardpan and gravel isn't really wide enough; to change the wheel she's going to have to get right out in the roadway with her hindquarters waving in the traffic.

What traffic? One pickup truck in the last two minutes. The hell with it.

The jack is an odd-looking device with a crank handle and at first she can't tell how it's supposed to work. She opens the door and gets into the car. It has become a furnace in here. She opens the windows before poking into the glove compartment, hoping to find an owner's manual that will have illustrations and instructions.

No such luck. Nothing in the glove box except the Pennsylvania registration and the maps she put there herself. Startling her, a drop of liquid falls onto her wrist—sweat from her own forehead.

A huge truck goes by: a semi at great speed. The blast of its wind nearly knocks her off her feet. As it gnashes away she's thinking about the likelihood of the truck driver's calling in on his CB radio to alert the world of her predicament— thinking no doubt that he's doing her a favor.

Must get out of here.

She studies the jack and the car. There's what looks

like the open end of a pipe directly under the door post at the side of the car. Is the jack meant to fit into that? Why not give it a try.

It fits, a male member into a female receptacle. She turns the crank and is pleased enough to smile when the side of the car begins to rise.

Another cluster of traffic goes by. She doesn't ask for help; no one stops. After they're gone she puts her weight against the crank handle and soon both left wheels are off the ground. She locks the crank in place and pries the hubcap off.

One of the lug nuts is so stiff she has to stand on the handle of the tire iron to break it loose but finally she has all five nuts in the upturned hubcap and she horses the flat tire off the car. Her hands are filthy and she's ruined the damned dress.

She hears the crunch of gravel and looks up.

It pulls to a stop on the shoulder just behind her car: a Jeep or a Bronco, one of those outdoorsy four-wheel-drive vehicles—high and boxy, forest green. A man gets out of it.

His face is hidden inside a trim brown beard streaked with grey. He's chunky and muscular in faded jeans and an olive drab tee shirt.

"Need some help?" His voice is pleasant enough. At least he's not a cop.

She rises to her feet. She has the tire iron in her hand.

"I think I've got it licked. Thanks all the same."

The man looks at the tire iron. He seems a little amused but she's not sure—it's hard to see what's going on under the beard.

He says, "I had a flat tire on one of these Interstates a couple years ago. Discovered I didn't have a jack. I waited seven hours for help and what I finally got was a ripoff artist in a tow truck, charged me fifty dollars just to borrow his jack and do the work myself. Ever since then, I see somebody broken down by the road, I see if I can do something."

She's trying to look icy. "Thanks for stopping. I really don't need any help."

He says, "I'm not a rapist, you know."

"I hear you saying it." She shifts the tire iron in her grasp: not an ostentatious movement but enough to remind him of it.

She says, "I appreciate the offer. It's very kind of you. But I'm sure you're on your way somewhere and I wouldn't want to delay you. I'm fine. I'm not in any trouble."

He watches her. She keeps her voice calm. "Please go."

He looks at the tire iron. "I guess these days there just isn't a whole lot of point trying to be a good Samaritan." He turns with a reproachful snap of his shoulders and climbs back into his vehicle.

When he drives by he looks at her and she feels she can read his thoughts: independent liberated feminist bitch.

No good explaining it's not because you're a man and I'm a woman. It's not even because you're a stranger.

It's because I don't trust you. But you didn't need to take it personally.

It's not you. It's me. I can't afford to trust anybody at all.

6 Los Angeles. A place for getting lost.

Is that a mistake? Why not Oregon or Idaho or Wyoming—somewhere miles from the beaten track?

The allure of somewhere rural and unpopulated is a

valley of temptation; but on cooler second thought it would be much too easy for them to track her along those untrod paths. Newcomers never escape notice in such places, where gossip travels with the speed of a prairie fire.

Besides, she spent half her childhood in an Iowa plains village and they may expect her to return to such a setting.

Better to be swallowed amid the crowds. Better to leave one pair of footprints among the millions. Better to go to ground in the urban tangle with a thousand exit routes and ten thousand places to hide.

Hasn't she always made excuses not to go along on trips to the Coast? Hasn't she made a point of her contempt for Southern California? Citing at every opportunity Dorothy Parker's (or is it Fred Allen's?) line—"It's a great place to live. If you happen to be an orange." And Woody Allen's dictum: "Los Angeles is a place where the chief cultural attraction is that you can make a right turn on a red light." And the jokes she's overheard somewhere and adopted as her own:

"How many Californians does it take to change a light bulb? Eight. One to change the bulb and seven to share in the experience."

And: "The difference between yogurt and Southern California? *One* of them has an active culture!"

A week ago she concluded that it will be safe for her in Los Angeles precisely because they all know how much she reviles and ridicules the place.

Besides, she needs the big city's facilities. There is so much to do and she has so little time. She's got a deadline and it looms alarmingly close. If she misses it—

Let's not think about that.

The city, then: Los Angeles. No further debate. Can't afford doubts.

Yet misgivings corrupt her. Will they know what she's planning? Are they one step ahead of her?

Quit it. Stop jumping at shadows. Get a grip on yourself.

Anyhow—face it, Jennifer-Dorothy. You turn up in East Tumbleweed, Utah, and you'll draw the stares of every drooling bumpkin in town.

She has examined this from every angle and she is persuaded it has been a cool decision, not swayed by vanity: it makes sense that if you're an unusually striking woman looking for a place to hide then you'd better seek out a place where there are a great many beauties, some of whose faces—like your own—have appeared in the ad pages of mass-circulation magazines.

7 The damnable wig has served well to disguise her on the road but it doesn't go with her coloring or with her grey blue eyes. It's hot and it itches.

Her hair is naturally sandy and usually shoulder length but she's worn it waved and blond for years; now she means to cut it short and let it hang straight and revert to color. At the moment the roots are showing and she's going to have to help the naturalization process along at first with a good beauty shop coloring job to cover up the yellow past. Meanwhile the damnable wig.

But changing the hair back to normal won't in itself effect much reduction in the possibility of chance recognition. Some other aspect of her appearance will have to change. Lose weight? No; any thinner and she'd look anorexic. Gain weight, then? No; she's too vain: she needs to go on liking herself.

For a day on the highway she entertained the idea of plastic surgery but discarded it because she wouldn't have time for the bruises to heal, and in any case it was a foolish idea and her life just now has quite enough melodrama in it without that.

Happily there's no town anywhere in the world where disguises can be obtained more readily than in Hollywood.

A few blocks from Vine Street, beginning to wilt in the heat, she finds a parking space two blocks from her destination. Hollywood Boulevard has gone to seed and she must thread a pedestrian traffic of hookers and dangerous-looking adolescents and ordinary people going about their ordinary business.

In the theatrical costume supply shop she tries on a pair of eyeglasses with plain clear lenses. She knows the lingo because some of the girls at the modeling agency in New York were always trying to make it as actresses. "I've got a callback for a workshop play—just a walk-on as a tough, no-nonsense secretary."

The clerk, a tanned blond young man with the pretty face and resentful pout of an actor between jobs, knows exactly what she requires; he simpers helpfully and goes to a drawer.

The frames have uptilted corners and give her the severe look of a self-important office worker. She is very pleased by how markedly they change her appearance.

"And I think a dark red wig, don't you? Something I can do up in a tight bun at the back."

He says, "I've got just the thing, dear."

8 Studying the map, she sits in a booth over cottage cheese and a diet cola. The glass shakes in her hand but all the same there is a singular fascination in having the freedom to choose not only where to live but who to be.

She tries to recall what she learned about the area during her brief trips years ago. Not much comes to mind; but she's heard enough casual talk in her lifetime to recognize some of the place names on the map.

She knows, for example, that Malibu and Santa Monica are on the sea, that Bel Air and Brentwood are where the movie stars and million-dollar executives live, that the extravagant shops of Rodeo Drive are in the middle of Beverly Hills, that East Los Angeles is the barrio and that Marina Del Rey is where the boat people go—the sort of boat people who own 36-foot cabin cruisers and make an annual half-day voyage to Catalina Island and spend the rest of the year parked at the dock sitting on deck attired in tee shirts and shorts, swilling beer and watching ball games on color television.

Through sunglasses her eyes explore the map. Not downtown Los Angeles: too slummy. Not Orange County: too stifled. Not West Hollywood or Beverly Hills or Santa Monica: not much likelihood someone from the past might be in town long enough to recognize her, but no matter how long the odds it is a risk to be avoided.

But there. Just over the Hollywood Hills to the north— the San Fernando Valley.

A hundred suburbs vainly in search of a city, indistinguishable but for their howler names: Burbank, Studio City,

Highway Highlands, Calabasas, Universal City—even, for God's sake, Tarzana.

There is the promise of anonymity in the very nickname: the Valley.

She drives toward it: north on the freeway through Sepulveda Pass, over a crest and down a long hill from which she can see across miles of gridded streets and low buildings. It is like the view from an airplane, the smog so thin she can see layers of tan purple mountain ranges beyond.

Quite beautiful, really.

Turning off the freeway she keeps her attention on the rear-view mirror. Maybe it's silly; it's implausible; but she still hasn't been able to shake the conviction that they are back there and gaining on her.

At first she'll have to stay in a motel. You can't rent anything else without identification.

She finds one on Ventura Boulevard between an Arco station and an Italian restaurant. The motel has flyspecked stucco and there's no swimming pool but it hasn't yet reached the next stage of decline, when it will begin renting rooms with closed-circuit adult TV by the hour.

All the same, the old woman at the desk gives her a sharp look of disapproval and a veiled lecture couched in threadbare euphemisms about neighbors, trouble and police.

She assures the old woman that she's not a hooker. Just a divorcee from Chicago seeking a place to start over. Looking for a job and an apartment.

She can't tell whether the old woman buys it. The woman's face is an immutable prunelike mask of skepticism. But it won't do to embroider the story any more: she doesn't want the old woman to pay attention to her.

The room is a bit shabby and vaguely Spanish in flavor except for the framed print above the bed, which depicts a French village in Impressionist fashion—maybe it's Barbizon—and she has a moment's amusement from the realization that she feels as incongruous as that thing looks.

It is now time to proceed with methodical care. She sits on the bed with a telephone directory in her lap and begins to make notes.

9 It no longer surprises her how much information you can get from bureaucrats simply by asking for it. After two hours at a pay phone she knows the easiest order in which to obtain identification.

She applies for a Social Security card, using the birth certificate from Tucson, and when the clerk seems puzzled that she's never had a Social Security number she explains that she has spent her adult life nursing her invalid mother, who recently died.

"I've been taking extension courses at UCLA but I've never had a regular job, you see, so I never applied before, but the people at the employment agency told me I should come and fill out an application. . . ."

The clerk stamps the forms, uninterested in hearing any more.

On her way out she slips another application blank into her handbag.

The card for which she's just signed will be mailed in about ten days to the street address of her motel. In the meantime there's a great deal to do.

On the Tuesday after the Fourth of July holiday she removes the red wig in a restaurant ladies' room and drives down to Orange County to have her hair done in a place where they'll never see her again and never remember her. "So hot this summer," she says. "I'll be cooler if it's cut short, don't you think?"

The hairdresser is an inquisitive man, sixtyish and overweight, gay and garrulous: Haven't seen you before, my dear; such lovely cheekbones; do you live around here?

She has to think. Now who am I going to be today?

She becomes the wife of an aeronautical engineer who's been unemployed for nearly a year and finally just landed an aerospace job here in Santa Ana so they've just moved down from Tacoma. Two kids and they are fighting the bureaucracy of school transfers this close to opening day. . . .

It is the sort of thing she's done for idle amusement in the past when she found herself on an airliner seated next to a stranger she knew she'd never see again.

From childhood on she's taken pleasure in harmless lies: they exercise the imagination. Now it is a talent she is going to have to cultivate permanently. That's an aspect of this thing that frightens her especially: the chance that she'll slip and misremember her own lies.

It means she needs to stay aloof—no efforts to make friends or steady companions. Not until she is comfortable in a new identity with a past so well rehearsed that it comes to mind as readily as if it were real.

The hairdresser sends her away in a wheeling cloud of advice about the most fabulous little places to shop and the most divine sushi restaurant.

10 She has destroyed her old credit cards but still keeps the old driver's license; she'll need it one more time.

The plan is based in part on the cautionary advice with which she was endowed inadvertently by that dreadful little investigator, what was his name? Something aquatic, like his sharkskin clothes . . .

Seale, that's it. Ray Seale.

From the outset she has implemented the plan with businesslike thoroughness and she's applied a ruthless concentration to the details—because she can't afford to make mistakes, and because for at least some of the time it keeps her mind off her fears for herself and for Ellen.

Much of the time she feels as though she is trying to walk underwater. There seems to be a haze over her vision: a translucence that separates her from reality. The things that she requires of herself are things that she accomplishes with prompt inventive adroitness but it is as if someone else were accomplishing them. Feeling dreamlike, trancelike, she knows she must keep moving briskly because, like a bicyclist, she'll fall down if she stops.

11 Wednesday morning there is rain but she drives to Van Nuys Airport anyway. The storm has brought road oil to the surface and she feels the car slide when she makes the turn into the parking lot, going too fast. A blast of wind strikes; the car shudders and she has a queasy sensation when the seat seems to pitch to one side under her.

There is the throat-tightening awareness that the car is out of control. She sees the metal chainlink fence skidding toward her in the rain; she remembers to lift her foot off the gas and waits in dread for the tires to find their grip.

Managing narrowly not to hit the fence, she rolls into a parking space and sits precariously still with the windshield wipers batting, wind rocking the car, afraid to breathe while she waits for the pulse to subside and reminds herself that none of this is going to be any good if she totals herself in a stupid careless accident.

If you can't remember to care about yourself, she thinks, care about Ellen.

She sucks in a deep lungful of air and waits a while, hoping the rain will quit or at least let up; she has no umbrella. It's a long way to walk and she doesn't see a parking area any closer than this one. Between gusts she recognizes the place down the field from his description on the phone: "I've got a little office in the hangar next door to the Beechcraft Agency. You can see it from the parking lot."

She remembers his voice now: coarse, a whisky-cigarette baritone with a rough resonance of barrooms and card games; on the phone it made her think of lumps of rock

22

rattling down a metal chute. She'd telephoned five flying schools and in each case she'd asked to talk to the instructor. She's picked this one because he answered his own phone and his intonation suggested he might not mind doing something a little out of the ordinary for a price.

He says his name is Charlie Reid.

The rain doesn't look as if it wants to depart. She makes a face and gets out of the car, fashions a tent over her head with the morning paper and runs toward the hangar, trying to dodge the puddles.

The open runway area presents no obstacles to the wind, which gropes for her in gusts, blasting rain into her face under the newspaper. By the time she reaches the door the newspaper is disintegrating and her hair is a sodden mat.

She hopes it is the right place. She goes in.

A man sits in a swivel chair at a cheap metal desk. Steam drifts from the Styrofoam cup in his hand; coffee makes a strong smell in the tiny office. The sign appended to the wall is in cardboard and appears to have been lettered with crayons by a meticulous child: "Reid Air Service and Flying School." Nearby are Visa and Mastercard emblems.

He is huge and unkempt in work boots, dungarees and a faded mustard yellow shirt with the sleeves rolled halfway back to his elbows. There are bags under his eyes; the lived-in face is creased and amused. It is evident he's been watching her through the window. He says in his rumbling voice, "You must want to fly awful bad."

"I do."

It elicits his skeptical grunt. He lifts a large metal wastebasket onto the desk.

She drops the sodden newspaper into it. "Thank you."

"Don't mention it." He secretes the wastebasket under the desk. Then he stands up. He is big.

Six-two, she thinks; probably six-four if he'd stand up straight. He towers. The shoulders belong on a water buffalo.

"You're ten minutes late," he says. "Not that it matters. Nothing out there flying right now except a few skate-boards and umbrellas."

"I don't want to fly today. I want to *learn* to fly."

"I know. Usually I take 'em up the first day. See how they like the feel of it. Half the people that go up with me never come back for lesson number two." He has a bellicose grin that surprises her because it engages her.

She thinks: I don't wonder they don't come back. One look at him and most sane individuals would think twice about going up in an airplane with him.

He says: "Some people just don't take to flying upside down, that kind of thing. How's your stomach?"

She is brushing herself off—ineffectually. Her feet are soaked and around them grows a puddle at which the man stares with a widening one-sided grin. All his expressions have a sardonic tilt.

Wet to the skin and miserable, she replies with tart defiance: "My stomach's all right. You might offer me a towel."

"Bathroom's in the hangar next door. But you have to go outdoors to get there."

"I don't suppose you have an umbrella."

"Never use 'em." His leer is a bit lewd. She wonders what it is about her that amuses him so. She doesn't feel a bit funny.

He is putting on a hat—a baseball sort of cap. He says, "Well shit," and clumps past her to the door. "Wait here." He goes out into the rain.

She feels she's achieved a petty victory. She glances through the jumbled papers on his desk and has a quick look at the documents that are thumbtacked to the wall under the crayon-on-cardboard sign. Beside an old map of Angola—what's that doing here?—she spots his private pilot's license, dated 1951, and his commercial licenses—single-engine and pilot-instructor, both dated 1974—and a certificate from the State of California permitting Charles W. Reid to operate a bonded school for the training of private pilots in single-engine dual control aircraft. There is the inevitable *Playboy* calendar nude. Off to one side she sees an Air Force certificate: he retired in 1972 with the rank of lieutenant colonel, which probably means he'd been serving as a major—not a very high rank after twenty years' service. Most of the documents are dirty and have gone ragged around the edges; none is framed.

Thumbtacked on the side wall above the desk, where he'll see it when he is sitting down, is a color snapshot of a nine- or ten-year-old boy with masses of brown hair and a big jaw like Reid's.

Wind slams the door open and he lunges into the room with a wadded towel in one hand and a Styrofoam cup of coffee in the other. He kicks the door shut behind him. All his motions are big and rangy: he moves like a large predator with total confidence in his own physical authority. He sets the coffee on the desk and proffers the towel. "Here you go."

"Thank you." She makes her voice softer than before. "It was stupid for both of us to have to get wet. I'm sorry—I didn't think."

"I've been wetter than this and survived it, I guess."

She scrubs her hair with the towel. "Is that your son?" She indicates the snapshot.

"Got to be. Looks like me, doesn't he. That was taken nearly ten years ago, when he made that sign. He's a sophomore at Stanford. Studying East European languages. Damn fool kid wants to go into the diplomatic corps. I can't talk to him any more."

But you're fond of him, she thinks. That's good. You'll know what it means to worry about your child.

She says, "When he gets a couple of years older he'll realize you're not as stupid as he thinks you are." She wraps the dank towel around her neck; there's no point trying to fix clothes or make-up—everything is ruined.

She reaches for the coffee, pries the lid off and tastes it. "This stuff's terrible."

"Yeah."

"Why do you drink it?"

"I get it from the machine next door," he says. "It's better than the stuff I make."

"Then I hope I never have to taste yours. About these flying lessons now—I thought maybe you could give me some books to study, and don't you people use those phony airplanes inside a hangar where you simulate actual flying for the students?"

"Link Trainers? That kind of thing? I'm not that rich. Maybe you aren't either. They use those to train professional pilots. If you intend to take up commercial flying for a living, maybe you ought to go apply to Pan Am or United Airlines."

"I just want to learn how to fly a small plane."

"What for?"

It takes her aback. She didn't anticipate that one; she hasn't prepared an answer to it.

When she hesitates, Charlie Reid says, "A few women take it up because they're lying out in the back yard by the swimming pool with nothing to do in the afternoon and they see a bunch of light planes buzzing around and it looks like a lot of fun. Glamour and freedom and something to do in the afternoons. And then there are the ones—the divorcees—that figure maybe it's a way to meet a man. You one of those?"

"No."

"Well then." He waits.

She says, "I've been up in small planes. As a passenger. I like it. I like the feeling. I can't explain it any better than that."

"Well, it's your money," he says. "You don't get the sample ride today but I can start you in on basic principles and paperwork."

"Good. Let's get the red tape out of the way and then

maybe you can give me some homework. I'll be away for a week or so. When I get back I'd like to start taking lessons three or four days a week."

"That's kind of pushing it."

"I'm in a hurry," she replies.

12 On Thursday she leaves at dawn and drives to Las Vegas.

There are several mail-forwarding services in town. On Fremont Street she picks one at random and signs up for six months, paying cash in advance. The man at the counter does not ask for identification.

In the coffee shop of one of the downtown casinos she orders iced tea. It is a drink she's never liked very much but it seems to be the thing to do in the Sunbelt and it fits in with her intentions to change her habits.

She is squirting lemon into the glass when a man stops beside her table. "Hi there. What's your name?"

Her breath catches. It is a moment before she can look up. She tries to make it steely. "I'm sorry. You've got the wrong table."

"I just thought maybe you'd let me buy you a drink or something." He is losing his pale hair on top and he wears flesh-colored glasses. Probably about her age. Slender, almost reedy. Type-casting him, she thinks of electronics—he looks as if he programs computers. An apologetic half smile shapes his mouth as if engraved there.

She says: "Thank you. No."

"You're very attractive, you know, and if you're by yourself—"

"I want to be by myself."

"I just thought—"

She says, "They have legal prostitution here. If you're horny—look, just pick up a newspaper over there and read the ads and find something you like and make a phone call."

The man says, "It just doesn't work for me if I have to pay for it." He turns his palms up in a gesture of abandonment. "But then I suppose we all end up paying for it one way or another." He wanders off. She ventures a guess that the ink probably hasn't dried on his divorce.

She feels compassion for the bewildered fool. There was a time when she'd have been happy to invite him to sit down and have a cup of coffee and tell her the story of his life. She's always liked people; she's always curious about them.

She wonders why her rebuff seemed to take him so utterly by surprise. Perhaps everybody assumes that an attractive woman who's alone must have a transparent reason to come to a place like this.

She doesn't want to take any others by surprise; it might make them remember her. When the next man arrives at her table and says, "Hi. You alone?"—it isn't more than five minutes later—she gives him a grim look and says, "I'm waiting for my husband. He's a police officer."

"Lucky for him. Too bad for me." The man goes away, good-natured, taking it in stride, searching with bright eyes for his next opportunity.

That one too, she thinks. Nice guy. For all you know all he wants is a friendly smile and a few minutes' conversation.

Dear God. I've always been such a nice person. I've always loved stray puppies—I've always been kind to my friends and generous to my enemies and trusting to strangers.

28

Is it possible to wake up one morning and make a snap decision that's going to change the rest of your life—and truly become a different person: someone you'd have hated?

There's got to be room for humanity. You can't just let yourself shrivel up into a suspicious crone.

And yet. . . .

You've got to think about Ellen. For her sake you can't trust anyone at all.

Let the poor sons of bitches find other girls to talk to. Right now you just can't afford the exposure.

Alone at the coffee shop table she fills in the Social Security application—the second one: Dorothy Holder's. Yesterday she stopped in an instant-printing shop and had Dorothy's birth certificate photocopied. She encloses the copy with the application and lists her mailing address as that of the mail-forwarding service.

She tries to make Dorothy's signature different from Jennifer's: bigger, rounder, heavier. She's practiced signing *Jennifer C. Hartman* night after night in a crabbed hand that is not at all like her usual flowing script.

She drops the application into a mail slot and a quarter into the one-armed bandit. It doesn't pay off and she goes back to her motel. It is six o'clock: a bit early for dinner and she isn't hungry anyway. She lies down on the bed, just to relax for a few minutes; maybe she'll go in the swimming pool in a little while to cool off, and then tackle some of the home study program Charlie Reid gave her—instruments, controls, regulations. . . .

When she awakens it is past midnight and she sits up feeling sour and hung over. Exhaustion, she thinks. It isn't the hard work of it all; it's the strain—the tension of knowing she needs to make only one misstep and it all will be useless and they'll come down on her like a falling safe.

Desperately tired, she can't get back to sleep.

It occurs to her at some point in the endless drag of the

night that never before has she known how dreadful it is to be truly alone. It's all a blank slate now: no past, no friends—not even the prospect of friends. Nobody at all.

Ellen, she thinks.

But Ellen can't help her fend off the terror; not now.

She opens Charlie Reid's spiral-bound primer and tries to memorize the rules of flying.

13 In the morning she sells the car for $800 cash on a small used-car lot two blocks from her motel. The dealer, a man with a sunburned bald head and an expression of wry bemusement, must be accustomed to buying cars for cash: he's probably seen a hundred examples of the hopefuls who arrive in Las Vegas in their $20,000 Cadillacs and depart a few days later in $100,000 buses. Those big-spending high rollers must have their mundane $100 counterparts and this is precisely the impression she wants to leave: she wants to differ in no way from the multitude.

According to the radio on the bald man's desk the official temperature is 108° Fahrenheit—and it isn't even eleven o'clock yet. The dealer sees her expression and says, "Wait till August, you want real heat."

When she signs the bill of sale she has to show identification; that is why she's saved the old driver's license. He glances at it, comparing signatures, but he'll forget her name as soon as she leaves the shack and he files the papers away.

She is curious whether he feels much pain in his red burned scalp but she doesn't ask; she takes the cash and walks away, squinting behind her sunglasses.

Back in the air-conditioned motel she plucks the blouse away from her fried skin and makes a little ceremony out of burning the old driver's license and flushing the ashes away.

Nothing left of the old life now except a ring of keys.

At the cheap blond desk she begins to make a list on motel stationery: a list of all the things she knows about herself. It isn't the first time she's done it. The ostensible purpose is to check off the items she's changed and to see what remains to be done. The actual purpose is to keep from going insane.

At one of those political dinner parties last year a guest was the private detective whose specialty is skip-tracing. "Raymond Q. Seale," his business card announces, and if you ask him what the Q stands for he replies, "Questing," with an irritating smugness: a self-important little man slicked up in a tight suit. Phony smile and the sleazy artful manner of a cynic who insists that the world lives at his own gutter level. But she listened to him with interest; the pressures on her had kept increasing and by then she'd already begun to fantasize ways of escape.

She recalls how annoyingly self-confident Seale was— but knowledgeable. "Your teen-agers run away from home. Twelve-year-olds sometimes. Or even younger. Half of them pregnant. They're the hardest ones to find—no fingerprints on file, no credit records, no paper trail to identify them by.

"Grownups run out on their bills, mostly. Sometimes they just get tired of their husbands or wives—sometimes the guy just doesn't want to have to pay alimony."

She pictures him now—a mean man, amused by the misfortunes he's describing. "We work for the bank to find the guy and repossess the car, or the parents ask us to find the runaway, or the woman pays us to go after the husband and bring him back so she can hit up the poor guy for alimony, whatever."

She remembers hearing the investigator say: "Most people got no idea how hard it is to lose yourself." He was playing to his audience with the cunning of a seedy nightclub comic. "If we've got a client who's got a pile of money and plenty of time and he wants to find you bad enough, we can find you. We can find *anybody,* see?

"I mean, it's impossible for most people to disappear and stay disappeared. It'd take brains and a lot of hard work. They've got to change their whole lives. If they used to play tennis, they've got to take up bowling. If they used to go to ball games, they've got to start going to the opera. A guy that used to live in conservative business suits, he's got to start wearing loud sports jackets and leisure suits and Levi's. If they're stamp collectors, they've got to quit it—and remember not to subscribe to any stamp-collecting magazines. If they drove a small car they should buy a big car, or a pickup truck or maybe a motorsiccle.

"And they can't ever make contact with any of their friends or relatives. That's what trips most of them up. Sooner or later they get the urge to drop a postcard to Momma or make a long-distance call to Uncle Fatface. That's when we get 'em.

"See, it's not enough just to change your name and move to Florida. You've got to change everything. Every detail. You make a list of everything you know about yourself and you change every single thing on the list. You try and change the way you walk, the accent, everything. You've got to become a new person—a whole new type of person in a different social class. That's the only way to hide from guys like me. See, most people just aren't willing to make those kinds of changes."

That was when she thought: I am.

14 Going home from Las Vegas—home: she's realizing that never before has she truly understood the complexity or ambiguity of the word—she spends three days on various buses and trains; she isn't in a sightseeing mood but she wants to be sure her trail can't be picked up and followed from the car she's just sold and so she endures a roundabout tour of Lake Tahoe, Sacramento, Napa and San Francisco. At every stop she converts thousand-dollar bills into postal money orders and bank cashier's checks.

Finally she returns by air coach to Burbank in the Valley.

On the plane she studies her list. It seems important to keep the mind pragmatically focused on details; otherwise she has the feeling she may fly apart.

For this flight she has paid cash and assumed yet another new false name. By now she feels able to do this with a certain distracted aplomb. Not like the first time, when she nearly gagged with alarm—filling out a motel registration slip in Pennsylvania, scribbling a name she'd made up on the spot, concocting an address, paying cash in advance for the room, hardly daring to look the room clerk in the eye.

The clerk didn't even lift an eyebrow and that was when she began to realize that nobody has any reason to care. Nobody suspects you if you just behave naturally. The world is indifferent to the way you spell your name. As long as you pay the bill nobody gives a damn whether you're traveling under a *nom de guerre*.

She's thinking: Nobody even notices. Then why's my heart still pounding so?

15 During her absence the first Social Security card—Jennifer Hartman's—has arrived in the mail. She looks at it in a kind of wonder. It gives her the oddest feeling: as if she is giving birth to a new person, one piece of paper at a time.

She takes a cab to the Motor Vehicle office and stands in queues all morning and part of the afternoon filling out a driver's license application and taking the written test; she stands in front of a machine that takes her picture—short fair hair and glasses; and now they want to take an ink impression of her thumbprint.

"Do I have to?"

"Why? You got something against it?" The man has greasy black hair and suspicious little eyes.

She says, "We're all just numbers in somebody's computer, aren't we. I don't want to be fingerprinted and weighed and whatever else they do in prisons. I just want a driver's license."

"The thumbprint's for your own protection. We don't send them to the FBI or anything. It's just for identification in case of—you know, suppose the car gets smashed up and burned."

"If that happens I won't care much, will I."

"The thumbprint's optional," he concedes. "You don't have to do it."

"Thank you."

"Take this form over to that line and make an appointment for your road test."

She manages to take the road test the same afternoon: it takes pleading ("I can't afford to keep taking taxis all the way out here") and some batting of eyelashes. Nothing, she thinks, is beneath me.

They give her a temporary license and she telephones for a cab; she has it drop her a few blocks from her motel at the supermarket, where she buys provisions for the evening and several newspapers. When she lets herself back into the motel room she opens the papers to the classified pages and spends the evening making phone calls.

Next day she looks at four cars and buys a three-year-old air-conditioned Japanese station wagon from a woman in Reseda whose husband is hospitalized with emphysema. "We won't be needing two cars for a spell," the sad woman says, and agrees to take $3,750 cash for the car.

By then it is time to drive to Van Nuys airport for her lesson.

16 She's going to want two apartments: one that can be used as a vested lawful address; the other to live in.

For her legal residence she picks out a furnished room off Lankershim Boulevard. She chooses it mainly because it's cheap and because the mailbox, to which she is given a key, is in an oleander-screened passage around the side of the building. She can drive in by way of the alley and no one watching the apartment or the main doors will be able to see her when she checks the mailbox.

The rental agency is a busy office a mile away and that's helpful because she doubts very much that they'll remember what she looked like when she signed up. They won't see her again; she only needs to remember to send in the rent check once a month.

Hurrying through cheap department stores and thrift shops she buys a wardrobe of new and used clothing. The three pairs of shoes are two sizes too large for her and the underwear and clothes are chosen to fit a woman approximately three inches shorter and ten pounds heavier than she.

In Duttons' bookshop she picks up a carton of secondhand paperbacks, most of them Regency romances. She buys an old black and white TV set for forty dollars and a couple of timers that will turn the lamps on and off automatically; an assortment of inexpensive toiletries and cosmetics, none of them her own brands; two bottles of very cheap wine, a few frozen foods and juices, several cans of soup and a few boxes of crackers—a variety of nonperishable foods with which to stock the dummy apartment so that it will look lived in.

She makes the bed and squirms in it and then climbs out, leaving the top sheet and blanket turned back and the pillow dented and a romance novel open face down on the bedside table. It occurs to her to leave two windows narrowly ajar to permit air circulation so that the place won't feel stuffy and uninhabited. Then she hangs a set of towels on the racks, unwraps a bar of soap and a toothbrush, uses them and leaves them in the bathroom.

A couple of tissues crumpled in the wastebasket; a folded paper towel beside the sink with an upended coffee cup on it; let's see—what else?

It seems enough. Not much by way of evidence about the woman who lives here—but such as it is, it doesn't point to the real tenant.

The next thing to do is leave a forwarding address at

the motel where she's been staying. From now on, this is the legal and mailing address of Jennifer Corfu Hartman.

And now for her actual residence she investigates seven or eight advertisements and chooses a one-bedroom apartment at the back of a court.

The furniture is nondescript; you could find better in a second-class hotel. The place is dark because its windows are small and set high, insulation and privacy and security being more important than light or a better view of the swimming pool in the unshaded yard below.

Under the afternoon sun it is far from cool in mid-July even though the through-the-wall air-conditioning units are running at capacity.

It has no grace, no flavor—nothing left of the transients who must have occupied it momentarily on their way up or on their way down or simply on their way through.

She takes it because it is clean and it is furnished and the price is reasonable and it is available month to month for cash without a lease.

She doesn't expect to entertain here; with luck nobody will know she lives here; she doesn't intend to stay any longer than it will take to get her bearings and decide on a structure for her new life and find a residence suitable to it: one into which she may blend so precisely that she'll never arouse anyone's curiosity.

It all needs to take place quickly. Because of Ellen it is a matter of acute urgency: she has six weeks, no longer. But she can't execute the crucial part of the plan until the license with her photograph on it arrives in the mail from Sacramento.

That will take a fortnight or more. Time enough to set Jennifer Corfu Hartman up in business.

17 She finds the shop easily enough from the instructions on the phone. It's set back in a little Burbank shopping mall, hardly much bigger than a motel—she counts eleven stores in the U-shaped court.

When she emerges from the car it is like opening the door of an oven that someone neglected to turn off two days ago: the heat has accumulated in pavement and walls and cars from which it radiates in lancing slivers of reflected sunlight, as painful against the eyes as steel darts.

Everything is too bright, too raw. She scrutinizes the place with unease and a growing skepticism.

It shows painful evidence of a promoter-builder's efforts to be quaint. The shops have high wooden false fronts and the walkway is shaded by a veranda roof supported on posts and wooden arches—an imitation wild west movie set. The parking lot is decorated with wagon wheels.

There are a western wear shop, an ice cream bar, the Native American Crafts Shop, a one-hour photo store, a harness and tack outfit that features silver-tooled saddles; she makes a face at the hitching rail in front of that one. Next door a display window holds agate and turquoise jewelry under a wooden sign that hangs on chains and carries the legend The Desert Rockhound. On the corner by the curb is a restaurant where you may eat al fresco at rustic tables under big umbrellas, the dining area surrounded by a split-rail corral fence. Behind it the small windows are filled with colored neon signs advertising several brands of beer. That is—inevitably?—Buffalo Bill's Saloon.

It looks like bloody Disneyland, she thinks, and makes her dubious way toward the half-hidden corner shop that announces itself with a meekly faded sign as Books of the West.

Inside she finds the soothing relief of air conditioning and another kind of relief that the shop hasn't been decorated with cheap gimcracks: no framed plastic replicas of old guns.

The bookcases along both walls are filled with volumes most of which don't seem to be new—many are without dust jackets—and the bins and tables that crowd the center of the room are stacked high with oversized picture books and paperbacks and bargain selections: All Books On This Table $1.59.

The cash register near the front door is a genuine antique—brass keys and pop-up numbers behind glass. But she sees a computer screen on the shelf behind.

There is no one at the counter. Two men are deep in conversation near the back: the older one glances her way and speaks up: "Be right with you, ma'am."

"Take your time," she says. "No hurry." She smiles at his "ma'am."

He is white-haired: tall with a flowing white gun-fighter's mustache, a bit stooped, dressed in jeans and an outdoorsy red plaid shirt. The customer with him is younger—thirties or early forties, brown mustache, khaki poplin business suit.

She removes her sunglasses and replaces them with the clear-lensed ones and glances along the shelves. Hand-crayoned signs thumbtacked to the bookcases identify their subject matter: American Indians . . . California History . . . Colorado River . . . Gold Rush . . . Gunmen. . . .

The man with white hair separates himself from his customer and comes forward through the clutter. She sees that he is younger than he appeared at a distance; his smooth tanned face is interestingly in contrast with the color of his hair, which is abundant and well combed, and with the stoop of his shoulders, which at closer glance seems a symptom of scholarliness rather than age. He's nearer fifty than seventy. His eyes are a troubled brown behind silver-framed glasses.

"May I help you?" He pronounces it *he'p*. Texas, she decides.

"I'm Jennifer Hartman—the one who called this morning about your ad? Are you Mr. Stevens?"

"Doyle Stevens." His handshake is almost reluctant. He goes behind the counter and glances out the window and touches a corner of the cash register. He seems to go slack. His attention flits around the walls and she senses a furtive desperation. He utters an awkward laugh. "I feel tongue-tied," he says.

Then he punches a button: there is the jingle of the high-pitched bell and the No Sale tab flips up and the drawer slams open with a satisfying crunch of noise. It is a gesture: some kind of punctuation.

He says: "You don't look like somebody looking to get into this kind of business."

It startles her because she hasn't had the feeling he's scrutinized her at all. "I'm sorry. What should I look like?"

He flaps a hand back and forth, dismissing it. "You want to know how's business, I expect. I can tell you how it is. Calm as a horse trough on a hot day. Or, to put it another way, and not to put too fine a point on it—business is terrible. You think we'd be putting ads in the papers if we were earning a fortune here?"

He pokes his head forward: suspicious, belligerent. The mustache seems to bristle. "Mostly I get fuzzy-headed inquiries by phone. Investors looking for opportunities—want to know about inventory and volume of business. Traffic in the location, all that jargon and bullroar. I tell them if they need to ask those kinds of questions, this is the wrong place for them. I tell them it's a terrible investment for a real businessman. You could earn more on your money with a passbook savings account."

Doyle Stevens prods his finger into the drawer and rattles a few coins around and finally pushes it shut. It makes a racket.

Finally he stares at her face. "I get letters from folks in Nebraska. Retired couples looking to set themselves up in retail. Looking for something genteel to, I guess, keep them busy while they enjoy the winter sunshine. I tell them too—forget it, my friends, it's hard work and it's full time and then some. My wife and I work a six-day week. And most of our evenings on the cataloging and the mail order."

He squints at her. "You don't do this to make money. And you can't treat it like some kind of part-time hobby."

She says: "No. You do it because you adore it."

But her smile seems to exacerbate his anger.

She says, "You have to love the smell of old books."

"Don't romanticize it. I hate sentimentality."

Sure you do, she thinks. What she says is, "Do you and Mrs. Stevens work here together?"

"Normally. She's at the accountant's office this morning. Trying to untangle some of the shambles. Paperwork. Federal government, state, county of Los Angeles, you'd think we were right up there alongside General Motors. A small binness like this, the paperwork alone can—Aagh, doesn't matter."

He pulls an old-fashioned pocketwatch out of his shirt pocket and snaps its lid open and consults it. Oddly, she does not have the impulse to laugh at the affectation.

He says, "She's got a good head for that kind of paperwork. And she's saintly patient with the bureaucracies and their fools. I expect her back shortly, in time for lunch."

Then he peers at her. "Ever been in the retail book trade?"

"No."

"Then maybe you're a Western buff. Afficionado of frontier feminism or Indian folk medicine—one of these fashionable concerns?"

"I wouldn't know a frontier feminist from Martha

41

Washington. But I adore books and I'd like to learn."

Doyle Stevens doesn't try to conceal his suspicion. "Care to tell me why you called?"

"Will you answer one question first?"

He has the talent to cock one eyebrow inquisitively. For some nonsensical reason she has always admired men who can do that. Ever since her third birthday when Uncle Dave—

She shuts off the thought, slamming a door roughly upon it; she says: "'Investment opportunity for Western Americana bibliophile'—don't you think that's ambiguous? Your ad doesn't make it clear whether you want someone to invest in your business so you can keep it going—or whether you just want to sell it and get out."

He turns away momentarily. She guesses he's looking at the customer in the back of the store. The man is well beyond earshot, putting a book back on its shelf and taking another down to examine it.

Doyle Stevens says, "How many sane people you think I'd find, invest money in this loony operation to keep it going?"

"So you want to sell it and get out."

He waves a hand around, bringing within its compass everything in the shop.

"My wife and I owe the publishers close to ten thousand dollars in unpaid invoices. Another two, three thousand to the jobbers. Owe the bank sixty-five thousand in business loans, eighty thousand mortgage on our house. So you see the plain fact is, Miss Hartman—"

"Mrs."

"Beg your pardon." He takes it without a break in expression. "Mrs. Hartman. Plain fact is I could've filed bankruptcy but I'd rather not see a receiver take over this inventory. I kind of doubt we'd be fortunate enough to have it fall into the hands of a banker with a true hankering for Western books."

He folds his hands, interlacing the fingers, looking down at them as if making a religious obeisance. "I was hoping to sell to somebody who'd have—at least a certain respect for this collection. Here, look here."

He takes down off the shelf behind him a heavy hardcover with a pale blue dust jacket. It looks quite new. Stevens opens it with reverent care. "*Triggernometry*. Cunningham. The first edition, Caxton Press. Pret' near mint condition. You have any idea how rare and precious this book is to a true collector?"

Then he replaces it on its shelf and heaves his thin arm high, pointing toward the very top of the bookcase. "Up there—all those? Firsts. Lippincott. Complete works of General Charles King, starting with *The Colonel's Daughter,* eighteen and eighty-one. The first Western novel. The very first Western of all time."

He possesses a bashful wicked smile like a little boy's: peeking at you out of the corner of his eye, trying to get away with something when he thinks you're not looking. "That is if you don't count the penny dreadfuls and the Prentiss Ingraham dime novels and those God-awful stage melodramas of Buntline's."

She watches his face. He isn't smiling any longer. He says in a different voice, "Who the hell remembers General Charles King now."

"I'm afraid not I."

"Why, shoot," he says with a scoffing theatrical snort, "without Charles King there'd've been no John Ford, no John Wayne, no nothing."

He is glaring at her. "I gather that doesn't mean a whole hill of beans to you. So tell me, Mrs. Hartman. What are you doing here?"

She smiles to deflect the challenge. Liking him, she says, "What if you found an investor to back you with operating capital?"

He looks as if cold water has been thrown in his face.

He catches his breath. "What are you saying to me?"

"I'm asking whether you'd prefer to settle your debts and close up shop and go spend the rest of your days in a trailer park—or whether, given the chance, you'd stay in business here."

It evokes his ebullient laugh. "What the hell do you think?"

She turns a full circle on her heels, surveying the place.

He says: "It'd be very painful if I thought you were kidding around with me."

It's nothing wonderful, really. A self-indulgent novelty-specialty enterprise in a cutesy-poo shopping mall. A couple of walls of books, most of them of no interest to anyone whose interests don't include such arcane memorabilia.

No one from her past life will ever dream of looking for her in a place like this.

"I'm not kidding around with you." She faces Doyle Stevens. "How much do you need?"

"Thirty-five thousand for the moment. And no guarantee you'd ever see a penny's return on it." He says it quickly and takes a backward step, ready to flinch.

She says, "You're just a hell of a salesman, aren't you."

"I'm glad you're perceptive enough to recognize that God-given talent in me. Marian doubts I could sell air conditioners in Death Valley. God knows what ever got me into retail trade."

"Do you regret it, then?"

"I regret I'm not rich, yes ma'am."

"I doubt that."

"Do you now." His smile has warmth in it for the first time.

She asks, "How much does the business lose in the course of a year?"

"Depends on the year. By the time Marian and I take

our living expenses out—we can usually figure on breaking even more or less. But the last two years have been poorer than normal. Partly the economy. Partly that our customers keep getting older—the demographics would make a market researcher weep. Half our clients are geriatric cases. Sooner or later their eyesight goes bad or they pass away. Whichever comes first."

A motorcycle goes by with a roar calculated to offend, and the white-haired man glares toward the window. "Our new generation there doesn't give a hang about the old West. When was the last time you saw a Western in the movies? You don't see any horse operas on the tube any more. Was a time twenty years ago there'd be two dozen cowboy series on the television every week."

He looks grim. "Remember *True Grit*? When was the last respectable Western book on the bestseller list? It's a sad thing, you know, but there's a generation out there all the way up into their twenties who think the American myth has something to do with automobiles. They've never heard of Wild Bill Hickok or Wyatt Earp or Cochise."

A man's voice startles her from behind her shoulder. "Doyle, there's a bloody story in that."

It's the customer in the khaki suit. He has a book in his hand. "This any good?"

Doyle Stevens takes it in his hand. "*The Journal of Lieutenant Thomas W. Sweeny*. Westernlore." It brings out of him a reminiscent smile. "An absolute delight. Sweeny founded Fort Yuma, you know. Remarkable stories about the Indians down there. They had paddlewheel steamboats on the Colorado River in his day, did you know that?"

She remembers her brief stroll. "You could hardly float a toothpick on it now."

The customer sizes her up. "That's the bloody dam builders. You know a hundred and fifty years ago before it got overgrazed and before they bottomed out the bloody

45

water table with too many deep wells, a good part of what's now the Arizona desert used to be grassland. Green and lush."

"It's a shame," she says with a polite little smile, wishing he would go away.

Doyle Stevens says, "Mrs. Hartman—Graeme Goldsmith."

She shakes his hand. His eyes smile at her with more intimacy than she likes. He's odd looking, especially up close where his astonishingly pale blue eyes take effect. It's been too long since he's been to the barber; he has a thatch of brown hair just starting to go thin at the front and she thinks she detects a pasty hint under the camouflaging tan: likely he drinks more than he ought to.

"That's G-r-a-e-m-e," he says. "Nobody can spell it. My mother fancied the bloody name."

Time has faded the accent but he is distinctly Australian.

Doyle Stevens, about to burst, says, "Looks as though Mrs. Hartman's going to be our new business partner."

"That so?"

She says, "If Mrs. Stevens approves."

"Well well. Good-oh. We'll have to give it a proper write-up in the *Trib*."

An alarm jangles through her.

Doyle Stevens says, "Graeme's a reporter on the *Valley Tribune*."

"Not to mention I'm a stringer for the UPI newswire," Goldsmith says quickly.

She hatches a smile and hopes it is properly gentle. "I'd rather you didn't print anything about this. It's sort of a silent partnership."

"Any particular reason."

"I don't want publicity. A woman living alone—you know how it is. It's the same reason I have my phone unlisted."

"Okay, Mrs. Hartman. I can buy that." But she has seen it when he latched onto the statement that she lives alone.

Doyle Stevens says, "You want to pay for that book or were you just going to walk out with it?"

Graeme Goldsmith still has his blue eyes fixed on her face. "How much?"

She tries to keep her glance friendly when it intersects with the Australian's but after he pays for the book she is glad to see the back of him.

A reporter, she thinks. That's just what I need.

18 Every day she visits the mailbox of the dummy apartment in hope there'll be something to collect.

By July 25 nothing has appeared except junk mail and Dorothy Holder's Social Security card: it comes from the forwarding service in Las Vegas.

Taking a break from her on-the-job training in the retail bookselling business and from the flying lessons that take up a good part of every third afternoon she drives to Carson City where she applies for a Nevada driver's license in the name of Dorothy (NMI) Holder.

In these towns you don't go into the good restaurants and eat alone; some of them won't seat you at all and the others assume you're looking for a pickup. You eat instead in chain diners and coffee shops where your palate has become exceedingly bored with oversteamed vegetables and bland American provincial cooking.

By now she has memorized DuPar's menus and those

of the House of Pancakes. She has had one too many Open Face Hot Roast Beef Sandwiches With Brown Gravy. Walking into this particular Holiday Inn restaurant she is dreaming wistfully of Guido Tusco's fettucine al pesto, of Henri's Dover sole amandine, of the Manhattan chowder that Marjorie Quirini used to make from clams her husband had dug out of the Great South Bay that very day.

It is in that frame of mind, walking in and waiting to be seated, that she sees Bert and recognizes him.

Terror roots her to the spot.

It can't possibly be—can it?

He sits at the bar with his back to her, the muscles pulling his jacket tight across the wide lean shoulders, and his big long close-cropped dark head is cocked a bit to one side as he stirs the drink in front of him. He sits hipshot on the barstool with one leg dangling and the other propped stiff against the floor—his habitual posture.

Standing bolt still she tries to fight the panic.

What in the hell is he doing *here*?

Come on. Jesus. Get a grip . . . just sidle on out of here . . . *move.*

She's paralyzed. Pinpricks of fear burst out on her skin.

Her mesmerized stare is fastened to the back of his head.

Unwillingly her eyes crawl up to the mirror beyond him, the mirror behind the bar. He's looking right at her.

For a moment it doesn't register. All she knows is that he's staring at her.

Then she sees his face—it was there all the time, a pinched dewlappy face she has never seen before.

A stranger.

It's not Bert after all.

Relief is so powerful that when the hostess comes toward her with a menu she beams a radiant smile upon the bewildered woman. But by the time she slides into the Naugahyde booth she's gone faint and weak and she orders a double martini, extra dry, and sits shaking in all her joints until it arrives.

Not him at all. But what an uncanny resemblance from the back. The shape of his head, the cant of the wide slabby shoulders—even the waist-nipped cut of the light tweed jacket.

It's so easy to be fooled . . .

He was just like that, she recalls, the very first time she saw him. Propped tall against a bar stool with his back to her.

It was in—what was the name of the place? One of those tony discos in the Hamptons. Filled with groupers, of whom she was one that summer: two weeks of sharing a dumpy cottage in Sag Harbor with five other girls.

He was in lime sherbet slacks and a madras jacket. She danced with him. He was long-boned and awkward: a graceless dancer, but he had an attractive way of laughing at his own clumsiness. And his hard lean musculature made the other men in the place look like marshmallows.

The hoarse rasp of his voice intrigued her. He had a quick sense of humor.

"Your name's Matty, isn't it?"

"How did you know that?"

"Matty Sevrin, right? I asked your girlfriend over there. When you went to the Ladies'. What's it short for? Matilda?"

"Madeleine."

"Pretty name."

He said his name was Al. She asked if it was short for Alfred. No; his name was Albert.

"Then I'll call you Bert."

"Why?"

"So it will belong to me," she said. "It'll be my special name for you and we won't share it with anybody."

She was just kidding along at the time. Flirting with him. Harmless. It meant nothing.

49

He seemed an outsider here, a bit older than most of them, amused by the swirling racket. He bought her a drink and said he'd seen her in a magazine spread, modeling fashions. She was pleased to be recognized.

(Weeks later he admitted the falsehood. He hadn't recognized her from ads. He'd pumped her girl friend at the bar. By then they were an item and she forgave him the white lie.)

They danced again; he asked her where she was staying.

It was getting late and the disco noise was starting to get to her. By then she'd fended off half a dozen young men and maybe she was just tired of it or maybe she was impressed by his hard body and his good-natured mature self-assurance and the way he didn't come at her head-on with all guns blazing. She decided she liked him enough to give him the phone number of the cottage.

He didn't offer to drive her home; he didn't make a pass or even imply one and she found this refreshing and disappointing at once. But she thought about him constantly.

Two days later he drove up in a white Seville with his friends, a married couple he'd collected at the L.I.R.R. station—Jack and Diane Sertic; thirty-fiveish, all of them. Bert made introductions and she got in beside him, carrying her racquet and wearing her whites. The Sertics were in Ralph Lauren purple and Bert called them snobs.

She sips the second martini and it all floods through her recollection as if it has just taken place an hour ago. She remembers how they chatted on the twenty-minute ride about the idiotic tribal rituals of the Hamptons and the lobster salad at Loaves and Fishes for which you had to pay a scandalous $18 a pound that summer.

The road seemed to have been reserved for use by Rollses and Cadillacs, with the occasional BMW for levity. And then Bert drove them into the sinuous pebbled driveway of the eight-acre Stanford White estate he was renting. It had sixteen rooms; pillars and a porte-cochere and a fountain on the lawn that sloped down to the shore. She noted a red two-seater Mercedes sports car and an Audi sedan parked in the four-car garage.

Jack Sertic was impressed. "What do you have to pay for it?"

"Forty thousand for the season."

"Not bad."

She tried not to gape. Bert said, "Used to belong to one of the owners of the 21 club. See the dock down there? They ran liquor in from here during Prohibition."

"Nothing changes all that much, does it. Now it's coke and Acapulco gold." Jack Sertic grinned at Bert.

They played two sets of mixed doubles. The Sertics were good; she and Bert were better. Enjoying the victory they went on to lunch at the beach club.

They swam in the afternoon. A foursome of Bert's friends came by, played a raucous game of croquet, drank planter's punch and departed.

She flowed with it all, in a pink silky haze: it seemed so Gatsbyesque. A little high on rum she drowsed in the shade and listened to the others talk about Studio 54 and about a thoroughbred stallion that was being syndicated for a million five and about an Arthur Ashe–Jimmy Connors match that had taken place a week ago. Bert told a rambling story about two gangs of screw-ups, one employed by the CIA and the other by the Mafia, who he swore had actually gone to open warfare several years earlier, the battleground being Port-au-Prince where rattletrap Second World War bombers piloted by CIA dipsticks had tried to bomb Papa Doc's palace, only to have their aim thrown off by unanticipated antiaircraft fire from the palace roof.

"Papa Doc made a deal with Lansky to get him ack-ack guns in return for some beachfront gambling concessions he gave Lansky. All the bombs exploded in the harbor. One of the planes got nicked. No casualties. End of war. It's all true, you know. I got it from that skip-tracer over in Newark, what's his name? Seale. One of the people in his office used to work for the CIA before they fired him for laughing too hard or something."

She was pleased but not surprised when he insisted she accompany them to dinner. Philip Quirini, who worked for Bert, drove her home and waited outside in the car while she changed; and when she got back in the car she said, "Have you worked here long?"

"Four years. Or you mean the house. No, ma'am. It's just rented for July and August."

"I guess this is going to sound like a strange question," she said, "but what does your boss do for a living?"

She caught Quirini's eye in the mirror. He had a hard face—jowls, a round heavy jaw, tough dark eyes, hair getting thin and grey. He seemed amused. "You heard of AJL Construction, ma'am? That's us."

She'd seen the big signs all over New York on building sites.

Pushing things she said, "I suppose he's married."

A sharp look in the mirror; then a brief smile. "No. He was married once I guess. Before I came to work. I think it was annulled."

He brought her back to the manor where Bert handed her a wine spritzer and studied her best low-cut designer job. "You pass inspection," he said drily.

The Sertics were there; they went on to one of the restaurants—she doesn't remember now if it was Shippy's or Balzarini's or the Palm; whichever, Bert knew the maitre d' and there was no trouble about a table even though they hadn't had a reservation.

She remembers the relaxed savor of the evening: the way they included her, now and then going out of their way to explain a private point of reference, generally seeming to take it for granted she was grown up and sophisticated.

Not like what she was used to: a world that appeared

52

to believe she couldn't possibly have more than two brain cells to rub together.

It was the curse of the smooth skin and big eyes and the Goddamned bone structure that earned success for her as a model: often she'd be taken for twenty or twenty-one.

She'd learned there wasn't much to the men who went for girls barely out of their teens. One of them, suntanned and Nautilus-muscled and trying his best to look like a high-school jock, had propositioned her just two days earlier—in that same disco where she'd met Bert—and she'd been so bored with it all that she'd just looked the jock in the eye and said in her deepest go-to-hell baritone, "What do you think we'd have to talk about after the first four minutes?"

"Four minutes?" The jock feigned indignation. "I'm good for at least an hour and a half." He might as well have been flexing his muscles. "Come on. What do you want to talk about. Name it."

"How about Kierkegaard?"

He'd edged away from her.

Not that she was out for the presidency of U.S. Steel. She made good money modeling and spent it on rent and clothes and amusements; there was nothing ambitious or far-seeing about her life. She had no plans beyond the date she'd made to spend the Labor Day weekend with the parents of a girlfriend from the agency up in a cabin on one of the Finger Lakes.

This one now, this Bert—she couldn't fathom him. She'd catch him looking her up and down with a quick frank smile of appreciation but he didn't stare down at her boobs or shove a figurative elbow into her ribs with clumsy fatuous attempts to be sly and lascivious. He'd spent the whole day with her but every minute seemed to have been carefully chaperoned: they hadn't been alone at all. That did not seem to be an accident. Was he afraid of something?

He liked talking to her. He watched her face while

they spoke. He laughed at the right points; he listened.

She watched his profile beside her at the dinner table as he talked with forceful confidence and made lavish gestures with his big hands. He caught her looking at him; he stopped in midsentence and smiled. It illuminated his face: it was an overflowing smile that demanded a response in kind.

She can remember vividly the startling beauty of his smile—especially now because of the irony it engenders. She remembers the life to which he introduced her: hard young capitalists on the make, a jet-propelled world of expensive toys, midnight conference calls, ringside seats, luxury condominiums, show-business evenings, sudden trips cushioned by limousines and hotel penthouses and VIP lounges.

By then they were married. She remembers the way he phrased his proposal. At the time she wasn't sufficiently sensitive to its subtext. What he said was, "I want you to be the mother of my children."

19 The weather cools a bit. Finally on August 1 the California license arrives and she spends two days going from bank to bank in Long Beach and Inglewood and Culver City, breaking one or two of the thousand-dollar bills at each stop.

Then she returns to the Valley and opens a checking account with eight hundred dollars in cash—not enough to draw attention—and applies for a credit card, listing herself as a divorcee with a monthly alimony income of $2,500. On the application she attests to numerous lies. As her residence she lists the dummy apartment. For a reference she gives the name of a fictitious company president at the address of the Las Vegas mail-forwarding service. For a second reference she gives Doyle Stevens.

At various post offices she mails $500 money orders to herself; when these arrive she uses them to open an account in a savings-and-loan where they give you a year's free rent on a safety-deposit box for opening a new account. She puts the diamonds and most of the rest of the cash in the box.

Examining the driver's license for the 'steenth time she studies the color photograph of herself: slightly blurred (she must have moved her head a bit), unsmiling. Points of reflected light on the lenses of the glasses obscure the color of her eyes.

The cropped hair and glasses serve to harden her appearance: in the picture she looks—what's the best word? *Efficient.*

Actually she has always been efficient; it is only that until recently she hasn't had very much need to prove it.

She showers away a day's grit and wipes the towel across the bathroom mirror so she can scrutinize herself.

The body isn't bad for an old broad of thirty-one. Too bony if your taste runs toward Rubens nudes but she could still pose in a bikini if she wanted to and nothing sags perceptibly; the stretch marks aren't pronounced.

The face, absent the phony glasses and with the wet hair matted down, looks fragile and vulnerable—all eyes and bones and angles as if she'd posed for one of those child-girls on black velvet. Ironic that she looks so young: she is thinking, I don't feel a day over ninety-three.

There is a hint of haggard gauntness in that image. With a detachment that feels almost academic she wonders how long you can go on living on your nerve endings before you begin to disintegrate.

In the mirror the unmade-up lips are definitely too thin and wide; no rosebud here. She's always had trouble with the look of her mouth; it took years of experiment to find a proper way to paint it for modeling. It is a big mouth made for smiling; it doesn't take naturally to the expression that photographers seem to want: distant chill with a contradictory hint of seductiveness. That is one of the reasons (there are others, God knows) why she never became a top model—she only came as near as perhaps the upper section of the second class.

She studies herself with dispassion. What else wants changing?

There's the gap between the two upper front teeth. He said it was sexy, didn't he. He didn't want you to fix it.

Tomorrow she'll find a dentist and have them bonded to fill in the space.

She leans forward with belligerent challenge and speaks aloud:

"All right. Now who are you?"

20 The young woman in the phone company store has frizzy red hair and brown eyebrows, plump cheeks and a Spanish accent.

"You never had a telephone before?"

"It was in my ex-husband's name."

"But if your ex-husband still has a phone—"

"I don't use his name any more. I want to build up a credit rating on my own."

"You know, I can sympathize with that. Honestly. These laws and red tape just step all over a woman, especially that's, like, gone through a divorce or maybe she's been widowed or, you know."

The telephone woman gives her a smile that is startling for its openness. "But I just don't think you can get around it. I'm real, real sorry, Jennifer. I know exactly what you mean. Like, you're not trying to buy the whole telephone company—you just want a phone, right? Honestly I wish I could, you know, do something about it. These deposits are just ridic'lous, Jennifer, I know what you mean. But I guess the company just gets ripped off so many times they just got to have these big, you know, deposits."

She writes out a check for a whopping payment, still startled by the way the sales clerk keeps calling her Jennifer. She supposes she'll have to get used to the creepy ersatz intimacy with which these Californians instantly take to calling total strangers by their first names.

She thinks, At least it's getting me used to being called, you know, like, Jennifer.

It reminds her how Bert always insisted on calling her Madeleine. Never a nickname, never the diminutive Matty. Madeleine in full—and he treated you as if you were a fragile porcelain art work.

It's so easy now to recognize all the clues he left strewn about—how is it possible to have been so unaware for so long?

Something to do with what you're looking for, she supposes; something to do with what you want from the world.

When she married Bert that was the life she thought she wanted. Fast lane: the designer milieu, the tony friends, the money. Put it crudely then: Bert was on a power trip and you were callow enough to enjoy the ride.

It would have taken a saintly kind of wisdom to turn it down.

Face it, Matty-Madeleine-Jennifer, you were a young woman adrift and the shore was receding at a steady rate: you were happy to tie yourself to the towline that Bert offered.

For sure you weren't going anyplace else important at the time.

You started with plenty of advantages, didn't you. A beautiful child with a brain. Parents loving and just—but of the old school. Sometimes painfully embarrassing: remember when you were fourteen and Dad was assigned to cadre at Fort Ord. He'd taken you and Mom down to the Monterey beach that Sunday morning and you'd had lunch in Carmel and cruised some of the art galleries. You were in the eighth grade having trouble with plane geometry and still getting used to wearing a bra and interested in horses more than boys. On the way home that afternoon Dad was telling you about Appaloosa horses and how the Nez Perce Indians in Idaho had developed the breed—he knew a great deal about native Americans and he was convinced there was Indian blood in the family, somewhere vaguely back four or five generations.

Caught up in his Appaloosa discourse he didn't spot the Highway Patrol cruiser in time.

He made a face and pulled over. She heard the dying cry of the siren. The trooper walked forward with a hand on his holster and stooped to peer into the car. Dad kept both hands on the wheel. When the trooper saw the major's pips on the shoulders of Dad's uniform he drew back deferentially and began to put his citation book away but Dad glared sternly at him and said too loudly, "Absolutely right, officer. I had my mind on something else and I was going over the limit. You've got me fair and square. Go ahead and write out the ticket. It'll remind me to keep my eye on the speedometer."

Painfully obvious that all this was for your benefit. An act to impress you with the importance of honest confession and respect for the law. It was almost comical. Later you and Mom had a laugh over it.

But his performances and his lectures worked, didn't they. Growing up you had values. You paid attention in all those schools you went to, trailing around to Dad's stationings in Germany and South Korea and Alaska. You could figure out the square root of a four-figure number; you could dissect a frog; you could recognize a Rembrandt—or an O'Keeffe— and you could hum Bach melodies on key; and there was a time when you could recite Shelley from memory: "Look upon my works, ye Mighty, and despair!"

Of course you had to rebel against all that. Why must we all behave with such hackneyed predictability? You came to New York determined to put that staid middle-American goody-two-shoes personality as far behind you as you could leave it: you came determined to kick up your heels like some rustic rube farm girl coming to the big city in the flapper era and discovering speakeasies for the first time. You came in search of excitement and you found it; you came in search of a glamorous career and you found one.

It turned out to be not all that glamorous, really. But don't they all.

After all, you didn't abandon your upbringing entirely. You weren't enough of a rebel; not then. A year or two of mindless diversions—then you found yourself on a date in the Whitney and soon you were going to the ballet at Lincoln Center, listening to good music, reading books again—no longer because it was what you were supposed to do but now because it was what gave you pleasure.

You made friends easily enough. Both men and women. Most of the men were attached or gay. The eligibles were hard to find; some of them were frightened off by your beauty— others by your wit. Mostly they just seemed terribly immature and dull.

There was Sylvan, of course—forty-six and distin- guished, a cultivated marvelous man—it was Sylvan who took you to the Whitney—but he was married and not inclined to get a divorce and you couldn't bring yourself to rationalize being a kept woman.

There was Richard and then there was Chris. Several years apart. The memories now are jumbled: moving in, min- gling the furniture—later the break-ups, the bleak sad search for another lonely apartment. And the quest beginning over again: for passion or affection or just (settle for it) companionship.

All too suddenly you were pushing thirty and in the morning you'd look fearfully in the mirror expecting to find a new crease in the beautiful skin.

It began to occur to you that you couldn't go on living this aimless life. You didn't want to think about that but now and then you'd have a premonition: a vision of yourself at thirty-seven trying to get work posing for lingerie ads in cheap mail-order catalogs and accepting some tedious schlemiel's marriage proposal out of desperation, knowing it would be good—at best—for four or five years of domestic boredom and financial security and another few years of alimony: you even saw yourself thereafter, midfortyish and fifteen pounds overweight, working as office manager for a chiropractor and making reservations for ten days at a Club Med: over the hill and desperate.

In that context Bert looked like more than a good bargain. He looked like a heaven-sent dream.

Remembering marrying him—remembering *why* she married him—she feels soiled.

Then of course the other question: Why did Bert marry *me*?

He professed nothing cornball; you couldn't expect Bert to deliver himself of pronouncements of loving devotion. The nearest he ever came was that remark about wanting you to be the mother of his children. There probably was quite a bit of truth in that. He had his head full of pop theories about genes and heredity. More than once he brought out her album of family photographs (she remembers, with a pang, leaving it behind) and showed it to their friends and boasted, as if they were his own ancestors, about her handsome grandparents and tall regal Great Aunt Irma who'd lived healthily into her 102nd year. He'd exult: "Look at that bone structure!"

But there was another factor as well, one crucially important to the role he envisioned for himself. He was climbing to new strata and he wanted a wife: visible, presentable, cultivated, respectable.

He wanted you because you decorated his life.

Did I ever love him?

Yes, she thinks; let's be honest; you did love him. You'd have done anything for him. You'd have given your life for him.

And now?

Now it has been cruelly reversed. Now that you're no longer prepared to give it, Bert will gladly take your life.

If he finds you.

21 She keeps opening accounts with the money she's brought west. The forty bearer bonds are each worth $10,000 but most of the rest is still in wrapped bundles of $1,000 bills, awkward to negotiate because they draw attention.

The best she can do is to change no more than one or two bills in any particular bank.

The bearer bonds are easy to convert—she visits the financial houses and sells the first half of the bonds one or two at a time and uses the proceeds to open small trading accounts: insignificant stock portfolios.

Her tongue keeps prodding the bonding on her front teeth. The gap between teeth is gone but her mouth feels like a stranger's.

Exchanging her cash for cashiers' checks and money orders—she thinks of it wryly as laundering the loot—she sets about investing the money: buying treasury bills and certificates of deposit; opening interest-bearing bank accounts; going into three money market funds, each through a different broker because it is important to keep it all in scattered places and in sums too small to provoke anyone's interest. She even opens an IRA on the chance she may survive long enough to need a retirement account.

The thought provokes a cringe of desperation: barely a month now to the deadline and so much to do.

She has left about half the money in the safety-deposit boxes; in a week or two she'll take it along on a quick trip to Nevada and open accounts there in the name of Dorothy Holder.

Converting the first half of the money has used up tankfuls of gasoline and when all the transactions have been completed she has two safety-deposit boxes filled with bankbooks and account statements; there is no more than $20,000 in any one place but the total is short of $500,000 by only the few thousand she's spent since the adventure began.

There is still half a million for the Nevada accounts—and she hasn't touched the diamonds.

Those are Ellen's.

22 "A little more aileron. Left foot," Charlie Reid says. Then in exasperation: "Your *other* left, my beauty."

"Sorry."

She depresses the pedal. The plane has been sliding; now it banks and continues to turn.

She attempts to line up the nose with the mountain pass twenty miles away—she's learned by now that it is called the Grapevine—and the plane skitters disobediently. She still isn't comfortable with the unfamiliar feel of the controls.

Whoever said it's just like learning to drive a car is an imbecile.

Charlie is talking into the radio mike and she hears the tower grant clearance; at least she assumes that is what is being discussed. There's so much crackling noise in the head-set earphones that she can make out barely one word in five. They all sound alike and they all seem to understand one another perfectly but to her it is as much of a foreign tongue as it was on the first day.

Charlie says something to her.

She peels one earphone away. "What?"

"We're cleared to land. Go ahead."

She stretches her body up to lean to her left and peer down through the window. Where the hell's the Goddamned airport?

Everything looks alike. Cars and trucks are toys moving slowly along the monotonous grid of streets; the roofs, the yards, the trees, the bright blue swimming pools—thousands of them, all identical, and you never see anyone swimming in them.

She tells herself that's because the inhabitants are indoors struggling with their own strife-ripped dualities of darkness and light. Never mind the bright landscape from the air. Cowering inside the boulevard shops and tract houses are creatures of despair, seducing and beseeching and murdering one another. She's thinking: Count your blessings, Jennifer Hartman. You think you've got it bad? Look down there.

That's the sort of pep talk she's been inflicting on herself lately. It doesn't do a very good job of persuading her. It's hard to sympathize with strangers when you're only one or two jumps ahead of the men with guns.

Wouldn't it be funny, she thinks, if they weren't after

63

me at all? What if they've given up and written me off?

Suppose nobody's looking for me?

After all, there's no evidence they're there.

Suppose it's all in my imagination.

All this effort . . .

But she knows them better than that.

By the time she finds the airport she is nearly above it. She's forced to go around in a wide circle and try again. Charlie is on the microphone apologizing, explaining things to the tower.

The runway moves from side to side within the frame of the windshield. It is coming up at her and the angle looks all wrong. She feels disoriented.

"Easy now," he says. "Gentle down. You're all over the sky. Just point the plane like a rifle. Honey child, you ever done any shooting?"

"Yes."

"Aim it then."

"I wasn't very good at it."

He says drily, "Bring the nose up now and cut your power back."

She pulls the wheel toward her and is relieved when the angle of glide flattens out: it no longer has quite the feeling of going into the ground like a falling coconut. She reaches for the throttle.

"Slowly," he admonishes. "We don't want to stall, do we, dear."

The runway keeps wavering from one side to the other. The buzz of the engine throbs in her every bone; she can barely hear him when he says, "A little bit less throttle now. Put your nose down just a hair."

She endeavors to earn his approval but the dreadful machine fails to cooperate.

"Baby doll, try to straighten out. You're flying like some kind of pendulum. I'm getting seasick. Bet you forgot

64

what I told you, didn't you. Pretend the runway's a road and you're driving your car down a ramp to it."

The plane tilts. She tries to right it. It tilts the other way.

Charlie says, "Easy. For God's sake."

The ground is coming up fast again; she realizes it's too fast—the angle just isn't shallow enough—and then the airplane lurches into a trough that feels bottomless: her stomach pops right up into her throat and she hears his groan and then she feels the controls move under her hands and feet when he takes over.

Halfway down the runway the wheels touch and then he is slamming the throttle forward and the yoke comes back toward her and the acceleration presses her back in the seat. The plane bounces and roars. A quick red haze slides down over her eyes.

She feels it soar. Down out of her side window she sees the earth pirouette, spinning as it drops away.

He levels it off. "You want to try again now?"

Something comes up into her throat and she has to swallow.

He says, "In other words you don't want to do it again right now."

"Give me a minute to catch my breath."

"Darling, you can have all afternoon. You're paying by the hour." Then he speaks sotto voce to himself but she hears him distinctly enough; she is meant to: "And I can't imagine a bigger waste of time and money."

"I'm going to learn to fly this thing if it kills me."

"No," he says. "You mean if it kills *me*."

She draws a long breath. "Okay Charlie. Let's do it again."

"Shee-yit."

23 On the fourth approach he keeps his hands off the yoke and she lands the airplane by herself. To be sure it is one tire at a time: there's a good deal of bouncing and pitching but she manages. She even remembers to steer with the pedals instead of the wheel.

She brings it to a stop at the edge of the pavement. "Do you want me to take it in?"

"Thanks just the same."

He taps her hands. She lifts them off the controls. Charlie taxis toward the hangar and idles into the parking slot, fitting it neatly between an Aercoupe and a Bonanza and cutting the ignition. Then he sits tense and still with his eyes squeezed shut. His huge hands engulf the control yoke.

She says, "You don't have to make a comedy act out of it."

He pushes the door open and swings his legs out onto the strut. He needs to climb out carefully because he's so big; he tends to bang his head and he's always getting caught in spaces another man might negotiate with a foot of room to spare.

Without waiting to help her he drops down off the step and walks away toward the hangar.

She smiles slightly, knowing him a bit now. She's confident he'll go for it. He's as good as most—and as inconsistent—but he's not all bluff. And he's got his mercenary side.

A good thing too because time's getting very short. It's August 8. Four weeks from today they'll have left Fort Keene and it will be too late.

If Charlie refuses there'll be very little time to get someone else.

She's going to have to put it to him today. No later than tonight.

She watches him go into the hangar. The heavy rolling gait is peculiar to him: as though he were a sailor on a wildly swiveling deck. He seems to hesitate before planting each foot, as if to make sure first that there's solid ground under it.

After a moment she follows him through the hangar. Two of the Beechcraft mechanics are working on a plane; they both wave to her and she smiles back. She stops at the coffee machine and plugs quarters into it and carries two cups of the wretched swill around the corner into Charlie's sanctum. She finds him in the chair with his elbows on the desk and his face in his hands.

She puts his coffee in front of him and tastes her own. "I wouldn't've thought it was possible to get used to this stuff."

"I once thought it was possible to get used to anything," he says.

"What changed your mind?"

"You did, my love."

"Am I supposed to be flattered or is that another joke?"

He says: "Some people are born piano players and some people are born aviators."

"And I am not one of the latter."

"You don't have the instincts, my beauty. Listen. A few years ago my kid was in a rock band. High school combo. They played for club dances and things. A couple appearances on some local public-access cable TV channel.

"They were all eleventh graders except this one guy who played the Fender bass. He was a senior and he graduated and went back East to college, and Mike's senior year the kids had to find themselves another bass player."

His voice rumbles around the room, throwing ominous

echoes. She enjoys the sound of it but she knows how a man's deep voice can deceive by making him sound as if he's got answers for everything.

"They hunted around school," he says, "talked to the music teacher, all that, and it ended up they auditioned about five kids for the job. In my garage. I heard them all. Couldn't tell much difference—all that junk sounds the same to me. Kids' music always sounds like crap to a parent. I grew up on the jitterbug—I hear that stuff now, it sounds like crap even to me. We just couldn't have been that naive.

"Now there was this one kid they auditioned from the school marching band, played the tuba, but he knew how to play the bass and he was by far the most accomplished musician of the bunch. You give him the notes, he can play them—almost never makes a mistake. Mike said this guy was the best-trained technician he'd ever heard."

He goes on: "But they turned him down. They went for another kid instead. Because this guy, the earnest zealot with all the training, he stood there like a lump and just played the notes. He didn't have the music in his bones. He heard it—but he didn't *feel* it. How'd they put it? They said he just didn't have soul."

"I had a feeling there'd be a moral to this story."

"Honey sweet, you may be the world's greatest pole-vaulter for all I know but you ain't got the soul of an airplane driver. You study long and hard, you'll memorize enough to get you a license, but every time you go up in the air you're going to be scared of the aircraft. You're never going to have a feel for it."

"Why are you so anxious to do yourself out of a paying customer?"

He smiles briefly: he can be surprisingly gentle. "Baby love, you're not going to make a good pilot. And if you can't do it well, why do it at all? Take up water skiing or horseback riding or amateur theatricals."

She doesn't reply. She watches him. Charlie sips coffee and makes a face. "We having dinner tonight?"

"That depends."

He gives her a straight look. He has an airman's blue grey eyes and when he isn't being sardonic they seem morose. The random thought crosses her mind that if you were filming *The Charlie Reid Story* you could cast Robert Mitchum in the title role. Charlie doesn't carry his eyes at half mast and he doesn't really look like the actor but he's got a similar resonance and he presents to the world a rough facade that hides a good ear and an ironic intelligence.

Charlie says, "I wish I could tell when you're really mad. Everything's an act with you."

"When I'm really mad you'll know it." She perches a hip against the desk; there's only one chair in the tiny room and he's sitting on it. She glances at the ten-year-old snapshot of Michael above his head. The kid's big-jawed face has the same effect as Charlie's: a little shifty and a littly ugly but somehow you know that against your better judgment you're going to like him.

"Does he still play in a band?"

"They've got a little group. Sorority dances and such. Just casual stuff. They have fun."

"What instrument does he play?"

"Saxophone."

"Is he good?"

"Put it this way. He's enthusiastic."

She pictures the kid—tall now and hulking like his dad. Honking into a saxophone, trying to sound lyrical. Probably has girls hanging all over him.

She says, "What did you do in the Air Force?"

"Flew fighters."

"Vietnam?"

"I did a couple tours. You want us to talk about my war crimes now?"

69

"Did you commit any?"

"I made a deal with myself not to wear sackcloth and ashes the rest of my life. You get tired of examining the philosophy of what constitutes being a Good German and what constitutes being a normal human critter. You get tired of trying to define what's a crime in those kinds of circumstances. It's about as useful as counting angels on the head of a pin."

Then he adds: "I never was much on moral introspection. I don't feel warped about it. I don't think it turned me into a hero or a maniac. I went there, flew airplanes, did what I was told most of the time. Tried to keep my self-respect, stayed alive, came home."

"You retired as a light colonel."

He gives her a quick look and she realizes her mistake. No one must ever know she's an Air Force brat. She's not supposed to know the jargon.

She's relieved when he lets it pass. He says, "I was a major. Deputy squadron CO. They wanted to promote me to a desk. Said I was getting too old to keep flying. So then I took my retirement—I was thirty-eight. Maybe that is too old to fly jets. I like piston planes better anyway. They're for *fun*, you know?"

She points to the old map on the wall. "Were you a mercenary?"

"I flew in Africa a few times. You like asking questions, don't you."

"I'm curious about you."

He says, "I'm kind of curious too. I don't even know what you do for a living."

"I own part of a bookstore." She's pleased to be able to say it with such ingenuousness.

"You sure in hell don't look it." He's drinking coffee; his eyes over the rim of the cup are examining her body frankly. When he puts the cup down his eyes droop with

70

amusement and his mouth opens and he actually begins to laugh.

"What's funny?"

"Thinking about the first time you walked in here. Soaked to the skin."

She stands up. She remembers his lewd leer at the time. To cover her abrupt self-consciousness she says, "Why didn't you get an airline job?"

"I'm not rated for multiengine jets."

"You could learn."

"I doubt I'd like it much."

"You were born too late. You should have been a barnstormer."

"Sleeping out under the wing of my Jenny. You think I never dreamt of that?"

Then he says: "Let me recommend Chez Charlie Reid. One and a half stars in the Michelin guide. It's a dump but the cook does a pretty good patio barbecue. You like rib steak?"

24 It is about half an hour's drive from the airfield to Doyle and Marian's bookshop in Burbank. She has made a discovery about the Valley: wherever you start from, you're half an hour from your destination.

That half hour conveniently is the running time of one side of a standard audio tape cassette. The car has a built-in player. (Apparently every car in California has one.) For camouflage she has tuned all the buttons of the car radio to innocuous mood music stations but the player overrides the radio as soon as you insert a tape.

Now she carries in her handbag several cassettes—baroque music mainly, and Mozart—and she knows it's cheating but she can't bear the thought of giving up good music for the rest of her life. She's made a pact to listen to it only when she's alone.

In the East a car was transportation. Here it is a cocoon: Californians spend half their lives in their cars; they drive everywhere with windows rolled up and air conditioners blasting even in mild weather—you see them jammed up on the freeways alone in their cars, sealed in, shouting soundlessly, gesticulating to the beat of the programs they've turned up to top volume. When you glimpse them it's always startling: they're like mime characters in an absurdist fragment of silent film, the plot of which hasn't been revealed to you.

At the interchange she's looking in the mirror while she negotiates the exit ramp from the San Diego Freeway to the Ventura Freeway. Two cars behind her take the same turns.

When she merges into the eastbound traffic she uses side mirror and indicator to ease over into the far right lane. The two cars are still back there: a rust red one and a boxy black sedan. They seem to hover in the mirror.

The traffic is clotted here, moving fitfully, backed up behind the exit for Van Nuys Boulevard, and it is only out in the far left lane that things move smoothly.

She watches the two cars go by in the fast lane. One of them has four teenage Valley Girls in it; the black sedan is driven by an old man with a scowl. He's gesticulating with one hand and talking to himself. It looks like a violent argument.

That's all right then.

She moves back into the faster lanes, listening to the *Magic Flute* overture, thinking wryly of a stale joke: help—the paranoids are after me.

Sometimes it seems so silly. Is it all only a melodramatic fantasy?

Maybe—maybe.

But suppose you choose to behave on the basis of that hypothesis—and suppose the hypothesis is incorrect.

It'll be a little late to change your mind when they've dragged you back to him and he's killed you.

She thinks about stopping at the apartment on Lankershim for the mail. Too hot. Do it later.

Poking along on the freeway she's remembering her visit to Ray Seale last winter. That was the day when anxiety finally drove her beyond speculation into decision.

For the umptieth time she rehearses it in her mind: has she forgotten anything he told her? Done anything wrong?

She tries to review the details of the meeting.

25 It must have been not long after New Year's Day. She remembers how she contrived it to look like a coincidental encounter.

She drove to Newark early that morning and went into the building where Ray Seale had his office, examined the building directory, and chose from it Dennis Nobles, D.C., P.C., and made a mental note of the suite number: 1127.

She got the number from Information and made an appointment from a pay phone in the lobby and then she took the elevator down two flights to the garage level and got in her car and locked the doors.

She waited more than an hour and had started to decide he wasn't coming to the office today when she saw him drive in and park the Eldorado in the slot with his name on it. He waved to the garage attendant and walked toward the elevator.

It was ten after ten. She got out of her white Mercedes and went after him.

He was wearing a narrow steel-colored suit. His hard heels—Italian leather—struck the concrete floor with a crisp echoing that made her think of dice. He pushed a finger into the depressed plastic square and it lit up and he waited for the doors to open.

She came up beside him and gave the button an unnecessary push. She didn't look at him; better to let him make the discovery for himself.

At first he gave her a surreptitious sidewise glance. Then a more direct look: surprise and recognition. Then hesitation—he'd be thinking about whether to speak or hold his tongue.

If he'd been less brash he'd have let it go. Knowing who she was he might have been afraid to speak to her; he could have pretended he didn't recognize her—they'd only met once, after all, and it had been a crowded dinner party.

But she was counting on his nerve and he didn't fail her.

Big beaming grin. "Hi. Mrs. LaCasse, isn't it? Hello there."

She gave him a startled look and one of those polite smiles you use when you're accosted by someone you don't recognize.

The elevator door opened and he held it for her. "Ray Seale? We met a few months ago at the Sertics'?"

"Of course." She let the smile grow broader. "You're the detective."

"You got it." You could see how pleased he was that she remembered him. He punched a button.

She said, "Would you push eleven please?"

"You bet."

The doors slid shut and his eyes drifted restlessly down her body, unclothing her. She put on the polite smile again. "Are you—'on a case'? Is that how you put it?"

"No ma'am. Just going to work. My office is on twelve."

"Why, I didn't know you were in this building. It's my first time here. I have a little trouble with my lower back . . . someone told me Dr. Nobles is a very good chiropractor."

"That so? I've got a little back trouble myself now and then. Good to know."

The car stopped on the ground floor and several people boarded. She moved back into the corner and watched Ray Seale. He seemed uneasy; at first he gave her a little smile but then he stood with his head thrown back, watching the illuminated numbers climb. He didn't speak again until the last of the other passengers got off at the ninth floor. Then he waited for the doors to close and said in a voice that was too offhand, "If you feel like it come on up and visit the office when you get done at the doctor's."

"I wouldn't want to disturb you."

"Be a pleasure to have some distraction from paperwork and telephones." The doors had opened; he held his thumb on a button to keep them from closing. "Come on up. Show you how the real investigators operate."

"Well, thank you very much. If you're sure it won't be a disruption."

She stepped off the elevator and smiled at him until the doors shut.

On the remote chance that Seale might decide to check up on her story she made good on the chiropractic appointment, spent twenty minutes filling out a detailed medical history form, read part of an article about the world series of poker in an old *New Yorker* and submitted to half an hour's chaste examination by the bald doctor, who listened to her complaint about recurring pains in the lower back and pre-

scribed a number of exercises she could do at home and told
her to come back Monday morning to begin a program of
traction-machine treatments and chiropractic manipulations.

She thanked him very much and went out to the desk
and made a Monday appointment that she would cancel later
by telephone if she got everything she needed today from Ray
Seale.

It was half past eleven when she went up to his office.
The black legend on the frosted glass panels of the double
entrance doors was in big bold lettering to inspire confidence.
Seale & Edwards—Confidential Investigations.

The opening of the door made a bell jingle. There was
a bullpen—eight desks behind a wooden railing. It was half
occupied: three men and one woman on telephones and typ-
ing and reading stapled documents.

Most of them glanced up when she entered. The jingle
of the bell above the door drew Ray Seale out of the private
office across the room; he smiled when he recognized her.

An acned receptionist at a desk, fat rump overflowing
the seat of her chair, was on the phone:

"I'm sorry. That's Mr. Edwards' special field. No, I'm
afraid we haven't got anybody else in the firm who can handle
that kind of thing. Mr. Edwards? No, I'm sorry, he's away on
an important case. No telling how long he may be gone . . ."

She hung up and winked at Ray Seale, who came forward to greet his visitor. As he passed the reception desk and
opened the low gate in the railing he said, "Who dat?"

"Some woman wanted us to find her Pekingese. I told
her Mr. Edwards was away."

"Old Edwards does spend a lot of time away, don't
he."

He turned and welcomed her with a gesture and explained: "There's no Edwards. Never has been. Seale & Edwards is a corporate name I just made up when I went into
business for myself. In the event of complaints it's useful to

have a partner to pass the buck to. And there's always the cases you don't want to take."

His smile was sly; his mannerisms were lubriciously ingratiating. He was narrow and slight with pointed shoulders and the small clever dark eyes of a ferret. His hair—possibly a hairpiece—was the color of dark stained oak, combed carefully into a high prow that jutted forward above his forehead; he probably thought it made him taller and more attractive. The face was boyish and unlined but there was a crosshatching of creases at his neck under the chin; he had to be well up in his forties, trying to pass for thirty-five. You got the feeling about him that there was an excess of oil in his skin and his hair.

He swept an arm around, indicating the bullpen. "Here's where we do the job. You see four desks unattended. That's because I've got a kid and two ex-cops out chasing leads this morning. That fourth desk belongs to a redheaded girl never turns up before ten-thirty, eleven, but that's all right. Girl's got the most amazing telephone voice—she can seduce more information over the phone than you can believe."

He dropped his voice to a confidential level. "She's got beady crosseyes and ugly buck teeth but you can't see that on the telephone. She can come in at four in the afternoon for all I care, long as she keeps producing the kind of results she's been getting. Well come on in the private office here. Gloria, this is Mrs. LaCasse."

The name made its impression on the receptionist; she all but stood up. "Pleased to meet you, ma'am."

Ray Seale showed her into the office and shut the door. It was redolent of stale essence of cigar. Halfway to his desk he hesitated. "I hope you don't mind. I always keep it shut. No point having the employees think I'm spying on them."

She gave permission by not commenting on it. She

said, "So this is where you work," as if it mattered to her.

"Yes ma'am. How's your back? That chiropractor do you some good?"

"It was just a consultation. I gather he'll have more to tell me next week, after he's done some X-rays."

"I hope it works out all right. Nothing worse than back pain."

"Thank you."

She looked out through the sooty windows at the Newark skyline. There were piles of half-melted snow on the rooftops.

Ray Seale followed the direction of her glance and said, "Town always manages to look like Dresden right after the Allies got done bombing it. Not a terrific view, is it. I'd move away like a shot if business wasn't so good here. But if your trade's repossessing cars and televisions, skip-tracing characters that run out on their creditors or their families, ain't no place better for business than a city where *everybody's* behind on their payments."

"It must be fascinating work."

"No. Mostly routine. Have a seat there. Can we get you some coffee or something?"

"No thank you. I really can't stay. But I do think it's very exciting, the work you do."

He was watching her with a peculiar intensity when she sat down. Then he said: "It's really kind of uncanny, you know? You look just like a woman I saw in Atlantic City, must've been three, four years ago. Could that have been you?"

"No. I've never been there."

"Strangest thing." Ray Seale leaned back in his swivel chair. "I remember some guy was on a hot streak and she'd been betting against him and she'd lost her stack and I watched her walk away from the table. She didn't seem to be with anybody. But I was on a case—I had to take over for one of my men that got sick. And the subject was right there at the dice table and there wasn't no choice, I had to wait him out and then keep following him around town until the guy led me to the Olds or the Buick or whatever it was the bank was paying us to repo.

"Funny thing. I don't even remember anymore whether I got the car back. I do remember going back to the casino and looking for that blond lady. The floor manager remembered her all right. So did a couple of cocktail waitresses and three of the dealers I talked to. But none of them ever seen her before and nobody knew anything about her.

"So I just had the one glimpse of her. Saw her maybe thirty seconds out of my whole lifetime but I still remember her and you are absolutely a dead ringer for that lady. Isn't that remarkable? You mind me talking this way?"

It sounded like a variant of the archaic "Haven't I seen you somewhere before" gambit but she didn't think that was it. He was a feisty little rat but she was sure he was too sly to risk insulting Mrs. Albert LaCasse.

She presented to him another of her cool smiles, one calculated to remind him of his station relative to hers. She said, "I'm sure it wasn't me you saw. I don't gamble."

"You must have a twin sister then."

"No. Just coincidence, I suppose—like my being in this building today."

"Must be," he agreed. "Hard to believe there's two like you walking around. You're a real good-looking woman, Mrs. LaCasse. I hope you don't mind me saying so. Your husband's a real fortunate man."

"Nice of you to say so. I suppose in your business you must come across quite a few cases of unusual resemblances. Mistaken identity."

"Oh sure. Nothing less reliable than an eyewitness. Look how I just mistook you for someone else. Happens all the time."

"That must make it fun when you're trying to find someone who's disappeared."

"Well—sometimes that's a fact, yes ma'am. In fact I recall a case . . ."

She heard him out—a rambling tale—and when he beamed so she could appreciate the punch line she said, "I like to read detective stories but I gather there isn't much truth in them. Tell me something—I'm fascinated by what you do—suppose someone, oh, let's say a woman like me. Suppose I disappeared one day without a trace. How would you go about looking for me? What do you call it again—skip-tracing?"

"Yes ma'am."

He gave her a smile that tried to curry favor. "That would depend on whether you disappeared on purpose. Some people meet with accidents or foul play. That's a different matter. When a person disappears, first thing you do is normally check all the hospitals, emergency services, friends and relatives of the subject, business associates. Thing is, is that you'd be surprised how many people go away on a business trip—something just came up, you know, spur of the moment—and maybe they forget to tell the wife about it. Half the time you just ask the guy's secretary, she knows exactly where he is, what hotel he's staying in, all that stuff. Case closed. See, the first thing you do is just ask sensible questions."

"Of course," she said, "but let's suppose someone has deliberately disappeared. Say you're looking for a woman who's married to a drunk or something. Say he beats her all the time and she's just got to get away from him—far away, where he'll never find her again. And say the husband hires you to bring her back. How do you find her?"

She knew people tended to be flattered when you asked them about what they did. She'd learned that in a previous life. And it proved easy to draw him out. He sat back and lit a small cigar—it didn't occur to him to ask if she minded—and said, "Well, first you'd go back to the public records. You find out where she was born, the family background, where she went to school. You check out voting registration, driver's license, credit files. All this is perfectly legal, you understand. Public records are open to the public. Anyway you build up this jacket on the subject—that's a fact file. Have you got time, Mrs. LaCasse?"

"I have a luncheon appointment but I can be a little late. Go on. I'm intrigued."

"Let's see. Okay, you check with the subject's doctor and dentist. Family and friends. Chances are some of them have heard from the subject. People have to have their medical records forwarded—for insurance applications or maybe they go into a hospital for some disease and the hospital needs a history on the patient. Whatever. Sometimes people just can't help getting in touch with their mothers or fathers or sisters or brothers. Or their children."

"But some of them must be smart enough not to get in touch with people that way."

"Some are, sure. There's still ways. A lot of skips seem to figure all they need to do is move to another state and they're safe. It's such a big country, you know, two hundred and forty million people, seems so easy to lose yourself out there. A lot of skips don't even bother to change their names. It's a hassle, changing your name. You got to start all over with fresh documents, new identification from scratch—it's hard work. So a lot of people just keep their name and their Social Security number and all that. They move someplace halfway across the country and they apply for a driver's license and open a bank account and *bang*, it's in the computer and we got 'em.

"Credit applications, that's another one. We buy the subject's old credit applications from companies that the subject got an account with. We just keep developing facts that way. A friend of mine, investigator out west in Marin County, he likes to say the thing about facts is, is that you put them together and it's like sex, they produce more facts. So you work the facts. You contact the oil companies and half the time you find out the subject left a trail of gasoline credit card charges all the way across the country right to the new doorstep. You get in touch with the company, you give the subject's name, you say you're the subject. Maybe you act angry. You complain you haven't been receiving your bills and you don't want to risk your credit rating. You think maybe they got the wrong forwarding address and you ask what address the bills are being mailed to."

The thin cigar had grown a tall ash. He tapped it into a glass tray on the desk.

He'd warmed to the subject just as he had that night at the dinner table. He said: "Around Christmas, New Year's, if it's a priority subject and a real dead skip—I mean one where all the leads have turned up empty—sometimes in the holidays we'll post people on stakeouts or we'll drive around and do spot checks on the relatives. A lot of skips just can't help going home for Christmas. Sometimes we just offer a reward and tell the relatives about it. You'd be surprised how many people turn in their own brothers for a thousand dollars.

"Sometimes we try to use the Internal Revenue. They're not supposed to give out information but sometimes you can get through. You tell them you're on the bookkeeping computer at ex-wye-zee company, you've got a W-2 or a 1099 form that you need to send to this person but it came back address unknown and maybe does the IRS have a forwarding address for this person so he can get his taxes straight. I've used that one a dozen times. It's illegal, of course, but I guess we all know you don't get much done if you don't bend the regulations a little, just now and then."

She remembers how his sycophantic wink made her feel soiled. The cigar had gone out; he relit it with a plastic lighter. "If you've got some idea what part of the country the subject may have headed for, you call the phone company out there, you ask for the New Listings Operator. Sometimes that gets you an address.

"You keep tabs on the subject's boyfriend or girlfriend

if there was one. A lot of people, especially women, skip out because they've been having an affair with a married man and he plans to take off in three weeks and meet her in Yucatan or Hawaii or something. So you ask around, secretaries and whoever the subject used to work with, and if you hear rumors about an extramarital affair you keep tabs on the boyfriend.

"Now you'll get divorced people where one of the parents doesn't like the court's ruling on child custody, so the parent steals his own kids or her own kids. Cases like that, where the kids are school age, we call up the school where the kids used to go. I say I'm the principal out here in Tulsa and I'm inquiring about the transcripts for these kids. And usually I'll find out the transcripts have already been sent out to a school in Boise, Idaho. Bingo.

"Even the worst cases get solved sooner or later. Most of them.

"See, the thing is, is that people tend to stay with the same social level. They're comfortable with their own kind of people and they seek out those kind of people. Eventually, see, there's going to be a coincidence. Eventually they're going to run into somebody from their old life that recognizes them. Maybe right away, maybe five years down the road. But it'll happen. It always does. There's only one way to prevent it, and that's when they make themselves over into a totally different person. New interests, new social class, new everything. And there just aren't a whole lot of people capable of doing that.

"And even *then* we get them sometimes. People make mistakes. And that's what we look for, mistakes."

He poked the cigar in his mouth, squinted through the smoke, spread both hands out with palms up and gave her a nasty little smile. "That's how we do it, Mrs. LaCasse. And notice at no time do my fingers leave my hands."

He chuckled at his little joke and she managed to smile appreciatively before she said:

"It's utterly fascinating. I don't—look. Let's take it from the other end for a moment. Just hypothetically. It's just so interesting. Do you mind? Suppose you take an ordinary housewife. Suppose one day she decides to disappear without a trace, and suppose, oh, let's say she knows her husband is likely to hire someone like you to find her and she wants to make sure she doesn't get found. How would a person go about disappearing so completely that even you couldn't find him?"

"Ordinary woman, ordinary husband? I guess she might get away with it if she knew how. But of course that'd be different with somebody like you, Mrs. LaCasse. Somebody with a husband like yours, I mean."

"That goes without saying." She smiled yet again. "But I *am* curious."

"I'll tell you then. Your ordinary housewife in South Orange, you mean. There's a lot of things she might do.

"For openers she'd have to clean out her bank accounts in cash and then throw away her checkbooks and all her credit cards.

"Best way to do that's put it all in a wallet and let somebody else lay a false trail for her.

"How she does that, there's a dozen ways. Railroad station's pretty good. Trailways depots are okay. Airports aren't so good because people tend to be a little more honest about lost possessions.

"Anyhow maybe she just gets on a turnpike in the direction opposite to the direction she's really heading. She'd stop in one of those service area Howard Johnson's and leave the wallet in the ladies' room. Make it look like she left it behind by mistake. You know how women empty out their handbags when they're trying to find the lipstick.

"The wallet may get turned in and returned to the husband, in which case he's got a lead in the wrong direction, but people bein' what they are it's more likely somebody steals the wallet. Next thing you know they'll be passing bad checks and running up credit card charges two hundred miles away, laying down a beautiful false trail for you. Am I boring you?"

She gave him another smile and tried to hide its insincerity. "If I get bored I'll yawn. Go on, please."

He did.

26 Getting off the freeway at Pass Avenue she is looking in the rear-view mirror again. It has become a habit too strong to break. And she's thinking it would be a tasty irony if Ray Seale has been hired to find her: an irony because his life will hardly be worth a thimbleful of dust if it ever gets out that he's the very one who taught her how to vanish.

It's half-past three and hot. Doyle and Marian are sitting at one of the outdoor tables in the corral of Buffalo Bill's Saloon, having what is probably not their first drink of the afternoon.

Graeme Goldsmith is with them.

Damn.

As she parks in front of a wagon wheel someone meanders into the bookshop and she sees Doyle get up from his table and carry his drink toward the shop. Mustache twitching in anticipation, he waves to her as she gets out of the car, then disappears inside in hope the customer is more than a browser.

She leaves the windows open and the car unlocked. There's nothing in it worth stealing and if you close the windows it's a furnace when you get back in.

There's no graceful escape. She joins Marian and the Australian in the shade of the table's umbrella.

Graeme lifts his beer toward her in a casual welcoming gesture. Coming from him it is at best a meaningless courtesy. He's made it clear enough that he doesn't like her. Perhaps it's her personality; perhaps he just doesn't like women.

In either case she feels no obligation to change his sentiments.

As she sits down, George, the aged waiter, saunters out from his post in the shade. Marian says, "An iced tea for herself, honey."

"That's lemon, no sugar, right?"

Jennifer—she thinks of herself as Jennifer now—confirms it with a nod and George retreats.

Marian says, "So anyway—sorry, Jennifer honey, just finishing the story—anyway," she says to Graeme in her prairie twang, "Nick used to come around once in a while with a jug and his ukulele. He had a great tenor voice, you know. He and Doyle used to tie one on, sing those old songs, we had a ball in those days, and that's how we first learned those bawdy tunes. We got the lyrics from Nick. You want the real lowdown, I think his widow's still got his song collection. Maybe you ought to call her. She's in the book."

Jennifer has made the discovery recently that a vast part of ordinary human conversation is made up of idle memories. People spend more time telling one another shaggy dog anecdotes about incidents from their past than they seem to devote to any other social activity.

It makes things awkward when the only past you can admit to is one you make up as you go along—and then have got to remember forever.

Marian is still reminiscing. "Nick used to know Reagan pretty well back in the actors' union days and when Reagan started running for governor I remember Nick just shook his head in wonderment. He'd always say, 'Trouble with Ronnie is, you ask him the time of day, he'll tell you how to build an

Elgin watch but the trouble with Ronnie is, he don't *know* how to build an Elgin watch.'"

Both of them laugh and Jennifer joins in it. Marian is drinking something blood red with a stalk of celery in it. Her pert face is sleepily content under the tight helmet of salt-and-pepper hair. She's forty-eight and her skin is brown and crosshatched by a fine netting of lines but she's an attractive woman: tiny, tidy, slim, with the abrupt sure movements of a bird. Behind the dark glasses are brown eyes that twinkle more often than not.

"This is my second bullshot," she says. "We're celebrating. You remember that idiot collector in Spokane?"

"The Wyatt Earp nut?"

"Uh-huh. The one with the voice like a nuclear explosion." Marian pronounces it "nucular."

Jennifer feels the heat of Graeme's eyes upon her. Marian's talk drifts by:

"We got a catalog phone order from him a couple hours ago. About blew my ear off. Complete set of Alfred Henry Lewis. Bound volumes of the *Tombstone Epitaph* and a couple dozen outrageously overpriced first editions—Stuart Lake, Billy Breakenridge, Walter Noble Burns, that kind of whitewash stuff. Take us half the weekend to pack it for shipping but it pays the rent for the whole month and then some."

"Congratulations."

Graeme says, "Looks like the value of your stock just went up a point."

She gives him a lazy glance through her sunglasses. Why is it that everything he says sounds like an accusatory innuendo?

George brings the iced tea. Graeme says, "I'll have another beer."

She tastes the iced tea and makes a face. "Can't you just make real tea and put ice in it? This powdered junk is dreadful."

"Use a lot of lemon." George hobbles away.

Marian shouts, "Grouch!" at his back.

The waiter takes no notice.

"Top of everything else he's going deaf," she says to Jennifer.

Graeme says, "How's the shrink?"

It takes her by surprise so that she has to think a moment. Then she says, "All right," rather irritably and flicks a sharp look at Marian, who pretends an abrupt keen interest in her drink, wrapping both hands around it and peering down into it with an attention so studied it's comical.

She's explained her afternoon absences to Doyle and Marian by saying she's been seeing a psychoanalyst to find out why she loused up her marriage. Evidently they've passed the confidence on to Graeme. Marian is right to be embarrassed. Jennifer makes no gesture to take her off the hook. She's wishing they hadn't told Graeme—and she's wishing Graeme would stop asking so many questions.

She hasn't told any of them about Charlie Reid or the flying lessons; she hasn't told anybody anything—she feels like a spy, parceling out information on a need-to-know basis. She's compartmentalized everything.

Graeme says, "I went to a shrink once. He told me I was full of shit. Hell, I already knew that."

Marian laughs with him. He goes on, addressing Jennifer: "Bless 'em all—Freudians, Jungians, gurus, messiahs— must be a thousand bloody schools of thought and every single one's got the corner on truth. The one true religion. Mob of charlatans, you know—all of 'em. They haven't got any answers. Just questions. You ask them what something means, they come right back at you with a question—what do *you* think it means?

"But then I suppose it's something to spend the alimony on." His smile, with a lot of white teeth, is as warm as a Times Square whore's.

Jennifer says, "I take it you went through an expensive divorce."

"Two of them, darling."

Perhaps that explains his animosity; perhaps not.

Graeme drinks from the bottle. "I think of alimony like buying gas for a junked car. I'd like it a lot if once in a while maybe she'd pay for *my* bloody doctor appointments. But it doesn't work that way, does it, ladies."

Marian says, "He's in a mood, as you can tell. He had to get up early to cover an unpleasant story. Somebody had the indecency to get murdered at five o'clock in the morning."

A moment's alarm. "I didn't know you were on the crime beat."

"Sure. I cover the organized crime types. You didn't see my series about the mob in Hollywood?"

"I must have been out of town."

It seems to take him a moment to decide whether he's been subtly insulted. Finally he lets it go. "The bloody phone at half-past five—they told me to get right round there. Could have committed murder myself just then—on the bloody city editor."

Doyle comes out of the shop with his customer. The sun's angle has changed; the reflections seem even more painful and the heat is a tangible weight. Jennifer holds the iced glass against her forehead. Marian looks pleased because Doyle's customer has a bulky parcel under his arm—a large paper bag full of books. Another day's rent taken care of.

Doyle comes to the table and pulls a chair out and waves his empty glass at George. In the meantime Graeme describes his early-morning murder:

"Button named Petrillo. Thirty-seven. Fat bloke, hairy as a gorilla. I'd seen him a few times. They hadn't loaded him into the ambulance yet because the medical examiners were still taking flash pictures. Cops held us back but I got more of a look at him than I wanted. He'd been shot three or four times—somewhere else, I'd guess. Dumped on the curb downtown where he'd be found."

Graeme sucks in a mouthful of beer, flutters it around

inside his cheek, swallows. The pause is purposeful. Finally he drops the punch line:

"Whoever did it wanted him to be found. He's a mess. They've ripped his bloody tongue out."

Marian's face changes: revulsion, then withdrawal—she doesn't want to hear this. Doyle says, "God almighty."

Graeme seems pleased by Marian's infestivity. "There'd been a rumor Petrillo was making some sort of deal to turn state's evidence and get immunity from prosecution."

Doyle asks, "Prosecution for what?"

"Cocaine. Petrillo had connections with the Cleveland mob. Allegedly, as we investigative journalists say, he was a conduit for distribution to Ohio. Anyhow, looks like he got his tail in a bloody crack and he was ready to name names to a grand jury and allegedly a contract was put out and he became the victim of a bloody mob hit a block and a half from the courthouse."

Graeme's grimace is actorish. "When they tear out your tongue it's supposed to be a warning to anybody else who may be thinking about finking on his pals. The Mafia are like those bloody fundamentalist Moslems—you steal from a don, they leave you lying around with your bloody hands chopped off. You spy on the wrong people, they find your corpse with no eyes in it. Explicit and expressive, the bloody Cosa Nostra."

Jennifer pretends to maintain a polite and discreetly shocked interest. In fact her heart pounds painfully and she clenches her muscles against a feeling of faintness. She has never heard of this man Petrillo, but Graeme unwittingly has just dashed her in the face with exactly the images she has tried vigorously to keep out of her mind.

27 What surprises her about Charlie Reid's place is that it isn't a hole-in-the-wall apartment.

It's a decent respectable little house in a cul-de-sac in Reseda. Electronic garage door opener. Azaleas and rose bushes on the front lawn and citrus trees in the high-walled back yard where he does his barbecuing.

In the kid's bedroom there's an 8×10 glossy of Mike and the other kids in the band—Mike hunched over his saxophone looking vulturish, pale eyes hooded like his father's. Thinner than she'd expected; but the shoulders are wide and he'll fill out.

She strolls through the house with a drink in her hand. He's out there cooking the steaks and the foil-wrapped corn and potatoes. He doesn't seem to mind leaving her alone to her explorations. Does it mean he has no secrets?

She makes her way back to the patio. He's peering skeptically at the coals. Then he hears the door and looks up at her and likes what he sees: his face brightens. It gratifies her that he approves of her appearance; she spent a bit of careful time deciding what to wear. She's got on a torquoise squaw blouse and a casual khaki-hued prairie skirt and sandals to match. A Zuñi necklace of silver and stones; a beaded belt. She didn't want to look severe or glitzy or too anxious: but she wanted to draw his eye and she has succeeded.

He says, "Be a while yet. I like to cook them slow."

"Everything's so neat and tidy."

"Cleaning lady was here yesterday," he says. "I should've moved into a smaller place when Mike went away.

Probably could get a fair penny for this dump. But I can't be bothered. Eight percent mortgage and I couldn't find any place cheaper to live and at least the kid's got a place to stay if he feels like coming home to see the old man between semesters."

"Does Mike fly?"

"Some. He got his license two years ago. It's not a passion with him. He'll be a Sunday flier."

"Do you mind?"

"I don't make the mistake of thinking of him as an extension of myself. He's got his own life."

He's flipping the steaks over. There's a lot of sizzling. She can smell hickory smoke from the chips he's sprinkled on the coals.

"What happened to his mother?"

"She was someplace up in Oregon last I heard. Waitressing in a lobster place." His shrewd glance flashes toward her. "I guess you want to know why I got custody of Mike. She's a drunk. Happens to a lot of Air Force wives."

You don't have to tell me about that, she thinks. My mother and my sisters were just about the only sober women in the—

Stop it. You haven't got any sisters. Your mother was a housewife and your father was a plumber and you grew up in Phoenix and Chicago, and they died twelve years ago in a four-car pileup. You have no family. For Ellen's sake—remember that.

"Does Mike ever see his mother?"

"He tried to. For a while. I never put restrictions on it. But it got so he couldn't stand seeing her boozed up. He writes to her now and then. In a letter you can pretend nothing's wrong."

She takes his empty glass inside and mixes him another bourbon and water.

On the kitchen wall hangs a ristra of red tongue-searing chili peppers. There aren't any curtains. It is unabashedly a man's kitchen.

She's still unnerved from this afternoon—the reporter's wallow in mob-style murder. She feels jumpy. Things keep blundering around inside her, hitting taut cords.

Through the kitchen window she watches him step back from the barbecue and clench his eyes against the smoke.

It's silly to be coy with him. What's the sense in delaying any longer? He's not going to be a pushover for soft lights and bedtime games. Whatever his answer would be then, it'll be the same now. Get it over with.

She's rehearsed it long enough: the story in detail. It's part truth, part fabrication. There ought not to be any questions that can take her by surprise. There's no excuse for procrastination except fear; and she's got to set fear aside out of concern for Ellen and the deadline, less than a month now, that hangs over her like a boulder perched on the lip of a cliff.

At the edge of the flagstones there's a patch of mint. She breaks off a sprig; rinses it with the garden hose and pokes it down amid the ice cubes in his drink.

He tastes it and shows his approval.

She moves to one side to get out of the smoke; the wind keeps pushing it around. She senses he is aware of the sexual tension. She reclaims her own glass from the redwood table and thinks about another drink.

But that would just postpone it. And let's not forget the rules of the new game: never drink enough to make the head fuzzy or the tongue loose.

Come on. It's Ellen's future you're farting around with. Blurt it out.

She says: "I had a motivation for learning to fly. It wasn't just for fun."

"No?"

"There's something I need to do and it requires an airplane."

Her abrupt determination seems to amuse him. "Smuggling wheelbarrows?"

"What?"

"Sorry. Old joke. Go ahead."

She takes a breath. "I've got a daughter—fourteen months old. I'm having a custody fight with her father."

"Must be painful." An upward glance: the concern is genuine. "Sorry to hear it."

She tries to decide how to phrase it. Prompting her, he says, "Your little girl got something to do with learning to fly a plane?"

"I wanted to be my own air rescue service. My daughter's."

"You're serious now."

"The son of a bitch has got my kid, Charlie. I want to get her back."

28 The steaks are seared; she watches Charlie crank the grill higher so they will cook more slowly. She can't decipher his expression. All he says is, "Go on."

"Last year we separated and I moved out here. I thought I'd get settled and then go back and collect Wendy. As soon as I'd established California residency I filed for divorce here. But then I found out he'd filed at the same time— back in New York."

"And?"

Now more lies: "There've been custody hearings in both states. California says I get the child. New York says he gets custody."

"He's got possession of the kid?"

"For the moment."

He pokes the steaks with a long fork. Fat dripping on the coals has started a fire and he sprays it with water from a hand-pump bottle that used to contain window cleanser. Out here he's startlingly different from what's he like at the airport or in the plane. His domesticity seems wildly out of place.

She says, "It's not altogether selfishness on my part. He's not a fit father. She can't stay with him. She just can't."

"Well—you're talking about kidnapping now."

"She's my own daughter. My child!"

"Love, I'm talking about the law."

"It's kidnapping in New York—it's honoring a court order in California. Depends where you're standing."

"Forget the legalities. The baby's in New York with her old man? Then—possession being nine points of the law and all—you're talking about kidnapping. You get caught, that's what they'll arrest you for."

"I know that."

"I think you belong on a funny farm." But he says it with gentle humor. "What kind of guy is the father?"

"You won't get an objective opinion from me."

"Granted. Tell me about him." He's taking the steaks off the fire.

"On the surface very charming."

"He'd have to be, to get you to marry him."

He's not looking at her just then and she wonders how he means the remark to be taken. Is it the casual flattery of a man on the make or a compliment meant sincerely?

"He's dangerous." Then abruptly she stops, feeling awkward. She didn't mean to put it that way. It seems to reveal too much. She doesn't want to scare him off.

She continues quickly: "He can be unpleasant."

"Yeah, well we all can be unpleasant." He's plucking potatoes and corn on the cob out of the coals, using the long barbecue fork to peel the foil off them.

"What's his name?"

"Bert. Albert. Some of his friends call him Al."

"Albert what? Hartman?"

"Of course," she lies.

Is it her imagination or did he notice her instant's hesitation?

His face gives nothing away. His eyes are squinted against the smoke. "We're about ready here." With deliberate care he breaks the leaves off the corncobs and removes the silk. He slides the potatoes deftly off the fork onto the plates and when she carries them inside there's a corner of her troubled mind that appreciates the precision with which he effects all these little accomplishments: he only *looks* disorderly.

He shakes up a decanter. "Salad dressing. My recipe. English mustard in it—hope you don't mind."

And he actually holds her chair for her.

When he sits down opposite her she's grateful to him for not lighting the candles. That would be carrying it too far.

She says, "Wendy's not in the city. They're at our—his summer house in the Adirondacks. Outside Fort Keene."

"That in New York State?"

"Yes. Near Lake Placid."

"Mountain cabin?"

"You could call it that. It's got twelve rooms."

He gives her a sharp sidewise look and pours the wine—something red from a California vineyard. She tastes it and it makes her tongue tingle pleasantly. Must be careful—ration herself to one glass.

She says, "They'll be going back to Manhattan on Labor Day. So I've got a deadline and it's less than four weeks away."

Now she lets him see her distress. It is genuine enough. "Doesn't look as if I'm going to be an accomplished pilot by then, does it."

"No."

It provokes her quick smile. "One thing about you, Charlie, you certainly don't believe in polite lies."

"I try not to lie to my friends, honey bun."

He hasn't started to eat yet. He points with his fork toward her plate. Not until after she begins to eat does he pick up his knife. He's a strange fossil, she's thinking. The last of his breed.

He asks, "What makes Labor Day the deadline?"

"In the city I wouldn't have a chance of getting near her. We live—they live in a condominium with its own private elevator. One apartment per floor. It's a top-security building. Guards all over the place. Even the doormen are private police. And you can be sure they've been warned about me."

"But you think you can get out of this house in the country. Even with her father right there?"

"I know how to do that. Things are more casual at Fort Keene and anyway he's not always there. Sometimes he commutes to the city during the week."

"I've got to tell you something," Charlie says. "This isn't exactly the dinnertime conversation I had in mind for tonight."

He ruminates on a mouthful and reaches for his wine and otherwise busies himself with actions that fail to conceal how industriously he's employing the time to absorb and to think. From his expression there is no way to tell how he feels about what she's told him.

Eventually he says, "Why an airplane? What's wrong with a car?"

"There's a seventeen-mile road in to the house. It's not a private drive—there are other houses—but it's the only road and it takes at least forty minutes to get out to the highway. He'd have the police on it before that—he'd just telephone."

"Cut the phone wires."

"Wouldn't help. He's got CB radios in the cars."

"Those can be disabled."

"I suppose they can. But there are always three or four cars in the lean-to and around the driveway. It would be hard to bash in all those radios without being noticed. They can see the driveway from the house."

"You've worked it out, haven't you."

"I've tried to."

He's cutting a piece of steak; scowling at it. He sits for a moment with knife and fork poised over the plate and she has the feeling he's making a decision but in the end he only asks another question:

"Three or four cars. What are you guys—the Kennedys of Hyannisport? How many people around the kid?"

"There's the housekeeper and her husband. He's sort of all-around caretaker and handyman, gardener, mechanic, so forth. And my husband's hired a practical nurse—a nanny to look after Wendy. And most all the time he'll have two or three of his partners and business associates there. They play cards and spend half the day doing business on the telephones. They like to hunt, even out of season," she adds pointedly.

"I guess you're telling me old Albert ain't poor."

"He's in the construction business."

"Yeah. What does he build? Skyscrapers?"

"Sometimes."

"And he and his buddies like to hunt. So there are guns around the place."

"Yes."

"You haven't gone so far as to say it's an armed camp, honeybunch, but would that be a fair conclusion?"

"No." Try to calm him down now. "It's not a fortified stronghold, Charlie, it's just a big rustic summer house. All wood—varnished, not painted. Mostly cedar. Big picture windows—a lot of glass. There's a cathedral ceiling in the living room, open beams, I guess it's forty feet high at the peak.

You could seat eight people at a table inside the fireplace if you wanted to—I've never seen a fireplace that big anywhere else. The house is huge but it's not a fortress."

"How do you expect to get in and get Wendy out?"

"I know how."

"That's reassuring," he says a bit drily. "What about an airstrip? Something to land on."

"There are two or three places."

"All of a sudden you're being evasive."

"I think I've already told you too much. Maybe it's the wine," she lies.

"Come on. You want me to fly the airplane for you. Don't you." He starts to chuckle. "Why not quit beating around the bush?"

"Oh dear. Am I that transparent?"

"I wish you wouldn't bat the big blue eyes at me. It just makes my heart go all pitty-pat."

She puts the corncob down and cleans her fingers on the napkin. Without raising her eyes she says, "I'm sorry I've turned your romantic dinner into a business meeting. Sometimes my timing's not very good."

This time he doesn't smile; he doesn't let her off the hook. He says: "I expect it's time I asked what's in it for me."

By leaping ahead of her he has taken her by surprise and as she watches him gnaw corn she reassembles her thoughts and chooses her words:

"It's become painfully obvious I can't fly the plane myself. I suppose I could try—but I don't want to put my child's life in that kind of danger. So it looks as if I can't do this without you, Charlie, and I guess that means you can pretty much name your own price."

"And lead us not into the valley of temptation," he murmurs. "You like some more wine?"

"No, thank you."

The steak is blood red. He shaves it in slivers to eat it,

she notices; no big hunky mouthfuls for him. He likes to savor what he's eating. She's practically finished and he's hardly started.

He says, "Special occasions like this, I get the meat at a little Italian butcher shop in Encino."

"It's very good. Everything's delicious. You'd make somebody a terrific wife."

"Yes ma'am."

She says, "How much is fair, Charlie? What would you say to five thousand dollars?"

"Probably not enough. On the other hand ten thousand sounds like too much. Why don't we say seventy-five hundred?"

There's an interval during which she is acutely conscious of the bashing of a pulse behind her eyes. She finally dares to say, "You mean you'll do it?"

"Sure, my sweet love. Why not. I haven't had a good silly adventure all week."

His grin is at once reckless and mysterious. He lifts his wine glass in toast. "To Wendy. Her very good health."

She drinks to that. To Wendy Hartman A/K/A Ellen LaCasse. She can smell the baby now: she has a tactile memory of tiny fingers clutching her own: she hears the burble of Ellen's laugh and the strident demand of her outcries. She can see the wonderful smile that crumples the little blue eyes into happy wedges. She can feel her child's warmth.

29 Driving away she feels by turns elated and confused: uneasy, at intervals, because too often Charlie seems to have that ability to take her by surprise—as he did ten minutes ago when, dishes washed and cognac swirled and lights turned down, he took the glass out of her hand and kissed her as she had not been kissed in longer than she could remember—flicking tongue and hard body pressure—and then lifted her to her feet and steered her toward the door.

"Peaches, I'll delight in making love with you and I hope we do it soon but right now neither of us could be sure it isn't just putting the signatures on a business deal. I don't mind doing it out of sheer adrenaline. I don't even mind a gratitude fuck. But I don't like screwing for business. Big bad Charlie may be a pretty loose fellow but he ain't yet standing in doorways."

As it happened he was standing in the doorway when he said that. It made them both laugh a bit.

Then he said, "I don't know where you're coming from. I've been around you a month or so and I still haven't figured out whether you used to be a librarian or a high-priced call girl. Now just on the off chance it's the former, I don't want to feel guilty if you wake up in the morning hating yourself, you should pardon the expression. So let's take a raincheck."

She kissed him on the lips—she can still taste it—and when she drove away she saw him in the mirror standing under the street light, not waving, just watching her go.

She likes Charlie. It's easy to become fond of such a man. But when there may be an enemy lurking around every corner you learn to distrust the unexpected and those who purvey it.

Charlie may not have been a wise choise. There's too much captain in him and not enough crew. And the sexual attraction doesn't make things any easier.

But there's not much she can do about it now.

She's going to have to be very careful in deciding how much of the truth she can reveal to him about Albert. If she tells him too little he may not take the dangers seriously enough; if she tells him too much it may discourage him.

She's thinking: I can handle it. I can handle him. You know I think it's going to work. I honestly think this ridiculous scheme is going to work. You hear me, Ellen? Don't give up. Momma's coming, darling.

30 A beige Datsun sports coupe is parked in her numbered slot behind the building. She finds another space.

The Santa Anas are starting to blow. Dust whips along the alleyway. Straight overhead she can see stars quite clearly: the Santa Ana is an ill wind that brings dry heat and pollen off the desert, stirs up dust and spores, carries misery to allergics and fans brushfires in the canyons—but it clears off the smog.

Alongside the oleander hedge she unlocks the mailbox. The skirt flaps around her knees. A gust nearly rips the mail from her grasp. She goes around the corner in the lee of the building and sorts through the sheaf.

Amid the mail order catalogs she discovers an envelope containing her new bank credit card.

Jennifer C. Hartman. She rubs the embossed letters with the pad of her thumb; gets out a pen and signs the back of the card and slips it into the transparent window of her wallet opposite the California driver's license.

They look so preposterously *real.* It's an eerie thrill—this feeling that Jennifer Corfu Hartman is actually beginning to exist.

She glances up the outside stair and along the railed balcony. A light glows through the lowered blind of the furnished room. The lamp is on a timer; it will switch off at eleven-thirty.

It has been more than a week since she's had a look inside; may as well dump the junk mail in a wastebasket, make a bit of noise for the neighbors' benefit and move a few things around—just in case the superintendent or some repairman has had occasion to let himself in. No point encouraging them to believe the premises have been deserted. How ironic it would be if the well-intentioned concern of neighbor or janitor led the police to issue a missing-persons report on Ms. Hartman.

The wooden stair clings tentatively to the building; it gives when she puts her weight on it.

When she goes along the upstairs balcony the footing is uneven and she walks slowly in the bad light.

The television in the next-door apartment casts blue illumination against the slitted Venetian blinds and she can hear the laugh track of a situation comedy as she fits the key into the door and enters and catches a man in the act of pawing through the clothes that hang in her closet.

31 He's heard the door; he's looking over his shoulder.
His expression is a comic exaggeration, like that of
an animated cartoon character taken by surprise.

She recognizes him immediately and realizes now that
the Datsun 280Z out back is a car she's seen before, parked
near the bookshop.

The reporter.

Graeme Goldsmith.

32 Indignation—rage—terror: for a moment her reac-
tions trample one another and she only stares.

Then a swift instinct takes charge. You've got to behave like a real person.

Indignation, then.

"What on earth are you doing here? How did you get
in?"

"Well." A furtive smile; he withdraws his hand from
the closet and faces her. "I didn't think you were going to
turn up."

"Obviously." She says it with bite.

Then she steadies her voice: "You've got about five seconds to explain this before I call the police."

He's trying to regain his composure: straightening up, rearing back on his dignity. "I don't think you want to do that."

"Why shouldn't I? You're breaking and entering. What in the hell is the meaning of this?"

She's glaring at him with unfeigned animosity and she's thinking:

You've got to play this all the way through. Stay innocent. Don't let the son of a bitch rattle you. Find out what he wants—find out what he knows—but don't give away a thing.

He lets the silence go on a beat too long. She says, "All right, Graeme, I'm calling a cop," and turns as if to go.

"Don't do that, Miss Jennifer nonexistent Hartman."

Anticipating the effect of the statement he attempts a smile. It is too sickly to achieve the swaggering effect he intends.

He says, "I've come by here four nights running. You don't live here. Nobody lives here."

He waits for her response. She gives him none—only a hooded anger.

"It's a front—it's a blind." His voice is rising. "I want to know what for."

She watches him bleakly. If you've ever thought fast in your life, do it now.

She says, "You make a habit of burglarizing people's apartments, do you?"

"I haven't stolen anything. I thought I'd find out something. And I did." He gestures toward the open closet. "Those things don't even fit you. You must've bought them so fast you didn't bother to see what size they were."

"For a reporter you're not very observant."

"No? Very well—then just for fun let's see you walk around the room in any of the shoes in there. Go ahead. Show me."

Her heart is skipping beats; she's faint now. She covers it by crossing to the island of the kitchenette and resting her weight on an elbow on the pretext of poking into the fridge; she takes out a can of vegetable juice and pops the ring top off it and slams the fridge door and drinks.

When her head stops swimming she says, "I don't owe you anything—least of all explanations—but I'm tired and I want you out of here. All right. I don't suppose it's occurred to you there may be some significance in the fact that they're all the same size, even if it's not *my* size?"

She slams the can down on the counter and wheels to face him with virulent wrath. That much isn't feigned; but nor is it uncalculated. She knows she's got to take control and hold it.

"Listen to me. I'll try to do this in simple language that even you can understand. I'm subletting to a friend and she's out of town and I just stopped in to pick up the mail and check things out."

She moves toward the door. "So much for your mystery. Now if you're all through sniffing around in that closet—"

He shouts at her: "Where do you live then, ducky? Where do you hang your pretty little hat that you're too bashful to use it as your legal address?"

"Where and how I live is none of your business."

He continues to shout, trying by sheer volume to intimidate her. "Who's paying your rent? What's the guy's name? I çan see him—the thousand-dollar suits and the Rolls-Royce—some honcho with a society wife at home and a ten-million-dollar image to protect. Tell me the bastard's name, ducky. Tell me his fucking *name*!"

The very question pegs him: now she understands. He smells a profit in this. He sees his chance to blackmail someone.

Well then—why not let him think it? Let him go right

on assuming she's the well-kept mistress of a politician or movie mogul. Let him put his nose to the ground and follow that lead as far as he'd like: let him outsmart himself.

She says: "I owe you nothing—least of all information. I know the law. Would you like me to tell you the penalty for breaking and entering? It's a felony, you know."

He's not meeting her glance. She puts her hand on the doorknob and goes on, driving it in: "You're slime. I can't stand the sight of you. I don't want to see you ever again. I don't want to hear from you. If you want to hang around with Doyle and Marian, do it when I'm not there."

"Your name doesn't even need to come into it. You're a confidential source. Nobody'll pry your name out of me, not even with a writ. Now all I want to know is who he is."

"Believe me, you can't afford to know the answer to that question. It could kill you."

"Don't be melo—"

"Get out *now*, Graeme—or I call a cop."

His mouth begins to assume a disgusted expression of defeat; he even slouches a few paces toward her—toward the door. But then cunning returns.

His mouth curls into a smile that is more like a snarl:

"Go ahead and phone. I shouldn't be surprised if they're just as interested as I am to find out how come Jennifer Hartman was born two months ago. How come there isn't a trace of her in existence before that. No credit rating, no Social Security account, no driver's license in California or Illinois. You did say you came out here from Illinois, didn't you, ducky?"

He leans forward to peer furiously at her. "I think there's a story in you. Quite possibly a big story."

She manages somehow to give him a slow cool smile. "Even if your ridiculous suspicions were true, there's no crime in any of that. On the other hand you broke in here and I ordered you out but you're still here . . ."

She walks wide around him, making her way to the telephone, watching him, knowing she's got to carry the bluff all the way.

He pivots on his heels to keep her in front of him. She picks up the receiver and dials the operator and meets his eyes icily while she listens to it ring.

"Operator? Get me the police, please. It's an emergency."

"Put it down," he says. "I'm leaving."

But she holds it to her ear. A voice comes on the line: "Police Department. May I help you?"

"I'd like to report a breaking and entering in progress. The address is fifty-one sixty-sev—"

By now he's got the door open and he's gone through it and she watches it slam behind him. She hangs up the phone and realizes she's hyperventilating but she has the presence of mind to walk unsteadily across to the window and pry the blind back.

He's halfway down the stairs. He doesn't look up.

He descends out of sight. A few moments later she hears the slam of a car door and the belch of a sports car muffler.

Oh dear God. What am I going to do now?

33 She drives west on Chandler. The street is divided by railroad tracks and trees. It's after midnight; there's no traffic.

No evidence of headlights behind her but she feels a crucial need to be certain and so she makes three right turns in succession, switches off the lights and coasts to a stop at the corner, keeping her foot off the brake because she doesn't want the taillights to flash.

She waits at the corner with the engine idling, watching Chandler in both directions, watching the narrow street behind her—watching everything.

A few cars pass under the street lights. None of them is Graeme's Datsun.

An instinct compels her away from her natural course; she turns south on Van Nuys Boulevard and drives up into the canyons, up Beverly Glen all the way to the top of the rugged spine that divides Beverly Hills and Bel Air from the Valley. She runs west on the ridge, hairpinning slowly along the tight twists of Mulholland Drive, here and there glimpsing a startling thirty-mile panorama of urban lights; up here on the thin strip of road corkscrewing through rocks and brush she has the atavistic feeling she's been flung back into primordial wilderness.

The road swoops across a graceful bridge span, crossing above the freeway in Sepulveda Pass, and she continues to pursue the westering half moon, concentrating on her driving, putting everything else out of her mind except steering wheel and brakes and accelerator: the car and the road and the constantly shifting sliver of the world that is illuminated by her headlights.

There's a clump of buildings on the left—a posh private school—and just beyond it is a wide graded pull-out where half a dozen cars are parked facing the sparkling view of the Valley. She comes slowly through the bend; her headlights sweep across the parked cars and she catches a sign of movement as two heads duck down behind a car seat. Lover's lane.

Soon Mulholland Drive peters out. She wonders whether to take the steeply descending road to the right or turn around and retrace her course.

What the hell. Why not explore.

Down to the right. The road keeps curving back on itself; it becomes a residential street—one of those high canyon suburbs, houses perched on land-fill outcrops so that each site commands a view. You pay for the houses by the square foot; for the views by the square mile.

The streets intersect one another without pattern or reason. She keeps turning from one into another, always choosing the street that leads downhill. Now and then she finds herself in a cul-de-sac and has to turn back and try another turning; but you can't really get lost up here—you can see the entire Valley asprawl below and you know you only need to keep going downhill until eventually, like a tributary rivulet seeking its main stream, you're bound to flow into Ventura Boulevard.

She needs this sort of distraction right now: she needs to clear her mind.

A sudden bend makes her brake. The lights traverse a dark thicket and now there's an animal caught in the blaze. It stands frozen, its eyes radiating phosphoric yellow. She stops the car.

Dog? Fox?

Then she realizes: coyote.

It stares at her, pinned by the headlights, ears up and bushy tail down, an emaciated grey yellow creature with bony spine and a swollen abdomen and its mouth peeled back in a proud smile.

Doyle says they're becoming increasingly bold. Feral. The developers and their cancerous urban growth have depopulated the coyotes' natural hunting ground and they've started coming down from the hills to slash Hefty bags and poke through garbage. They're attracted to back yards by dog food that's left out overnight unfinished. Sometimes they'll attack family pets. Not long ago in Burbank one of them killed a six-month-old child.

The coyote stirs at last: turns and trots away toward

the brush, exposing a new angle of view that makes it quite evident that the beast is pregnant.

Fleeing alone through the night with no society to protect her. Trying to safeguard her young; trying to stay alive.

The animal vanishes. One more flick of yellow light reflects from its eyes—or is that just a trick of her vision?

I feel as if I've been given a sign. I wish I could tell what it's supposed to mean.

She finds her way down off the mountain and drives to within a few blocks of her apartment and waits five minutes in the mouth of an alley in deep darkness with windows rolled up and doors locked.

We're going to get a dog, she decides. A female. We'll adopt it from an animal shelter. When Ellen's old enough we'll breed it and Ellen can watch it bear puppies and she'll learn to raise them and care for them. We'll—

No. Let's not dream about the future just now. There's something more pressing to decide.

She's waited here long enough. There's no one following. That's for sure.

Like a kid playing hide-and-seek. She hears her own giggle.

Don't go all hysterical now. It's hardly a suitable time for flying to pieces.

She parks on a side street. Can't use the apartment building's carport any longer; if her car were identified there it could lead someone straight to her room.

Walking to the court she keeps looking over her shoulder. In these small hours the emptiness of the street is dreadful.

A shadow stirs; it makes her jump; she peers into the darkness—a lemon tree, a cinderblock wall, something moving . . . an animal.

It darts into an unpaved alley and she can hear its toenails click on stones.

34 She lets herself in and double-locks the door and slumps into the threadbare easy chair. Strength flows away as if a drainplug has been pulled.

Blood pressure, she thinks. That's all it is. A drop in blood pressure that follows shock's injections of adrenaline. The body feels it's safe now so it wants to relax.

Got to keep the brain working now: analytical, observant. No time for Victorian swoons.

A drink. A drink would help . . .

No. Coffee would be better.

She fills the kettle and sets it on the burner. For a moment it is good to occupy her hands with methodical functions: fit the paper filter into the Melitta's plastic funnel; dip measures of ground coffee into it.

Waiting for the kettle to boil she's imagining a knock at the door—seeing herself go right up the wall.

Crooks, she wonders: fugitives whose faces are pinned up on post office walls. How can they live like that—wanting to scream every time someone sounds the doorbell, desperate to run if the telephone rings, terrified if a stranger so much as looks at them twice?

She remembers the glittering eyes of the coyote. Not furtive but startled. Fear is nothing to be ashamed of. But how do you go on endlessly living with it?

Now we have got to think, children. Quickly and very clearly.

The son of a bitch took you by surprise and he threw a

hell of a scare into you. But how much of a danger is Graeme, really?

He's jumped to confusions: he doesn't suspect any part of the real truth.

What is he likely to do? What's his next move?

You can't predict that until you've figured out what he really wants.

If you assume he's eager to find someone to blackmail, then it's quite possible he'll give it up as soon as he realizes there's no profit in it for him; and he'll arrive soon enough at that realization because he isn't going to find any leads that will take him any closer to identifying the Very Important Person whose mistress he believes you to be.

Maybe he'll try to follow you around. He may keep an eye on the bookshop until you show up. Then he'll try to tail you to see where you're living.

You'll have to have eyes in the back of your head for a while: keep giving him the slip until he gets tired of it.

Isn't he bound to get tired of it? He's not likely to waste weeks or months on something that isn't paying off.

If it comes to the worst he'll trace you as far as this place. He'll ask questions—neighbors, superintendent—and he'll learn nobody's ever seen a male visitor to her apartment.

Maybe even then he'll still believe she's consorting with a tycoon or a movie star or a senator; but he'll realize she's too cagey for him and he'll have no name—no one to blackmail.

Graeme's an opportunist. He won't waste his time. He'll give up; go somewhere else and harass someone else. He's the kind who likes to exploit people's weaknesses. If you show him none he'll go away and find easier opportunities elsewhere. All you've got to do is remain calm and strong.

Just don't panic, that's all.

Realistically now: to what extent—if any—does he threaten your security or Ellen's?

The kettle begins to whistle. She pours water through the coffee into the mug. When it stops dripping she sits at the dinette table with both hands wrapped around the mug; it's now that she notices how cold she feels.

Trouble is, you know, you can't count on Graeme's perfidy. Just because you dislike him you mustn't rush into a miscalculation. Suppose he isn't a cheap blackmailer? What if he's actually doing his job?

Suppose he's looking for a front-page beat? A nice scandal over his byline?

Journalists. She's known a few of them. Self-appointed truth seekers who respect no one's privacy but their own—it never matters whose feelings they hurt or what damage they do: not so long as they can shove a microphone under a grieving widow's nose or catch a princess naked in a telephoto lens or photograph grisly blood-soaked victims of wars and accidents or fill two columns of tabloid newsprint with lurid headlines and yellow sensationalism.

News. The people's right to know. The Fourth Amendment.

Never mind whose life the story may destroy. A fourteen-month-old girl's? Too bad. C'est la vie. C'est la news.

I think there's a story in you. Quite possibly a big story.

The real risk isn't that he's a cheap blackmailing crook. The real risk is that he's just what he says he is: an investigative reporter.

He's already suspicious enough to have hung around four nights in a row watching the other apartment. Suspicious enough to have done a cursory job of tracing the backtrail and found out it led nowhere. Suspicious enough to keep looking? To find Jennifer Corfu Hartman's 1953 death certificate in the Tucson courthouse?

And then what?

You've done everything possible to break every point of connection that might have led them to trace you from

114

New York to here. But you didn't think about what could happen if someone tried to trace you backward, starting out from here.

What can he find?

Be reasonable. Don't attribute superhuman skills to him. He hasn't got X-ray vision.

But he does have contacts. If he's written lengthy articles about organized crime it means he must have developed a good number of useful lines of communication both in law enforcement and in the underworld.

Coincidences do occur—especially among people who share interests. Ray Seale persuaded you of that. If Graeme has informants in organized crime then you have to accept the possibility that he may happen to be acquainted with one or two of the very same people who've been instructed to keep an eye peeled for a woman named Madeleine LaCasse, five-foot-five, a hundred and sixteen pounds, formerly blond, grey blue eyes, possibly still carrying a suitcase full of diamonds and cash. . . .

They may even have photographs of her. God knows there are enough of those around. In the scrapbook she left in the Third Avenue apartment her face appeared full length or head-shot only in nineteen full-page magazine layouts and sixty-one smaller ads. They won't have had any trouble finding pictures of her to distribute.

She's changed the hair, exposed herself to enough sun al fresco at Buffalo Bill's Saloon to build a good tan, put on the glasses, changed her style of make-up. Anyone passing her casually in the street won't be likely to connect her with that model in the photographs.

But this is something else. If one of those pictures ever comes into Graeme's hands and he hears any part of the story that goes with the picture, he'll study it with a little imagination and put things together and he'll know whose face it is.

Granted, in constructing this scenario you're relying on

one or two far-fetched assumptions; probably no such thing will ever happen.

But it *could* happen.

And that means you have no choice.

For Ellen and for yourself, you've got to run again. Disappear again. Start over again.

She looks around the dismal kitchenette. The ceiling feels as if it's pressing down.

35

"Let us know if there's anything else we can do for you, Mrs. Holder." The officer at the New Accounts desk is tidy in a three-piece suit. "Thanks for coming in."

She gives him a distant polite smile and walks away; she's slipping the book of temporary checks into her handbag alongside four others and the Nevada driver's license. It's the fifth bank Dorothy Holder has visited this morning in San Diego.

As she approaches the pay phones she realizes that she has no retinal image of the bank officer's face. She remembers the dark suit and the neatly knotted tie but what color are his eyes? What shape is his face? Is his hair light or dark?

She picks up a phone and looks over her shoulder. Across the lobby he's leaning back in his tilt chair talking to the white-haired woman at the next desk and his waning hair is a nondescript shade of sandy blond. Round face. Possibly a mustache but if so it blends right in; even from only forty feet away she can't be sure.

Hot damn. I wish I had a face as forgettable as that.

She dials the number again. It's the third time she's tried. Most likely he's still taking some eager would-be Chuck Yeager through loop-the-loops and Immelmann turns. She listens to it ring.

An operator with a computerized voice speaks in disembodied words that are like a juggler's pins spinning through the air, each in its own orbit unconnected to the others. Please. Deposit. Eighty. Five. Cents.

She plugs coins in and listens to the bong and ping.

She's surprised when it's picked up. "Reid Air Service and Flying School. Charlie Reid speaking."

She keeps it light. "Hi Charlie. It's Jennifer."

"Hello there, doll baby." He sounds cheerful enough. "Where the hell you been?"

"Busy. Are we set for Tuesday?"

"Bet your bottom."

She's relieved to hear him say it.

His voice rumbles down the line: "I made some calls. Located a four-place Cessna for rent in Plattsburgh. That's about thirty miles northeast of Fort Keene. You're north of Lake Placid, right?"

"North and a little west."

"Got it on the map here. Mountains around there run to thirty-five hundred, four thousand feet. Lot of contour lines. You sure there's a place to set down an aircraft?"

"It may have cows in it," she says, "but it's flat enough to land on."

"Don't forget, love, you need more distance taking off than setting down. If the runway's a little short you can always stop an airplane against a tree but I never knew anybody who had much success taking off that way."

"They've landed planes there before. I've seen it. One of them had two engines. You know, the kind with the V-shaped tail?"

"Twin Bonanza? All right. Then it can accommodate a baby Cessna. But we'll have to do a recon. If the grass is too

117

high or the soil's too boggy we'll have to forget it. We'd be glued to the ground for the duration—bring your hiking boots."

"It'll be all right, Charlie."

"It's your charter. You're the boss."

"You didn't rent the airplane in your own name, did you?"

"Phony pilot's license, phony name. I've played that game before. I don't want to end up in jail any more than you do. Where and when do we meet?"

"Can you fly up to San Francisco on Monday night?"

"I guess. Why not."

"Good. I'll meet you Tuesday morning at San Francisco International. Make it seven-thirty. United Airlines."

"What flight?"

"I forget the number. It's the eight-fifteen for Chicago."

"Okay. In that case, my dove—you busy for dinner Monday?"

"I'll be in San Francisco . . ."

"Fine. I know a little place near the Embarcadero. Not a tourist joint. The waiters are surly but if you like pesto they grow the basil themselves in window boxes."

Instinct urges her to decline.

Keep your distance. Don't be stupid.

But she hears herself say: "Where is it—and what time?"

A few minutes later she's walking out to the car and she feels something like the beginnings of a jaunty bounce in her step and for a moment or two she enjoys it.

The car this time is a sand-colored Buick compact, five years old, a couple of dents and the paint chipped here and there. Drab transportation to go with the slightly frumpy style of the brunette woman she now portrays: thick sensible brown shoes, dull green plaid skirt, loose white blouse in need of ironing, pastel green scarf tied carelessly about the neck, hair drawn back from her temples with tortoise-shell combs. Nearly an academic look.

By the time she's driven two blocks she has brought herself back down from the momentary high.

Face the truth. If you didn't need him to fly the plane you'd have left him flat the same way you left Doyle and Marian; even as it is you'll never see him after Tuesday.

So let's don't for Christ's sake start looking *forward* to anything.

It can't be any other way. Ellen has to come first. Doyle and Marian—and Charlie too—they know you as Jennifer Hartman.

And so does Graeme.

That's the kicker. Graeme. Picture Graeme exchanging confidences with Ray Seale . . .

And by this time next week Charlie will know altogether too much about Jennifer Hartman and her daughter who's just turned fifteen months old and the summer place they come from in the Adirondacks. If somebody like Ray Seale gets the bright idea to start questioning licensed charter pilots . . .

It's the only way: after Wednesday, Jennifer Hartman must cease to exist.

36 The motel in La Jolla has become a welcome refuge. To reach the ocean she only needs to step out of her room and walk across the narrow street and climb down a steep worn little trail. There are bits and pieces of beach amid the massive dark eroded rocks.

At sunset she's there barefoot in a tangerine sleeveless blouse and frayed shorts made of cut-off jeans, sitting on a folded blanket with her back against a rock, holding a drugstore steno pad against her upraised knees, checking off items in yet another of her lists of things to do, things to get right.

You could live in a place like this. A kid could grow up here. Mild sunshine all year round. Ocean, mountains, the San Diego Zoo.

Maybe you shouldn't think that far ahead. Maybe you'd better not dare to hope.

There's a bronzed teenage couple on a patch of sand beyond the next lump of stone; she had a glimpse of them when she arrived and once in a while she hears the energetic vocalizations of their love-making between strikes of the gentle surf.

It brings up the thought that she didn't exactly have a celibate life in mind when she began all this but she supposes it could hardly be otherwise right now—it's only that she never stopped to think about it. She recalls how she used to envy some of the other models at the agency their hedonistic capacity to luxuriate in extracurricular evenings with randy photographers or half-drunk ad agency men or conventioneering fabric and fashion buyers. An expensive dinner; drinks in a skyscraper lounge with a view of the park; a hundred dollars for the powder room and a few hours in a hotel. Strangers before, lovers during, strangers after.

That was long before Bert. She was young and not confident of who she was; it seemed best to be one of the gang, to look as they looked and behave as they behaved. She remembers one veteran's acerbic counsel: "There's forty or fifty of us for every job. Think about it. You go along or you go under."

But she didn't go along. After the first few print-ad jobs she went her own way and found it didn't really make much difference. Maybe she lost a few shots here and there but mainly she still got the jobs, or got passed over for them—it depended mostly on what sort of face and body they were looking for. They'd make passes of course; that was part of the ritual; but most of them were grown up about it if you didn't put out. That was up to you.

She has never been at ease with one-night stands. Sexuality has never seemed that casual. Nothing feels quite so vulnerably intimate as sharing her naked body with a man: it's just not the sort of thing she can do comfortably with a stranger.

She's thinking now of Charlie. His burly gentle power. No longer a stranger; a father, a flyer, a barbecue cook. A friend; and the sensual pull is strong—clearly he feels it as much as she does.

But she knows another thing as well: that in a few days she'll be turning her back on him.

The thought stirs a restless unease. She should not have accepted his invitation. Dinner in San Francisco inevitably will lead to an invitation to his hotel room.

In the dusk she looks at herself in the mirror of her compact. The dark new coloring, the hairdo—is it enough? She's been scanning the newspapers for two weeks now, looking for Graeme's byline, expecting every day to see a blown-up telephoto picture of herself and a caption, *Do You Know This Woman?*

No one knows this woman, she thinks. Not even me.

But she knows someone else. Or at least she knows him this well: Charlie's no more easy with one-nighters than she is.

Whatever we might do, it would mean something.

It wouldn't be the kind of thing we could just forget.

I like you, Charlie. I really do. But I don't know what the hell to do about it.

37 In twilight the teenage lovers depart. The temperature drops quickly. She is startled when several people materialize from various nearby hidden pockets and climb the few yards to the road.

With the shore to herself she begins to feel chilled but it takes energy to move. This is such a lazy place. A sense of peace: something she hasn't felt in God knows how long.

Thinking reluctantly about stirring, she delays her ascent to watch ribbons of pink dwindle to grey on the horizon.

She feels very tired. So many things to make sure of. What has she overlooked?

She holds the steno pad against her knee and moves the pencil down the margin.

The diamonds? Check them off the list. Transferred to a safety deposit box in Capistrano Beach. In the name of Dorothy Holder.

Previous car? Sold for cash in Calexico. If Graeme's curiosity leads him that far perhaps it will give him the notion she was on her way out of the country into Mexico.

Back-up identity? Initiated ten days ago. Took an early plane to Salt Lake City. Obtained a birth certificate for Carole A. Fry. Applied the same day for a Social Security card and a Utah license.

She knows the drill now; she knows what lies to tell; they sound natural on her tongue—an advancement in glibness that pleases her perversely. She knows she ought to feel ashamed of herself. But it's far down the list of concerns.

God help me now—how many times am I going to

have to go through this? Is Ellen going to have to grow up in a new town every year—a new school and new friends every season and a new name to get used to?

Stop it. Got to assume there's room for hope. Must behave as if it's going to work this time.

Back to the list in the notebook: pay attention now. Hard to read in this bad light . . .

Jennifer's two apartments? Check; check. Both landlords notified of departure. One security deposit forfeited.

Bills? Current and paid. Nothing outstanding.

All this is important because it would be stupid to attract the attention of bill collectors or skip-tracers.

Doyle and Marian? That's taken care of, at least for a while. On the phone to them last week she contrived to sound breathless and a bit incoherent: babbling about going back to her ex-husband, a trial reconciliation, a long trip together to the Orient and the South Seas to see if they can't patch it up and get it working again—got to run now; got to catch the plane. . . . My investment in the bookstore? Let it ride, good friends, and keep me on the books and if you make any money put my share in an account. I'll be in touch when we get back—oh, it may be months, six months, eight, hell I don't know. Love you both. Must absolutely *run* . . .

A patchwork solution but it'll have to do for the moment; at least it'll keep them from calling out the Missing Persons squad.

And when they repeat the story to Graeme—as Marian inexorably will do—it won't give him leads to follow. What's he going to do, hunt all over Asia and the islands?

Must remember tonight or tomorrow to reserve a rental car in Plattsburgh. Have to do it in the name of Jennifer Hartman because it would be suicidal to leave traces of Dorothy Holder that close to the lion's den. Put it on Jennifer's Visa card and remember to send in a money order to cover it because you'll never receive the bill.

The car must be something with four-wheel drive.

Better do it tonight.

What else?

The hardest part has been making sure she wasn't followed during the three days in Los Angeles when she drove from bank to bank, clearing out Jennifer Hartman's accounts, taking the money in cash. Every last account emptied—even the retirement account, although the man gave her a look of stern disapproval and warned her of dire consequences from Internal Revenue.

Now the money is redistributed around this new city and its cluster of satellite towns. Jennifer Hartman's assets are gone: liquidated and untraceable.

It's so difficult to create a life—and so easy to destroy it. All it takes is a few signatures. Or a bullet.

A bullet . . .

She flashes on an image: Bert with his gun collection. Unlocking the chain, taking down a revolver, showing it to her, trying to explain its operation. His exasperation when she doesn't seem to want to understand it.

"What is this—Victorian times or something? It's not a feminine thing to do? What's this crap you're giving me? Come on. Your old man was in the military. What are you going into a swoon for?"

"I just don't like the damn things, Bert."

"Fine. Sometimes you need things you don't like. Suppose some creep breaks in here, comes at you with a knife?"

"I'd probably shoot myself in the foot."

"I'm talking about the baby now. I'm talking about protecting my kid."

"Bert, the baby's not even due yet for nearly six months."

"People in our position, the world's full of creeps looking to put the snatch on rich kids. They bury infant babies alive out in the woods someplace and they come after you for two million dollars ransom. You understand? Now pay attention. You get a good grip on the thing and you hold it in both hands—here, like this . . ."

So she let him teach her how to load it, how to aim it, how to shoot. At Fort Keene, five months pregnant, she was pressed into accompanying Bert and four of his friends on their venison safari. There was Jack Sertic, togged out in professional white-hunter khakis, and the helicopter pilot who was a crack shot, and two guests from Bert's growing show business coterie of chums. One of them was an actor who three years ago had been modeling in designer jeans commercials and subsequently had become the beefcake star of a hit TV action series; the other was a fat comedian from New York and Las Vegas who had the filthiest mouth she'd ever heard. She'd complained to Bert about it and Bert had agreed with her. "But he's a funny son of a bitch, you've got to admit."

She did—with reluctance. All the same she found it hard to hide her amusement at the ludicrously grim serious-ness with which these presumably grown men crept stealthily through the trees on their sponge-soled boots, stalking in grim slow silence like little boys playing Steal-the-Bacon, behaving remarkably like smirking renegade villains prowling toward their sinister ambush in some horrid silent movie melodrama.

She had a rifle. She knew how to use it. She saw a buck deer—bolt upright and staring right at her—and she just watched it until it wheeled and darted away, the signal spots of alarm showing white on its rump—and Bert came clamber-ing out of the trees to gape in astonishment. "You had him. You let him go. For God's sake, why?"

She looked him in the eye. "I hate the taste of venison. Didn't I tell you?" And walked away.

"Jesus H. Christ." He came after her: gripped her arm and turned her. "Hey," he said in a different voice.

Then he dropped his rifle and pulled her into the circle of his embrace. "Hey," he murmured. Then his gentle smile became a sybaritic leer.

It was one of the last times she can recall laughing with him.

An hour or so later she watched him fire a high-powered bullet that tossed a smallish buck right into the air and brought it down in a hideous somersault against the bole of a birch tree with force enough to shake the ground.

She saw the avid excitement in Bert's face—"Hey, hey guys, you see that? You see that?"—and she turned away.

As she walked off she heard the comedian say, "You sure that ain't somebody's cow? Fucker goes hunting, comes up to this dumb-ass farmer, fucker says I'm sorry I killed your cow, man, can I replace it? Dumb-ass farmer goes, I don't know, fucker, how much milk can you give?"

Male laughter.

She didn't laugh. She made the excuse of fatigue and made her way back to the cabin, leaning back in that ungainly way to balance her expanding abdomen.

She was changing into another person all the while. It was possible now to look back and see what must have been happening then. Even at the time there was a sense that day by day her life was becoming different but she attributed this to the baby that was growing inside her.

It's more than that, though. Perhaps it's a kind of growing up.

From a reasonably strait-laced upbringing she shifted as a young woman, without ever marking the transitions, to a life of self-centered trivialities and meaningless cosmetic surfaces.

Amazing how we fall into traps: how we begin to care—simply because other people, superficial people, purport to care—about so many things that don't matter. What's In—what's Out. Who's U—who's non-U. A Triumph? But my dear, that was *last* year's car. Wouldn't be caught dead with a man who drives anything but a Datsun 260Z.

And then she'd gone beyond that into Bert's world of

hedonistic luxury with its power trips and billygoat morality—aspects of which she was only beginning to discover.

In fact, thinking back now, she is distressed by the vastness of her ignorance about Bert in those days. They had been married more than a year. She shared his bed and his life. She didn't like most of his friends but she knew them—she believed she knew *all* of them.

She believed she was married to a construction magnate.

It wasn't until later—less than a year ago—that she found out about the rest of his business operations.

Troubled by her naivete of those days she has tried to reason it out:

I'm not an innocent . . . I didn't just parachute in yesterday . . . How the hell could I remain oblivious for so long? There must have been plenty of evidence. Clues all around . . .

You don't see what you want not to see. It's partly that. And it's partly that Bert has a compulsive way of compartmentalizing everything in his life. There was always that remoteness in him, right from the beginning: he made you aware that you were only seeing as much of him as he wanted you to see.

For a long time it was more than enough. Living with Bert was exciting: it was like watching a performance by a great actor—the unpredictably explosive kind who radiates danger. There've been times when he's put her in mind of Brando, of Robert Duvall—even when he's at rest there's an electric menace that hangs in suspension around him like heat lightning ready to strike.

You never knew whether a night in bed with Bert would be a seduction or a rape.

Not that he ever actually treated her roughly. Once they were married he behaved toward her in an Old World manner that was simultaneously reverential and condescending; always he was a conscientiously generous lover. Yet there was always the feeling that at any moment he might explode.

She remembers Jack Sertic, his mind a stagnant pond, saying to her more than once, "Al lives at the edge. Right at the razor edge."

She might have been a crystal statuette—an image that defined not only her status but the extent of her influence over Bert's decisions.

And the longer she lived with him the more she realized how little she actually knew about the nature and range of those decisions.

There were entire compartments of his life about which she knew absolutely nothing. When she first stumbled across clues to the hidden compartments she ignored them; when they persisted she became troubled; finally it was no longer possible to pretend they didn't exist. There was a world of evil—perhaps Bert inhabited it only part of the time but it dominated him, it described the way he was—it defined *who* he was. And the more she learned about it the more she feared him for the child's sake.

By the time the baby was born she knew it was no good: it was out of kilter. As the bureaucrats might say, this was not a suitable environment in which to raise a child.

The baby was hardly a day old when for the first time she saw Ellen in Bert's arms and the decision grenaded into her mind: *I have got to take her away from him.*

38 Monday morning she flies all the way to Texas to make telephone calls. At the Dallas–Fort Worth airport, watching automated tram cars move silently in and out of their stations like boats piloted by invisible Charons, she dials the number of the Third Avenue apartment and listens to it ring three times before the machine picks it up.

He hasn't changed the recording. The voice is still her own: "This is seven six six two. There's no one near the phone right now but please listen for the sound of the beep and then leave your name and number on the answering machine tape. We'll get back to you as soon as we can."

She hangs up without leaving a message.

At least he hasn't changed the number. Maybe he's still hoping she'll get in touch.

It was worth a try but the result is worthless. If he'd answered the phone himself she'd have known at least that he was in the city. If the nurse had answered it would have suggested that Ellen was there in the apartment. That's assuming the same nurse still works for him. But this way? Nothing.

She dials the number of the cabin at Fort Keene. It rings twice; a man's guarded voice answers: "Five four six one." She recognizes the soft bass growl—Philip Quirini's voice. She's hoping to hear background sounds—other voices—but nothing comes through. She hangs up on him. With luck he'll dismiss it as a wrong number.

Damn. Philip would be at the cabin anyway; he's there

all summer, he and his bovine wife in charge of the household. So you still don't know a thing, really.

You know you can't put it off any longer. This is the call you knew all along you were going to have to make. Come on—get it over with.

She places the call.

"Hello?"

"Diane? This is Madeleine."

"You're kidding me." Then: "Matty?"

"Yes dear. The same. The very same."

"Matty—are you all right?"

"I'm getting along."

A stretch of silence. "Well. Well, *well*." Then: "Where on earth are you calling from?"

"Just say it's long distance. How've you been?"

"Me? I'm all right. A little tennis elbow. Al and—we got wiped out last week in doubles."

"It's all right. You can mention his girlfriend's name if you want. I assume he has a new girl?"

"Several. You know Al—"

She can picture Diane: dark, long-limbed, tan, big brown eyes flashing with excited speculation.

"Matty, what the hell happened to you? Where are you? My God, if you knew the—"

"I can imagine. I'm all right. I'm fine. I won't go into detail. He earned it, you know. He asked for it."

"Al?"

"Of course. Who else?"

"He was awful mad, honey. He didn't say it but you could see—"

"That's hardly surprising. Nobody bugs out on Albert LaCasse. I walked off with his pride. How are the boys?"

"Fine, fine." Diane is nervous; her laugh is off key. "You know teenagers. The last week before school starts again. They're staying with a rowdy crowd in one of those

130

grouper beach houses on Fire Island. Screwing all the girls and drinking all the beer. My God—you remember when we all first met, out in the Hamptons? Jesus. Think how much things change."

"How's Jack?"

"Jack's all right. Up at the cabin right now with Al. I guess they've been shooting venison for the freezer."

Bingo.

Passengers hurry by; she can't help smiling at them. Into the phone she says, "Nothing's changed much, I gather," and watches a uniformed steward push an old man in a wheelchair toward the boarding gates. The old man is listening to a Walkman and conducting an invisible orchestra—sealed in a private world of music that no one else can hear. A loudspeaker blares: "Mr. Emil Schnarf, Mr. Emil Schnarf, please pick up a white courtesy telephone."

In as casual a voice as she can manage she says to Diane, "How's Ellen? Have you seen her?"

"Not lately. He's had her up in the mountains all summer. I guess they're coming back to the city next week. Good *grief*"—Diane's voice soars and squeaks—"you've got to tell me what you're up to. Where you are. What you've been doing. I'm just *dying* to know. Come on—give!"

"I'm doing fine, dear. I've made a new life for myself down south here. You wouldn't believe it but I've been going with a cop. Big enough to dismantle Bert by hand. But a real gentleman all the same."

"Hey, hey. Tell me more!"

She pictures Diane in her big apartment on Central Park West—probably wearing a designer outfit that's the ultimate in summer's day brevity, surrounded by her collections of porcelain figurines and miniature paintings, some of them hardly an inch square and painted with a one-hair brush. Acquisitive Diane with the fullest acreage of clothes closets you've ever seen.

131

"He's a nice cop," she invents, "believe it or not. Poor as a churchmouse. He's got three kids by the former wife. Adorable brats."

She's thinking: How amazing I ever thought of making the gift of my friendship to Diane. What a pathetic creature—her boundaries defined by pretentious brand names and that Park Avenue shrink with his clientele of Valium addicts. You could trade a hundred Dianes for one Charlie Reid or even one Marian or Doyle Stevens and you'd still be incomparably ahead of the game.

But in those days you didn't know any better. You had no Marian, no Doyle, no Charlie to compare her with.

You haven't missed Diane once. Or any of that crowd. And here you're already missing the Stevenses and you feel like hell about Charlie even though you'll see him again within twenty-four hours.

My God. How is it we become so damned valuable to one another—so painfully important?

Into the phone she says quietly, "By the way, do you remember Stan what-was-his-name, the one who published those fashion magazines?"

"I remember him." Diane's voice has gone chill. "What about him?"

"I just got a glimpse of somebody who looks just like him," she lies. "Do you ever see him any more?"

"No." Very curt now.

"Too bad. Must have been terrific while it lasted. They say he's a real stud."

"I wouldn't know about that."

"Sure you would. You used to meet him in the after-noons in that apartment he keeps on the floor above his offices. You had what they call a torrid affair with him for nearly a year. It always amazed me Jack never found out about it."

Diane's voice is nearly inaudible now. "How'd you know about that?"

"I did print work up there before we all met. I saw you in the building several times. You didn't know me then—you wouldn't have recognized me."

"You never said anything . . ."

"I know how Jack is about that sort of thing."

"He'd break my arms and legs. Just for openers."

"You must have known that when you were seeing the guy."

"Of course I did. But that was part of the fun of it. I mean, nothing's fun if you don't take a few chances, right? I mean, right now you're taking a hell of a chance just calling me on the telephone—you know that."

"I'm pretty sure you won't tell anybody about it. You won't mention I called. You haven't heard from me at all."

"Well of course, Matty. If that's what you want."

"If Bert finds me because of anything you might let drop—I hate to do this, dear, but you understand I might have to talk to Jack about you and Stan."

There's a beat of silence; an audible indrawn breath; finally Diane says, "I see."

"I thought you'd understand. I'll probably call again sometime." She puts on a Texas drawl: "You have fun now, y'hear?" And hangs up.

Turning away from the phone she's feeling bleak and angry with herself. All right: you were never truly friends; you never liked Diane. World's largest aggregation of expensive make-up. Brings a whole new meaning to the word "shallow." Always primping in mirrors. Flirting with anything in pants—including Bert—whenever she was out of Jack's sight and thought she could get away with it.

All the same it's a cheap shot: a shabby way to treat a woman who's never done you any harm.

But it'll keep her quiet. And you've accomplished what you came here to do: you've confirmed that Ellen is at the cabin.

She looks up at the airport clock. Forty minutes to spare before the flight to San Francisco.

She's thinking: Charlie, you may not be a cop with three adorable kids but I do believe you're big enough to dismantle Bert by hand. Question is, would you have the guts for it?

39 The feel of his body is good. He's as accomplished a lover as she might have expected: relaxed, confident.

She could close her eyes and imagine anyone. Replace Charlie in her fantasies with someone else. But she doesn't want to. She covets no one but Charlie.

She knows it is a perilous way to feel. The danger signals are up; these qualms are sounding the alarm.

At the moment she just doesn't care.

She watches him, watches everything he does. She wants his hands and his mouth to be all over her. It's been so long since . . .

But finally there's no more time for languid reflection. Accelerating sensation whirls her. She's losing her bearings. Afraid at first; but she abandons herself to it and rising ardor becomes a hungering breathless impatience: she craves him with an unsuspected greedy voraciousness.

She hears herself cry out, full voice. It is an impetuous sound of vehement joy: the frenzied triumph of an escape to freedom.

Climax.

"Oh God, Charlie. Oh God."

40 On the plane to Chicago he's businesslike: plans, routes, timing. But then impulsively he seizes her hand, kisses her fingertips, gives her an astonishingly shy smile.

Christ, this is no good. What have I got myself into?

The steward comes by, topping up coffee cups, and the captain's voice blares from what sounds like a torn speaker: "For you passengers on the right side of the plane, we've got Lake Tahoe coming up a few miles to the south in just about a minute here."

She says, "Story of my life. I'm always on the wrong side of the plane to see anything."

"I'll fly you over Tahoe any time. After we get back."

It makes her look away. Broken clouds below the window; the mountains are a deep green, almost black.

He says, "You still haven't told me why you went and changed your hair. I liked it better before."

She is thinking: what if I level with him? Why not tell him the truth? The whole truth and nothing but the truth. Charlie'll listen. He'll understand.

She turns to look at him. He's got his nose in his coffee. She studies his face. Her scrutiny draws his attention, then his frown. He says, "What's the matter, my pretty?"

She shakes her head in reply and looks out the window again.

I'll tell him, she decides. But after Ellen's free and safe.

41 Connections are not the best and it is after dark by the time they arrive in Plattsburgh. And it's starting to rain.

They check into a Holiday Inn as Mr. and Mrs. Charles Reid. Her pulse is racing—not because of the deception at the registration desk but because Ellen is hardly thirty miles from here and by tomorrow night at this time with a little luck it all will be accomplished: reunited and the dangers behind them.

If all goes well.

He carries the bags into the room and kicks the door shut behind him. "We mustn't keep meeting like this." He sets the bags down. "Lovey dove, you want to get a drink and some dinner or do you just want to get laid?"

Sex ought to be the farthest thing from her mind right now. So many details to think about . . .

She reaches for his hand. "Undress me. We can eat and drink later."

42 It's an atavistic hunger. She can't remember feeling this way before. She can't get enough of him. They make love before dinner and again after dinner; and with the dawn she's at him again, pestering him until he wakes up laughing and takes her in the massive circle of his arms.

But it's subdued this time and as she lies beside him catching her breath she recognizes the thing that has been disturbing her: the rattle of a hard steady rain on the roof overhead.

He peels the blind back from the window. It's sheeting down out there. Reaching for the phone he gives her a glance expressive of quizzical distaste.

He talks and listens, hangs it up and leaves his hand at rest on the cradled receiver. He glances at her. "Stationary low. The front's stalled right here."

"Then we can't fly today."

"Not even a balloon."

"What about tomorrow?"

"God knows. What happens if we can't fly until the weekend?"

"I don't know. Probably Bert and his crowd will arrive from the city Thursday afternoon. For the long weekend."

"So it'll be harder to take Wendy out of there."

Feeling absurdly unconcerned she says, "But it's only Wednesday morning. It can't rain forever. Come here."

He doesn't move. He sits on the edge of the bed with one hand propped stiff-arm against the phone; he's looking down at her over his shoulder and he says, "I feel as if I've wandered into one of those one-act plays that nobody understands. It's time for you to trust me."

"What do you want me to do?"

"Tell me what's going on. Tell me what you've got in mind. In full."

She says, "If we don't show up on time you're free to take off without us. If we do, you can fly us to Canada. That's all you have to do."

"Just a taxi driver."

"I just don't want to get you involved."

"I'm involved, honeybunch. I'm involved." He hikes a

hip back on the bed and lightly with a fingertip begins to trace rosettes around her nipple. In a musing voice he says, "The minute old Bert knows we've used a plane he'll be on the horn to every airfield around. We'll have no place to set down. You sure you've thought this out, sugar doll?"

"We won't land at an airfield. You'll pick a farm or a country road. Up in Quebec Province somewhere. Drop us there and take off again, by yourself."

"What happens to you and Wendy?"

"We'll walk. Hitchhike. If we pick our spot sensibly it won't take long to get to the nearest city. Wendy and I will lose ourselves in the crowd. We'll take our time back to California. Please don't worry about it—we'll be fine."

To prevent him from asking more questions she hurries right on: "You can fly back to Vermont or New Hampshire. Land in a field and tell the farmer you had engine trouble— ask if you can leave the plane for a couple of days until you can get a mechanic out to fix it. Then you could make your way to Boston or Albany and drop a postcard to the people you rented the plane from—tell them where to find it. And then," she lies, "we'll meet you in Los Angeles."

His fingertip draws a line from her throat to her belly. She reaches for him. "I'd like to make love now."

He lets her pull him toward her. His face looms above hers. Not altogether admiringly he says, "You're kind of a clever bitch."

"Trying to save my kid. Necessity," she says. "You know. The mother of invention."

They make love in oddly affectionate silence. But afterward he's still got the knucklebone of suspicion in his teeth and he won't let it go: he stands at the window and glowers at the rain. "You want to tell me the truth now about you and your kid and your husband?"

"What do you mean?"

"I get the feeling the truth is you just took a walk.

138

There aren't any child custody rulings, are there? Did you ever file for divorce?"

She broods at him. "What gives you that idea?"

"Your evasiveness, mostly, and a picture I'm compositing of your husband. The macho deer hunting stuff, the way you've gone to such extremes to cover your tracks—maybe I'm making unwarranted assumptions but he doesn't strike me as a guy who'd take kindly to being served with a divorce action."

"You're very perceptive, Charlie."

"Yeah. But you're going to let me go right on wondering, aren't you."

"I just don't want to get you in unnecessary trouble," she says. "Trust me."

"I do, my little valentine. Question is, when are you going to vice the versa?"

43 He awakens her with soft kisses to her forehead and the tip of her nose. "Rise and shine, love of my life. I want to have a look at this crate we're renting."

"What's it like out?"

"Grey. Dewy. Clearing up."

He climbs out of bed and she watches him pad to the bathroom. She lies back with her eyes shut, listening to the splash of the shower and watching a display of bright fireworks explode across the insides of her eyelids; she is thinking this ought to be a moment of guilt because she oughtn't to feel so bloody good: it seems somehow a betrayal. This has got to be Ellen's day . . .

But why shouldn't it be my day too?

She sits up, beaming. "It's going to work. I know it is. Nothing can go wrong today."

Filled with adrenaline she goes charging into the bathroom, singing at the top of her voice, and opens the frosted glass door and climbs into the shower with him. Charlie laughs at her and she tickles his ribs and in retaliation he's all over her, soaping her down, sliding his hands over her body.

She reaches up to clasp her hands behind his neck; she stands back at arms' length and lets him look down at her and she feels good when he likes what he sees.

He has been full of quiet passion: considerate and attentive and easy with a confidence that is not yet quite proprietary.

"You like my boobs, Charlie?"

"I do love them."

"You don't think they're too big or too small or too high or too low or something?"

"Passion flower, your boobs are the most perfect little boobs I've ever seen in my life. Just absolutely positively perfect."

"What do you mean *little,* you son of a bitch?"

Laughter explodes from him. They struggle for the soap.

When he's finished shaving and she's putting on makeup she says, "There are some things I've got to buy in town. Child things. You know. Diapers and such. I don't imagine we want wet upholstery in the airplane. I'll take a taxi. Meet you at the airfield no later than ten-thirty."

"All right. That'll give me time to do the paperwork, make sure the crate's topped up and ready to go."

He's dressed now. Flying boots and khaki chinos, a lumberjack sort of shirt. He finishes shoving things in his suitcase and comes to her; he rests his hands on her bare shoulders and watches her in the mirror. She leans her head back against his abdomen.

"Are you going now?"

"Get dressed and close up your suitcase and I'll take it with me."

"I feel strange, Charlie. Like there's something wrong with me. I ought to be scared to death right now and worried about my kid. I just want to leap back in bed with you."

"Natural enough, honey sweet. Biology of the beast. Primitive instinct. Happens when we're just about to go in harm's way. We get scared and that sets all the juices to flowing. Battle anticipation—combat nerves. Why do you think the birth rate booms in wartime?"

She gets to her feet and turns into his arms, wanting to be held.

44 She knows she'll be lucky to pluck Ellen away with as much as the clothes on her back. There'll be no time in that house to stop and gather blankets or toys. She's going to need everything: baby food and spoon and bottle and toddler clothes sufficient to last several days. She's got some of these things in her suitcase but there didn't seem any point weighting it with Gerber jars or thick packages of disposable diapers.

Speeding on the hypodermic of nervous energy she whirls through a supermarket tossing things into a wheeled basket.

Now then. Stop. Breathe. Think. Forgotten anything? To hell with it. If I did it'll just have to wait.

There's only one register open and she has to wait in line behind two matronly customers who are comparing at length the excellences of their respective teenage sons. Each of them has a cart piled high with purchases enough to equip a family for the entire season; and the check-out girl appears to be suffering from a case of terminal inertia.

She has to restrain herself from screaming at them but actually there's loads of time; it's only half past nine when she emerges from the store with her loot and settles into the back seat of the taxi.

The driver says, "That was quick. My wife never gets out of there in less than an hour."

It's turned into a clear summer's day, a few cirrus clouds floating high; good flying weather at last.

A few minutes after ten the taxi decants her at the seedy little flying field. The rented Jeep, painted a dark forest green, is parked next to a motorcycle in the shade of what passes for a hangar; the place looks as if it may have seen previous service as a cow barn. Beyond it she sees Charlie in a row of pegged-down light planes, talking with a skinny little man in a cowboy hat. She waves to Charlie, pays off the cab driver and lugs her packages across the dewy grass runway. By the time she reaches the parking area her feet are soaked.

The man in the cowboy hat turns out to be not much more than a kid—Adam's apple, peach fuzz and acne; he gives her a startled bashful grin of white buck teeth, nods his head several times with jerky nervousness and plunges toward the nearby glass-sided shack in full ungainly retreat.

She says to Charlie, "The grass is wet. Do you think we'll have trouble?"

"Probably."

The flat tone of his voice brings her eyes up to his. There's a mask down over his face; she doesn't like what she sees.

He says: "You didn't tell me we're going in against the fucking Mafia."

142

45 The shock of sudden fear makes her furious. "What did that kid tell you?"

"He said it may rain again tomorrow."

Charlie is very cool. He's got his arms high, testing an aileron at the back of the wing, moving it up and down with his hands, watching the control yoke inside the plane move from side to side in response.

She keeps her voice low. "What about the Mafia, Charlie?"

"Says he never heard of any Albert Hartman. But one Albert LaCasse fits the description—twelve-room house, so forth. The kid says everybody knows him. Seems they know him just well enough to stay clear of him."

He drops his arms to his sides. His eyes are narrowed; he's fuming. "Who is he? Who're *you*?"

"Names don't matter, do they?"

"Jesus. The Mafia."

"He's not Maf—"

"For God's sake don't do a J. Edgar Hoover number on me and pretend there's no such thing as organized crime."

He walks around the nose of the plane to the far side and performs the same experiment with the aileron there. She follows him around.

"I'm trying to tell you he's not in the Mafia. He's not even Sicilian. Do we need to talk about this? I've been trying to forget all of it. Hell. Albert and his friends—they're people who do business together."

"That sounds like his words. Not yours. Rationalization."

"You couldn't call it an organization. It isn't the Mafia."

"Drugs and murder. That kind of businessmen."

She hesitates, then gives way. "All right. Yes."

"But it's not Mafia. It's not Syndicate." He makes a face.

"There are thousands of people smuggling drugs, Charlie. This isn't the twenties or the thirties. They're not just thugs and gangsters. They're normal people."

"Normal?"

She can't decipher his expression. In front of the wing strut he kicks the right-hand tire and then gets down on one knee to inspect its tread.

She says: "You probably won't believe this but I didn't know he was involved in anything besides building construction. Not until after Ellen was born. I only found out by accident."

At the tail he stoops to inspect the elevator surfaces. He's not looking at her when he speaks. "You married the guy and you didn't know who he was?"

"I thought I knew. I didn't realize how much I couldn't see."

"Funny. Everybody up here seems to know about him."

He moves the rudder from side to side, feeling for cable tension and smoothness of movement. He glances at the sky.

She says, "I'm not trying to excuse my stupidity but all this is beside the point. It's got nothing to do with you. You won't have any contact with him. They'll never lay eyes on you. He's probably in New York today anyway."

"Sweet Jesus." He closes his eyes and draws a deep breath. "Ellen. That's your kid's real name?"

"I'd planned to call her Wendy from here on."

He walks forward, ducks under the strut, kicks the second tire and looks back at her. Having followed, she tries to touch his hand but he retreats a pace and bangs his head on the strut; he utters an oath and wheels out from under the wing, sidestepping to keep his distance—as if he can't stand the smell of her.

"Charlie, doesn't it help you understand why I have to get her away from there?"

"You could've told me, you know. You could've."

"Why? So you could lie awake worrying?"

"Come on. You were afraid you'd scare me off. You had to have me to fly the fucking airplane and you calculated just how much you could tell me without risking that I might take a walk."

She says slowly, "Yes, that's true."

One side of his mouth curls up.

She says, "I'm sorry. I didn't know you well enough then."

"Nobody likes to be used. Don't you know that yet?"

"She's fifteen months old and defenseless, Charlie. That's what I know. I never set out to hurt you. I didn't tell you any lies that mattered."

"Leaving out the undigestible parts isn't the same thing as telling lies?"

"Haven't *you* ever rationalized something? I haven't done you any harm. And you've been paid. I expect you to keep your part of the agreement."

He glances toward the radio shack with its tall loran pylon; the kid is in there behind glass reading a comic book. Charlie turns a full circle on his heels, scowling at the trees. "The last couple of days—I thought we were getting to know each other. Now I think you were just sinking the hook. One good fuck and I'd follow you anywhere—that the idea?"

"No. That's not the idea. It wasn't any part of my plans."

Charlie opens the pilot's door and reaches into the

cabin, prodding the yoke and then the pedals, watching the movements of control surfaces at wing and tail.

He says: "I'm vain enough to want to believe that. Let's say I buy it. Let's say I buy everything you're telling me the same way I bought the horseshit you sold me before." He isn't talking loudly but his voice makes her wince.

He says, "Let's say it's all true this time. What it comes down to, you want to take the kid out of that house and there's a pretty good chance you could get yourself killed, these guys being that kind of people."

"You won't be in danger, Charlie. I'm not asking you to—"

"You're missing the point, luscious one. I'm pretty good at worrying about my own hide. What bothers me is worrying about yours."

"Thank you."

"Wasn't fishing for gratitude. The thing is, you know—what happens if you die or something? How do I explain that to myself?"

"I'd be doing it with you or without you. Put your conscience away, all right? I can't afford it. What time have you got?"

He looks at his watch. "Ten-forty."

She confirms it against her own watch. "My feet are freezing. Are my boots in the Jeep?"

"Back seat."

"Are you ready to go?"

"Airplane is. Not so sure about you and me."

"Come on, Charlie, I can't fight with you all day."

"Go on. Dry your feet off. Put your boots on. I've got to pay Dennis the Menace for the gas."

By the time he comes back from the shack she's in the Jeep tugging her boots on. She feels it sway when Charlie puts his weight on the open door sill. He leans in, scraping his head on the top of the doorway, and levels upon her at close range a grave stare.

146

"Tell me about the landing field."

She's showed it to him on the map; he marked it. She says, "It's about a mile and a half from the house. On government land, I think. They put down the strip a year ago last spring."

"If it's a grass runway we'll need a long throw to get off the ground. It'll be pretty wet. Happen to know the length of the strip?"

"It's about three quarters of a mile, I think. In any case it isn't just grass. They laid down some sort of metal webbing. It came on big flat trucks in rolls."

He's astonished. "Marsden matting? That stuff costs a fortune. They used to use it to build temporary fighter strips during the war."

"I don't know what it's called. I know they've landed bigger planes than this there—even in the snow."

"If they spent that kind of money on the strip . . . I take it we're talking about smuggling now. What is it—cocaine?"

"I don't know. More likely heroin, wouldn't it be? I really don't know much about it. I suppose I made it a point not to know anything. I know the airplanes don't always bring things in. Sometimes it goes the other way. Sometimes he sends suitcases full of cash out."

"Out to where? Switzerland? The Bahamas?"

"Your guess is as good as mine."

"Doesn't matter." He's still watching her, head ducked under the door frame. He says, "I guess I believe you. How often do they use the runway?"

"Two or three times a month. That was last year, of course. I don't know about now."

"Just my luck to run right into one of their shipments."

But then he smiles in an odd way. "I seem to have decided to go through with this bullshit. Just for God's sake don't ask me why."

She knows why; he probably does too. It's because he

has an image of himself as a man who keeps his word, protects women and children, takes heroic risks.

She says: "You're a romantic, Charlie."

"I am?"

"You'll be there at one o'clock exactly."

"Yeah. I'll be there."

"You know that if you change your mind—"

"I'll be there." His paw locks around the back of her neck and pulls her forward: his kiss is hard on her lips.

Then he draws back and before he turns away he makes a silly face at her. "Jesus H. Christ. A fucking Mafia gun moll."

46 Driving the Jeep through town she is thinking: maybe there is some way Charlie and I can include each other in our futures.

She still can taste his mouth. Preoccupied, she nearly rear-ends a little car when it stops abruptly. Its bald driver begins to jockey it into a parallel parking space. Irritated, she leans on the horn when she pulls out to get past. Then she misses the light and bucks to an awkward stop and feels a flush across her face when in the mirror she sees a police car right behind her.

It follows her several blocks and she clenches the wheel until her knuckles turn white but finally the police car turns off behind her and she drives on out of town at a sedate speed, waiting for the tremor in all her fibers to dwindle.

Look, it could have been worse. Suppose you'd run the

red light? You could be spending the next half hour explaining things to a justice of the peace.

Quit jumping at shadows. You need to have your wits about you this morning.

The road forks and narrows; it's a darker day here in the trees. Climbing into the soft hills she feels a chill bite in the air. Strong scent of pine sap here.

Charlie . . .

No. One thing at a time. Ellen comes first.

She watches the mirror anxiously but there's nothing behind her. Never mind that; they'll be chasing soon enough.

The Jeep runs easily along turnings she knows by heart, carrying her across a range of wooded hills and down the length of a valley—a slow country road that undulates beside the stream. Birch forest here—in twenty minutes there'll be pines as the road takes her higher.

The air is emphatically clean, washed by yesterday's rain. Sunlight dapples the water and throws striking shadows across the white tree trunks that march beside the road. The day is aflutter with dragonflies; a chirruping of cicadas is loud enough to be heard over the grinding whine of the Jeep's heavy-duty transmission. Fields of merry goldenrod climb the slopes beyond the stream.

Got to think clearly now. All the things that may go wrong—the things she didn't mention to Charlie. What if there are new dogs? What if the locks or the burglar alarm have been changed? What if they've moved the nursery to some other room? What if Ellen isn't here at all?

What if it's like the last time and it goes crucially wrong? What if this time you don't get away at all?

What if they know you're coming and they're waiting for you?

Last time in a strange way it was easier than this because she hadn't been through it before and she hadn't really thought about all the things that could go wrong. The advantage presented itself; she acted on the spur of the moment. The decision itself had been premeditated but the timing of it was not—she was taken utterly by surprise by her own action.

She'd known for months that she had to rescue the baby: that they had to leave Bert and go in search of sanity.

She'd known it in the back of her mind since Ellen's birth but she hadn't been ready to face it squarely. Her feelings kept changing: she didn't know what she wanted or what she needed.

At first there wasn't sufficient evidence to support her sprouting apprehensive consternation. Instinct was all she had: an intuition of darkening evil. There was nothing to which she could have given testimony.

He didn't seem to have changed; he was still the same big hearty slab-hard hoarse sportin' man who'd swept her off her feet with his contradictory streaks of considerate courtliness and bizarre vulgarity.

Sometimes the excitement still overwhelmed her and in their fevered thrashings she'd find herself thinking *Yes, yes, my God, more—I want more* and she'd wonder how she ever could have dreamed of giving him up.

Yet her unease intensified. When she held the vulnerable baby in her arms the qualms turned into outright fear, even though at first she could not define it.

Then she found out about the drug business.

It wasn't a big dramatic moment. She didn't catch him with glass envelopes full of white powder. It was nothing more than the appearance of his name in a newspaper article. No accusation; just journalistic innuendo:

> Another name that has surfaced in the DEA's investigations is that of Manhattan building contractor Albert LaCasse. It is not yet clear what connection, if any, LaCasse may have to the unfolding story of drug-trafficking indictments. . . .

150

No more than that. But it was the last of many segments; when it fell into place the pattern came instantly clear.

Perhaps it always had been: sometimes she wondered if she hadn't deliberately avoided finding out, like an Albert Speer who wanted to be left alone with his architecture, not caring to know anything about Hitler that could compromise his relationship with his own conscience.

Bert came home that evening to the condominium on Third Avenue and she was waiting for him in icy calm and after one look at her face he said, "I see you've been reading the *Daily News*."

"It's all true, isn't it."

"No." He was hanging his coat in the hall closet. "Where are Philip and Marjorie?"

"She's in with the baby. I told him to go to the movies. I thought we'd better talk in private."

"I pity you, Madeleine, if you think you're ever getting truth for your quarter. They're not peddling truth. They're peddling newspapers."

"You're right to pity me. I've been such a pathetic fool."

He tossed his jacket on the couch and jerked his tie loose and strode toward the wet bar; then he changed his mind and came to her.

She was at the window by the balcony. Snow on the railing had melted a bit during the day, then refrozen; it had a hard sooty crust.

He didn't make the mistake of reaching out for her. He stood at arm's length and tried to stare her down. He said, "If they had any proof, don't you think I'd have been indicted by now? Listen—it's all distortions. I'm in this fight with the unions. They're animals. They'll spread any kind of lies to cut you down."

He continued to stare at her; he endeavored to smile.

"That's all it is—a couple of union buttons got paid to

151

peddle a bunch of garbage and the reporters ate it up like the pigs they are. You understand?"

Her stubborn silence argued with him. He threw his hands high in a violent gesture of exasperation and now the hoarse voice thundered at her:

"It's a bunch of fucking lies. I don't deal dope. You ought to know that. Have you ever seen me dealing dope? Come on. These creeps, I expect this kind of shit from them—but what hurts, what really hurts all the way down, it hurts me to see you believing this swill. That's what hurts. That's what I hate the bastards for."

She was afraid of the violence in him. And it was a good act, full of bombast, almost persuasive.

But she didn't believe him.

It all fitted too well. She'd spent the past two hours remembering things and putting them together. The suitcases full of cash—for "union payoffs." The twin-engine planes on the Fort Keene airstrip with their furtive Latin American pilots. The obsessive secrecy that always cloaked his expeditions out of town with Jack Sertic and one or more bodyguards. The guns everywhere—in the apartment, in his Lexington Avenue suite of offices, in the Fort Keene cabin. And the getaway preparations in the leather jacket he always kept in the front hall closet, its lining sewn with a passport in a phony name and God knows how many cut diamonds. She hadn't been prying; she'd been going through the closet yesterday looking for things to donate to the Armory benefit and she'd felt the hard flat passport in the jacket and its presence had made her examine the jacket more closely.

Strange how careless he could be about things like that when he was so cautious about other aspects of his security. Once a week a man with a heavy briefcase came in to sweep the apartment for electronic bugs. The unlisted phone numbers and the combination of the burglar alarm were changed at irregular intervals. All their cars were equipped with break-in alarm systems.

152

Yet he'd fooled her. Perhaps, albeit, with her subconscious connivance. . . .

After that there was no more ducking the decision. If only for Ellen's sake, the only thing left was separation and divorce.

Of course he wasn't going to like that.

She didn't see any method of approaching the subject by subtle misdirection; the only way to handle things with Bert was to put them out in the open. He wasn't tuned in to subtleties. You couldn't hint around; you couldn't ease up on him. To get his attention you had to hit him over the head.

She made the mistake of confronting him with it the night they returned to the apartment from the Armory benefit where they had shared the head table with the mayor and four Broadway–Hollywood stars and two noted philanthropists and their wives. Bert was in an elevated mood when they came home: his eyes were aglitter with a kind of vengeful satisfaction, for there was in him (she had discovered) a streak of childlike vindictiveness that was rewarded whenever he was treated like an equal by the sort of people who reeked of old money and spoke with Ivy League establishment drawls. Bert carried himself with a forceful kind of panache but there was no disguising the fact that he was a child of New Jersey, descended from lower-class immigrant Corsicans; he never pretended to be otherwise than nouveau riche but still it pleased him to dine not only with celebrities but especially with brahmins and aristocrats.

Seizing the chance to catch him in a good mood she evaded his embrace in the bedroom. "Let's talk."

"Later."

"No, Bert. Now."

"Come on. Let's fool around."

"I want to take the baby away for a while."

He tried to absorb that. "Aagh," he said, dismissing it. "I don't know what you're talking about."

"I need a change."

"For Christ's sake."

"Don't dismiss it like that. We've got to talk about this."

"Talk about what? You been smoking something or what?"

"We're going away. The baby and I. We're not staying here any more."

He watched her very closely. He hardly seemed to be breathing.

She plunged on. "We're just going away for a while, that's all. Call it whatever you want. Say I want to get my act together. Say I need an ocean voyage. Call it a vacation. I need air."

"Call it leaving me. Call it walking out on me. What the fuck are you talking about? You're my wife. Ellen's my daughter. What's this you need a change, you need air, you want to go away for a while? What's this shit? Who the fuck you think you're talking to?"

"Please don't make a bigger thing out of it than it is. I just need a little space to breathe for a while."

He sat down on the edge of the bed and began to unlace his shoes. He kicked them off and stared at them. Finally he looked up at her and she could see his disbelief and she realized her tentative approach had been cowardly. It would have been better to tell him the truth from the outset.

She tried to make up for it. "All right. Let's have it out in the open. I'm leaving you."

He looked a little punchdrunk. She'd caught him so badly off balance she nearly felt sorry for him.

She pounded it home: "She's not going to grow up in a dope dealer's home. My daughter's not going to live in that environment. I can't allow that. I'm taking her away from here."

A deep breath: don't run out of gas now. Keep going. Finish it. "I'm sorry, Bert. You should have been con-

154

tent with the construction business. I can't go on living with the kind of thing you've turned into. I can't expose my daughter to that."

He stared at her, his face closing up as she spoke—and then his continuing silence made her break out in a cold sweat.

She felt a growing desperation. "We can do this like civilized people or we can do it the hard way, you know. If that's what you want I'll have to get a lawyer and believe me I'll get the nastiest bastard I can find. I don't imagine any court in the world would grant custody of a baby girl to a dope peddler."

She gathered up her handbag and the wrap she'd been wearing; still in evening clothes, stalking on high heels, she went toward the door. "We're going now. I'll let you know where to send our things."

"Like hell you will."

It wasn't his words; it was the low even rasp of his voice that stopped her.

He said to her back, "Just stay put. I need some time to think about this."

"Fine. Think about it all you want. I'll let you know where you can reach me when you want to talk about it."

"You want me to sleep in the other room tonight? Fine. All right. But nobody's leaving right now."

She turned to face him. "You can stop me from taking her tonight, of course. You're strong enough. But I'll just get a court order. Is that what I have to do?"

He shook his head—more in bafflement than in visible anger. "No divorce. No custody. That's all. Okay? Understand?"

"You're having some kind of Corsican dream. Let's talk about reality."

"I'll tell you reality. Reality is you don't take my daughter away from me. Reality is you don't walk all over me in a divorce court. You don't like it here any more? I'm sorry about that. But you made a bargain. You took my name, you took my money."

"You can have them both back. I don't need your money."

"Yeah. How noble. Okay. Reality, now, reality is you don't walk out on Albert LaCasse. And Ellen stays with her daddy."

"Jesus, haven't you heard a word I said?"

"Sure I heard you. Let's discuss one simple fact." He'd gone glacial; his enunciation became angrily precise:

"You file against me, you try to take Ellen away, anything at all along those lines, the whole thing comes to an end for you right then and right there."

She gaped at him. "Are you actually threatening to kill me?"

"Kill you? What the fuck am I now, some kind of murderer? Christ almighty. Who said anything about killing anybody?" The big shoulders lifted; the expressive hands gesticulated, then subsided. He had control of his alarm now.

He descended into dark weary sadness. It was only partly an act, an aspect of his voluble Corsican theatricality; it was also a manifestation of genuine pain and loss. He brooded; he scowled; he searched for thoughts he could express.

And finally without heat he said: "I don't think you have any idea how many subsidiaries I run, how many people owe me consideration."

He looked up. She was watching him, puzzled, not able to anticipate where this might be leading.

"I got a truck-leasing lot on Northern Boulevard and twenty percent of a cable TV outfit in Trenton, okay? I got a piece of a resort hotel down in the Bahamas. I got nursing homes in Staten Island I built and I own, you know that?"

He was sitting on the bed, elbows on knees; his hands dangled from the wrists. He wasn't looking at her.

156

"I got half of a little private hospital out in Amityville. What this leads up to, Madeleine, the point I'm trying to make, you've been acting very strange all of a sudden here and I think maybe you're having a little nervous breakdown or something, and if you were to go and see some lawyer or try to steal my daughter out of her home or anything like that, then I guess I wouldn't have any choice but to have you committed to a mental facility for observation and treatment. For however long it might take to straighten out your head."

Then he looked up and smiled.

It was a warm smile full of bright pleased triumph: it was the most frightening expression she'd ever seen on a human face.

After that it was a question of opportunity and even more of courage.

Neither came easily. She realized belatedly how stupid it had been to forewarn him. Now the baby was always under supervision: there were nurses and nannies around the clock. No one prevented the mother from being with the baby; no one limited the mother's freedom of movement—so long as the baby remained in view of employees—but the unspoken rules were manifest. She never doubted Bert had meant every word he'd said, quite specifically and literally. He was entirely capable of putting her away in a rubber room somewhere and locking it for the rest of her life.

He would grieve, of course. He would be mortally offended. He would be the suffering injured party, filled with pain. As the little girl grew up he would explain to her how her mother had gone mad and tried to break up the family and actually tried to kidnap poor baby Ellen from her loving daddy. . . .

She moved into the guest bedroom of the condominium. Bert allowed that much. He had enough dignity not to wish to share a bed with a woman who reacted catatonically to his advances; and he had enough concern for appearances to keep his liaisons discreet.

Evidently he convinced himself she was making her way through the confusions of some temporary emotional aberration. Every second or third day they'd cross paths or he'd seek her out; on those occasions he would say, "Come back when you're ready," and "Maybe you ought to talk to a shrink, what do you think? Might help you straighten yourself out," and "Must be kind of lonely in that guest bedroom," and "I'm not putting any pressure on. You let me know now, hey?" He had cast himself as the innocent, waiting for her to recognize her error—waiting her out with humble seraphic patience.

She was free to come and go. With acquaintances like Diane and with the few friends she had left from modeling days she kept up appearances because she didn't know what else she could do; but regardless of outward appearances of unrestricted freedom she was imprisoned—tethered to a chain leash that Bert might yank at any time.

Of course it was intolerable. You could go mad this way in no time at all. Soon if they put her in a mental home it wouldn't be a fiction.

The decision to escape was anticlimactic, really. There were only questions of when and how. She had to find, or design, a way to abduct the baby and to disappear so neatly that Bert could neither follow nor find her.

That was when she went to Newark and pumped Ray Seale about the mechanics of skip-tracing and disappearance.

After that she set out methodically to lay her plans.

They nearly worked. . . .

He may have forgotten she had a key to the front hall closet; more likely he had forgotten nothing but simply could not credit the idea that even in this estrangement she might steal from him.

The suitcase of cash appeared in the closet on the occasional Thursday or Friday, whence it would be taken to Fort Keene on the weekend. There presumably it would be handed over to a pilot at the airstrip.

Heretofore she had believed these clandestine shipments of cash to be headed for numbered bank accounts in tax-haven countries where they would be deposited in behalf of a union leader or building inspector or zoning-ordinance politician.

Bert had done nothing to disabuse her of the idea. She'd even confronted him with it once and he'd retorted with predictable rationalizations—that if you wanted to do business at all you had to do it this way; when in Rome, etc.

Now she knew better. The pilots were accepting that cash in return for shipments of narcotics.

You can go with the kid. Or you can go with the kid and a suitcase full of cash. It's Ellen's legacy—Bert owes it to her—and besides let's face it, disappearing with a year-old infant is going to be hard enough without having to scratch for a living at the same time.

So it needed to be a Thursday night when he came home from his banking rounds and locked the suitcase in the closet.

She was taken by surprise, therefore, when one Monday afternoon he came back from the office at half-past-three with Jack Sertic. She heard them in the living room; she heard the clink of ice in glasses and Bert's voice: "Here you go. Okay, we can leave about midnight, drive up there easy, no traffic, meet the plane six o'clock in the morning. Get back here by one, two in the afternoon."

"I think you're right. It's safer than sending errand boys."

"Aeah. Go on home, take a nap. I'm going to get some sleep myself. Can't keep the kind of hours I did when I was a kid. Meet me back here eleven thirty. I'll tell Quirini to put up a couple Thermoses of coffee."

She sat in the dining room ostensibly reading the *Times* until she heard Jack take his leave. Bert's footfalls thudded along the carpeted hall. He looked in at her. "How you doing?"

"All right." She returned his glance stonily, giving him nothing.

He gave her the benediction of a saintly smile—*Take your time, darling, I've got all the patience in the world*—and went away toward his room.

She decided to give it half an hour but the first twenty minutes took forever and that was all she could stand. She put her handbag on the hall table by the front closet, unlocked the door and looked inside. The suitcase was there. Locked—but heavy. No doubt of its contents. And the leather jacket with the diamonds sewn inside.

She hadn't planned it this way. She hadn't packed—not even a diaper in her handbag.

Hell, Matty, you can buy whatever you need. This is the bird in hand. Grab it.

Go. Run. *Now.*

She left the closet unlocked, left the handbag on the table, left her coat on its hanger; no point arousing the employees with clues. Unnerved and empty-handed she went back through the apartment toward the nursery.

When she passed the kitchen door she saw Philip Quirini emptying the dishwasher.

The nursery had been a second guest bedroom before Ellen's birth. Now it was brightly wallpapered and stuffed toys were strewn everywhere on the floor and in the crib.

Marjorie was with the baby, feeding her with upended bottle.

Don't hesitate. Look natural. Come *on.*

She swept right in. "I'll do that."

Marjorie surrendered the baby and the formula without remark and retreated into the corner with arms folded.

Cradling the baby, cooing while Ellen sucked at the nipple, she went out the nursery door with her pulse pounding so heavily it poured little black waves across her vision.

Past the kitchen door. Philip putting cups away on their hooks. Don't go straight down the hall now; might make them suspicious. Go into the living room. Keep talking to the baby. Make it seem aimless—a random wandering through the apartment.

The glasses, half full with the ice mostly melted in them, remained on the bar from Jack Sertic's visit. She carried the baby to the window and looked down at the avenue. Nothing remarkable down there: traffic crawling uptown in its usual afternoon snarl.

The subway was the best bet at this hour. There was an entrance just a block uptown on Lexington. She'd already decided that; she knew precisely where she'd go with the baby— down the Lexington Avenue line to Grand Central Station, change for the crosstown shuttle, get off at Eighth Avenue, walk two blocks to a car rental agency and hope they had something immediately available. If not, walk straight down the street into the Port Authority bus terminal and catch a bus to any town across the river in Jersey where they rented cars.

Speed was the trick. Get out of Manhattan; get into a car. After that there'd be time to breathe, time to find an open supermarket, time to study maps. But first she had to get the baby out of this apartment.

She carried Ellen to the front hall closet. The bottle wasn't empty but the baby must have sensed her distress. Probably felt the bashing of her heartbeat. Ellen spurned the nipple and began to cry.

She put the bottle down on the hall table, hooked her handbag over her wrist and reached into the closet: folded the leather jacket over her forearm and picked up the suitcase, cradling the wailing baby in one arm, and turned to struggle with the deadbolt on the front door.

A torrent of adrenaline slammed through her; her palsied hand was barely able to turn the knob.

When Philip Quirini cleared his throat she nearly dropped the baby.

Perhaps it was the tone of the baby's yelling; perhaps something else. Whatever it had been, she was caught. The

Quirinis, husband and wife, came down the hall with carefully expressionless faces, their eyes taking in everything: the suitcase, the baby, the half-open apartment door.

Philip Quirini said very politely, "Let me give you a hand with that suitcase, Mrs. LaCasse."

Marjorie contrived a sliver of a smile. "I'll take the baby for you now."

He had his hand on the edge of the door, blocking her exit; Marjorie was reaching for Ellen. Over the infant's howls Marjorie said, "The baby's not supposed to go out in this weather"—what weather? It was a normal day for early summer—and she saw Marjorie's glance fall upon the suitcase again and saw the determined set of Marjorie's jaw under the polite cool subservient smile and she knew it was no good: she couldn't get away with the baby but neither could she turn back now because within two minutes Bert would be told what she'd tried to do and her next stop, and last one, would be commitment to that rubber room.

No choice. None at all.

She surrendered the baby. "Tell my husband I'll be away for a few days. Tell him not to worry." And picked up the suitcase and took it with the jacket through the door. They didn't move to stop her. That wasn't included in their instructions. They only smiled and she watched the door swing shut, cutting off her view of the baby.

She could still hear Ellen's yowling when she crossed the vestibule and put her key in the switch that summoned the elevator. The sound dwindled as the baby was carried away toward the nursery.

Would they awaken Bert right away?

Probably.

Chances were she only had a minute or two to get away. Where was the damned elevator?

What else could I have done? There must have been something. Can I go back now and get her? Isn't there some way?

She scrambled feverishly amid the labyrinth of visions. But all of them were dead ends.

She heard the elevator mechanism. At least it was moving. But where was the car?

Back in the apartment she thought she heard a door slam.

My God. Come *on!*

Nothing to do but run for it. Hide. Set up a nest somewhere safe. Then come back when he's no longer expecting it and take the baby away from him.

Footsteps in the apartment. Pounding hard on the carpet. Coming forward. Bert's stride.

The car arrived; the doors slid open. She kicked the suitcase into the elevator, swung inside, jabbed her key into the slot.

The doors were closing and she just had a glimpse of Bert as he came plunging out of the apartment. He was stretching forward, trying to claw at the closing doors, but they came together before his hand reached them.

The car lurched and began to slide downward.

She wept and wept and wept.

47 All the way up the seventeen miles of one-lane blacktop she's tense and rigid at the wheel. If you get trapped on this road—if Bert's decided to come up a day early this week or if one of them is driving toward you from the house right now and recognizes you . . .

She remembers evenings on this road when you had to stop and wait for the deer to finish bounding across the road—counting them as they leaped: five, six, seven. One time, with Ellen hardly ten weeks old in her arms, she counted out twelve of them.

A car coming forward: she glimpses a glitter of sun reflection as it moves toward her beyond a bend in the trees.

Oh Jesus. If it's one of ours . . .

Every quarter mile or so there's a pullout to allow oncoming traffic to pass. This one happens to be on her left as she approaches it; that's good in this case because it will put her on the far side of the vehicle—harder for the oncoming driver to see clearly; and her door opens directly onto the woods in case she's forced to duck and run.

It comes in sight—a white Lincoln, muddy and bug-spattered. She pulls her head back into the shadows of the cab and peers through her sunglasses. The driver of the car—quick glimpse of a black man in a grey windbreaker—waves his thanks and drives by. The car has M.D. plates.

A doctor? No one she's ever seen before. Possibly from one of the other houses along the road.

Sweating, she drives on.

The gate is shut of course; it's always shut—a forbidding grillwork of steel appended to stone gateposts amid no-nonsense signs: Private and No Trespassing and Beware of Dogs.

Her palms are damp and she sits taut for a moment, gulping breaths, remembering how she never used to pay much attention to the gate; she always had one of those remote-control transmitter gizmos in the car—you just pressed it and the gate rolled open and you drove through it and it slid shut behind you with a silent assurance that made you feel safe.

She doesn't even remember which side the lock is on. Getting out of the Jeep she examines the left-hand gatepost, sees nothing on its mortared fieldstones, and crosses to the right-hand post.

There's the lock. A small brass plate; a keyhole into the mortar.

She's had these keys for three years. Certainly after she disappeared from the New York apartment two and a half months ago he would have changed all the locks there. But has he bothered to change them here as well?

She's riding on a big assumption here: that his natural arrogant carelessness toward mechanical details will have extended as far as this gate. Bert's a good driver but he rarely drives the car himself, especially here in the mountains; he's usually in the back seat of the limo talking on the phone or hatching plans with whichever of the boys have accompanied him on this weekend's trip to the cabin. The union bosses or the casino architects or the international bankers or the ones Bert never introduced to her.

So—count on the likelihood that, rapt in scams and schemes, invisible behind the tinted windows of the limousine, he usually can't be bothered to notice when the car stops for a red light or the opening of an automatic gate.

The key fits in the lock. She turns it against spring pressure. The gate begins silently to slide open.

Blinking with gratitude she climbs back into the Jeep and drives through.

Can't take the Jeep anywhere near the house; they'd hear it. Got to cut through the woods here. Stay on the downwind side of the house so the noise won't carry in that direction. Drive tangentially around to the far side of the place—intersect the rough-cut pioneer road back beyond the ridge somewhere.

That's why the four-wheel-drive vehicle is necessary.

She's driven these before but nevertheless she has trouble shifting it into the low range and has to break the instruction manual out of the door pocket. After a bit of study and several tries it finally gnashes into gear and to be sure of her bearings she checks the angle of sun shadows on the ground,

165

then tests the wind—a light breeze coming from her left—and goes bucketing to the right across a meadow, crushing flowers and knocking down saplings and trying to avoid the litter of hard New England rocks that could block her passage or puncture an oil pan.

It doesn't matter about the tracks she's leaving behind. By the time they're discovered and followed, either she'll be long gone with Ellen or it will have failed.

48 Thank God it isn't heavy primeval timber. There was a forest fire six years ago in the fall when nobody was in residence; that was during the reign of Bert's previous wife, Aileen, the one who fell in love with the headwaiter at the Englewood Country Club and eventually married him. She too had been a former model. The house that autumn was scorched but saved by air-dropped firefighters. By the time the fire was contained it had taken out most of the middle-sized trees. What's left is second growth that has sprouted around the occasional granddaddy tree that survived the blaze.

Mostly she follows game trails through the woods, splashing through puddles left by the hard rain. Where the track squeezes through gaps too narrow for the Jeep she backs up and finds a way around.

It reminds her of treks during hunting season with her father when she was nine or ten or eleven years old and he was trying to teach her to be a boy. He was very serious about knowing how to survive in the wilderness. When they were stationed at Elmendorf he'd been forced down twice by freak weather in the Alaskan wilderness; he came out on foot both times, to the amazement of experts who'd presumed him dead.

Backing up for the third time to find yet another way across a steep-sided creek, she is thinking, I wish I'd paid more attention to what he had to say.

Then she thinks: don't make a habit of recollecting things like that. You'll never dare repeat them to anyone.

Not even Ellen?

That's a question she hasn't answered: whether it will be safe someday to tell Ellen the truth.

There isn't much breeze. She's worried that the sound of the Jeep may be carrying as far as the house—it can't be much more than three-quarters of a mile off to the left.

Something stirs to her left. It draws her quick alarmed attention. She gets a glimpse of movement—tawny fur bolting into the trees. Doubtless a deer. There are quite a few of them in these woods, trapped on the property by Bert's brutal fence: they're born here and they grow up here and they die here, mostly from bullet and shotgun slug wounds inflicted by Bert and his hunting cronies.

It all seems to be taking much longer than it ought to. The boundary fence should have turned up before now. She's had time to cross the entire property twice over. It's only 320 acres, for Pete's sake.

Has she lost her bearings? Running in circles like a fool?

No. She checks tree shadows along the ground; the sun is there—that's the proper angle; she's still heading toward the fence. It ought to be right in front of her. She ought to have smashed into it by now.

So where in hell is it?

There. Just up the slope, concealed by brush.

She turns to the left, fighting the wheel, braced against the seat as the tires lurch across rocks and root systems and unexpected holes. The rough pitching flings her against the shoulder belt and at intervals it cuts into the side of her neck; by the end of this ride she'll have a welt there and a purpling bruise on the side of her elbow where it bangs into the door. Without the belt to hold her down she'd have smashed her skull against the ceiling by now. She feels shaken to pieces.

It isn't the sort of establishment into which an innocent party would wander by accident. The fence goes all the way around the property. It is nine feet high, a chain link metal barrier topped by an arrowhead pattern of electrified barbed wire strands. Once a week Bert's man has to walk the length of the fence with a pole cutter to trim back branches and leaves that threaten to drop across the line and short it out.

Be just dandy if he's making his rounds today . . .

Now she knows where she is. Anxious about the draining of time she vectors to the left across an open meadow and guns the Jeep to reckless speed.

At the top of the meadow she slaloms amid tree trunks, some of them jagged and blackened. Must be almost there now. Got to be . . .

Wheels spinning, engine whining, she bursts out of a tangled thicket into the rutted pioneer road. The front wheels plunge down and the Jeep nearly stalls.

Hitting the clutch, gathering breath, she remembers when they bulldozed the road through from the house to the landing strip: a rough pioneer track, unsurfaced, barely graded but sufficient for the Bronco.

Twigs and branches lie askew in the ruts now, some of them crushed. There are a lot of puddles. She sees dark grease stains on the bent weeds that make a spine along the hump of the middle of the track.

It's been used fairly recently, then.

Of course that doesn't prove they're still using the airstrip. It doesn't prove they haven't rolled up the steel mesh and taken it away.

If they have—suppose the strip has become boggy

168

from yesterday's rain: too overgrown for Charlie's airplane to land?

The worst thing is there's no time to find out.

She cranks the wheel sharp right and fits the tires into the deep tracks and drives the short distance to the back gate. It is a simple reinforced steel contraption that lacks the formality of the curlicued iron gate at the front entrance but makes up for it in solidity: the gauge of its mesh is such that no wirecutter short of an acetylene torch could breach it.

Holding it shut are two enormous padlocks, top and bottom, their hasps at least half an inch thick.

They gleam in the sunlight—the glint of new metal.

Her keys don't fit.

49 She switches off the ignition and stands beside the Jeep staring dismally at the padlocked gate. In the abrupt silence there are sharp pinging sounds—heat contractions in the engine.

Her watch: it's noon. She feels the terrible pressure of time. Charlie will land at precisely one o'clock but how long will he dare to wait for her if she's not there to meet him?

Charlie with his simplistic images of Mafiosi and his limp jokes about gun molls: what if he's not as brave as he pretends to be?

The padlocks are hopeless. You'd need a bazooka to break them open. She examines the other side of the gate. The hinges are thick steel straps belted around the upright

169

steel pole. Bolted together and the nuts welded in place to prevent anyone from unscrewing them.

It would take something a lot heavier than this Jeep to bust through that gate.

But she's remembering an odd snatch of conversation. It was Jack Sertic, wasn't it? Up here at the cabin one rainy afternoon; half a dozen of them sitting around the huge living room in boots and hunting shirts waiting with their rifles for the rain to quit so they could go out and prove their courage against a hapless fenced-in herd of deer.

They were talking about crime in the city: street crime and burglaries. They didn't think of their own activities as crime—not in that same sense. (She remembers confronting Bert with it; one of the last conversations they had; she was accusing him in a tight quavering voice barely under control and he replied arrogantly: Jesus, the way you talk you'd think we were some kind of thugs—I don't pull out a knife and ambush people on dark streets—I don't threaten innocent people with a gun—I don't break into anybody's home and steal things—I'm just a businessman, honey, so it's against the law, so's jaywalking, I just sell things to people who want to buy them.)

Jack Sertic that day was talking about a friend of his who lived in a penthouse on Riverside Drive, one of the post-war buildings with greenhouse balconies and interior fire escapes. The friend's penthouse had been burgled so many times that finally he'd invested a fortune installing a solid steel front door and doorframe with inch-thick deadbolt locks. The most burglarproof door money could buy.

"So the next time he's out of town for the weekend"— she even remembers the chuckle in Jack's high-pitched voice—"the burglars come back and they take one look at that bombproof door of his and they just laugh and pick up a sledgehammer and smash their way right through the wall next to the door. These buildings, Sheetrock wallboard, you can go through the walls like butter."

She still can hear the bray of his laughter and see Bert's scowl of disapproval. Muggers and burglars aren't amusing to Bert. He can be very righteous.

Recalling that day she thinks of Jack and Diane together and of her phone call to Diane a few days ago. Suppose Diane decided to go ahead and tell Jack about the phone call from the south? Or suppose she told Bert about it? Suppose Bert figured out what it meant—suppose he's taken Ellen back to the protection of the apartment in the city?

It's no good speculating. You've got to base your actions on your latest and best knowledge—and to the best of your knowledge Ellen is still here.

She walks off the road and moves close to the fence to examine it.

The top and bottom rails of the fence are pipes. The chain link mesh is attached on all four sides but each panel is at least ten feet wide. Designed to keep people and animals out; but what about Jeeps?

You may as well assume it can be done. Because you haven't got any choice. It's the only way out of here. Either you break through it or you're trapped inside this beastly fence.

But that comes later. Can't risk the noise now.

All right. No more time to dawdle. Leave the Jeep here. Take the ring of keys. Let's go get Ellen.

She walks back along the road: heading for the house. Alone and unarmed.

50 The house sits high on two acres of cleared ground. The lawn around three sides has taken hold this year: it looks rich and thick.

The helicopter like an engorged insect perches on its pad halfway between the side of the house and the edge of the timber. It's still white and blue. Still exactly the same. Funny; she feels she's been away so long that everything ought to have changed.

She remembers when he first bought the helicopter. They weren't yet married then. "Sick and tired of airport congestion," he growled in that perpetually hoarse voice that she'd thought so attractive.

For months the chopper was his favorite toy. He had to show it off to all his friends: take them for rides.

He hired and fired four pilots before he found one he liked—George Talmy, the freckled redhead who looked like a truant schoolboy with his twinkling eyes and snub nose. One night when everyone had a bit too much to drink she learned the boyish George had earned medals for flying gunships in Nam and had been arrested 'steen times for smuggling anything you'd care to name across virtually any border in the world.

She wonders if George is still around or if Bert has found himself a new chopper jockey.

She turns off the road into the woods and ducks under branches, placing her feet with care to avoid the worst of the mud puddles; angling to approach the house from the back corner where birches and evergreens crowd up within a few yards of the sloped padlocked Bilko door that gives access to the basement.

There are only two small high windows on the ground floor at this corner—the laundry room and the mud room porch. It's the only corner of the house you can approach with a fair likelihood of not being seen from inside.

Four wooden steps lead up to the back door. This is the old part of the house, still unpretentious; simple 2 × 6 boards for steps and rails. She stands at the foot of the steps looking up at the door and picking among the keys on the ring.

There are two tiny bulbs by the burglar alarm keyhole. One is red; one is white. Both of them are unlit—meaning the house is open and occupied, the alarm system switched off.

That's a small break. At least she doesn't need to find out if her old key still fits the alarm lock. She's had visions of forcing her way through the alarm system and setting off a clanging din that would awaken anybody within two miles.

The more important question is whether one of her old house keys will still fit the back door. If not she'll try the padlocked Bilko door but that's a noisy bugger to open.

Do these back steps creak? She can't remember. She puts a toe on the bottom tread and eases her weight onto it slowly. The stair feels a bit loose but it holds her without complaint. She tries for the second step.

She hears a low growl and turns in time to see the dog come rushing forward around the corner: big-framed German shepherd with massive chest and battle-scarred snout.

The dog snarls again and bears down on her, ready to start barking; she only has time to speak in a fast low voice:

"Down, Hoagy. Down."

It makes the dog hesitate.

"Take it easy, it's just me."

The dog cocks his head. Tentative wag of tail. She drops to one knee on the lower step and holds out a hand. "Come on, boy. Calm down. Just me."

Hoagy sniffs her hand and smiles. He lays his big head across her knee. She rubs his head, scratches his ears and speaks in a murmur: "You're a good pooch. Good pooch. My goodness, that rip in your ear is something new. Been tangling with that sheepdog again? Shame on you. Go on now, beat it."

Hoagy sits back and watches her, tail wagging.

"Go on. Back to work, that's a good pooch. Keep the burglars away."

She goes up to the top step. Hoagy finds a new interest and scratches industriously at his throat with his hind foot. Then he trots away.

She waits for her breathing to settle down. Then she tackles the door.

The key fits, thank God. She twists it soundlessly and feels the bolt withdraw on its spring; she thumbs the latch and slowly eases the door open.

Nobody in the mud room or the narrow service hall beyond. She shuts the door behind her. The wall pegs are hung with red caps and hunting coats and waders; there are boots on the floor.

She moves into the hallway, putting weight down slowly on each foot. Glances into the laundry room, sees no more than she expected to see, moves on toward the L-turn that leads past the back stairs into the kitchen.

At the corner she presses her back to the wall and listens before she peeks around.

She can hear the buzz of men's voices; can't identify them or make out words. No noise coming from the kitchen. The voices are beyond, in the big front room.

She looks around the corner. Past the narrow flight of open stairs she can see this side of the kitchen—butcher-block table, wooden chairs, heavy copper pots hanging from the wrought iron gizmo she remembers buying at a country auction—and part of the far wall with its stainless steel sink under the side window.

Nobody.

We are running in luck, kid. Just let it hold.

She moves in under the stairs and peers between the treads—a slightly wider angle of the kitchen from here. The steel door of the big walk-in freezer; lights burning in their shades—this part of the house has always been dark, even at noon on a bright day.

Hell, there's nobody back here. Let's get moving.

Out from under. Around to the foot of the stairs. Nothing visible up there except shadows. Someone laughs boisterously in the front room—she doesn't recognize the laugh but she does recognize Jack Sertic's high-pitched voice when he replies, "Bet your ass, man," and his distinctive bray.

Oh Jesus. If Jack's here on a Thursday then it's almost dead certain Bert's here too.

It's just what she's hoped to avoid.

Someone else speaks—it may be Bert's voice; too indistinct to be sure—and several voices join in the laughter. She hears the rattle and chink of chips on the table.

There's a whole damn *gang* of them in there. Jesus.

But there's nothing you can do about that and this is hardly a bright time to turn around and flee. You're almost home, child. Unless they've changed things all around in this house, Ellen is just up those stairs.

Let's go.

She goes up the steps quickly, surrounded by the familiar cedar smell of the house.

At the top there's one of those three-foot-high expandable gates across the doorway, the kind they use to prevent small children from falling down staircases. Rather than risk a noise by opening it she steps over it.

The rattle of poker chips always used to annoy her. It's one of those sounds you can't ignore. It used to keep her awake half the night.

On her left the gun room is unoccupied: bookcases

filled with Bert's big picture tomes on wildlife and ballistics; recliner chair, lamp, couch, gun rack bristling with weapons, big console TV under the shelves of pirated videocassette movies.

"You what?"

"Said I raise forty dollars."

"Marjorie?" Bert is hollering. "You want to go get us some sandwiches? Slice up some of that venison from last night."

"You gotta be out of your gourd, man. I got trip nines staring you right in the face."

"You want to play cards or just brag about your nines?"

The sound of a nearby door latch. In sudden alarm she wheels back into the den and flattens herself against the wall just inside the doorway; and hears footsteps march forward along the landing.

She sees Marjorie Quirini go past in the hallway; recognizes Marjorie's broad beam and the apron ties. There's some squeaking and snapping as the child gate is opened and shut: Marjorie's heavy feet plod down the stairs.

Christ. That was close.

She must have been dusting or something.

She goes back out into the hall. The bathroom on the right is empty. There are two possible routes here: through the bathroom to the master bedroom and then out into the landing; or forward to the landing and then along past the row of bedroom doors. But the landing is an open loft above the big front room and the voices are below that balcony. If the furniture hasn't been rearranged the poker table is in full view of the landing.

So she goes in through the bathroom and opens the connecting door a crack.

No one in the big bedroom. She looks at her watch. Twelve-twenty.

Get a move on.

176

She remembers the fourposter bed. Bert's previous wife bought it when they redecorated the place after the fire six years ago.

She goes past it to the door and softly eases it open.

This will be the worst part: the gauntlet between this door and the nursery twenty feet to the right along the balcony. Every step of it will be in sight of a good part of the big living room below.

"Look at that. The case nine. Four nines. I lose with jacks full. Can you believe it?"

"I told you not to mess around with my nines, stupid."

Then she realizes. Of course. All I've got to do is lie down and crawl. They won't see a thing.

She pokes her head out and looks both ways along the landing. Nothing stirs.

Someone coughs. "You want to deal the cards or just sit there looking stunned?"

She hears Bert's voice clearly for the first time: "I think the son of a bitch shorted us the two kilos on purpose. I think he got a better price from somebody else."

Feeling idiotic she gets down on her face and begins to crawl along the baseboard. Out under the railing past the edge of the balcony she can see the upper portion of the high plate glass picture windows that run across the front of the house.

Another voice now. Vaguely familiar but she can't identify it: "What's wrong with that? You get a better deal someplace, you take it. Hey—am I right or am I right?"

"Not after he agreed to the score." Bert is petulant. "We had a deal with the son of a bitch."

She's halfway along the wall now. Hope to heaven nobody comes up the stairs right now.

Through the picture windows she sees the helicopter and now she realizes whose voice that is: George Talmy the pilot. So he's still here after all.

She crawls as far as the nursery door. There's a big

cutout of Snoopy thumbtacked above the latch.

She opens it silently.

A big woman in a white uniform—a stranger—sits watching TV on a small portable color set with the sound turned way down.

The baby napping in the crib is only a bundle of sheets and a clutter of toys from here.

The big nurse is lifting five-pound hand weights. Up slowly and down again. Her biceps look like Muhammad Ali's.

Oh *shit.*

51 In the rack are six hunting rifles and four handguns. A heavy chain connects all of them, running through the trigger guards, fastened with a thick brass-frame padlock.

It's the same lock. Her key opens it. As silently as possible she pulls the links of the chain through the trigger housing of the Luger.

Despite its heft it is the smallest caliber revolver on the rack. Any of the others would be a lot more powerful and menacing but this is the only one she's sure she knows how to use because Bert forced her to memorize the procedures of shooting and reloading and cleaning the damned thing. If you're ever alone up here, he kept saying—as if she ever was up here in the woods without the company of Bert or the Quirinis or half a dozen of the deer-hunting fraternity and their ditsy wives and girlfriends.

It isn't loaded of course. She remembers his lectures about keeping loaded guns around the house. She unlocks the ammunition drawer and finds the box of .22 magnum cartridges; fumbles a bit loading the chambers but finally has it full; puts the box back in the drawer and locks everything up and carries the heavy revolver to the door.

She goes back through the bathroom and the master bedroom and out onto the landing. Belly-flat again she creeps toward the nursery.

"You want lettuce and mayonnaise?" That's Marjorie, her big voice echoing from the kitchen.

"I'm dealing. Seven to a possible straight. Three's, a pair. Nine on the flush, that's three clubs. And a jack on the table. Treys bet. You guys want mayo?"

"Sure."

"Why not."

"Marjorie? Mayo's fine, anything else you got. Maybe some horseradish."

Jack Sertic's voice now, reasoning calmly: "Hey, look Al, like he never gave us trouble before. He delivered three kilos on time. Good quality stuff."

George Talmy again: "What you gonna do, Al, waste the poor bastard just because he comes up short once in his life?"

And now Bert's reply, husky with insinuation. "George, the way you talk I get the feeling sometimes you believe you've been promoted from helicopter driver to partner."

Jack laughs at him. "The amount of money you pay him, he qualifies as *senior* partner."

George says, "You think I'm out of line, Al? I don't like to feel I'm just some kind of servant around here, you know. But all the same I know who's in charge. I don't give you any real lip, do I?"

"Al, you gonna bet those threes or what?"

She shuts the door behind her. She doesn't think she's made any sound but the nurse looks around—alarmed perhaps by some subtle shift in the light.

The weights are on the floor by the chair. The nurse sees her, sees the revolver in her hand. The nurse's eyes whip around past the crib to the table in the corner.

It draws her attention to the big pistol on the table.

"Don't. I'll use this if I have to."

"You're her, ain't you."

She moves across the room, keeping her distance, making a circle around the nurse. At the crib she looks down.

My God she's grown. She's beautiful. Radiant. My lovely child. Still got those funny freckles around her nostrils. They'll be cute when she grows up. Dear Lord—it hasn't even been three months but she seems twice as big . . . my darling . . .

She feels herself soften; as if her body is growing heavier. Tears flow into her eyes. I have missed you so much, my love . . .

Stop that!

She snaps her face around toward the nurse, who hasn't stirred. But you can tell by the shrewd narrowing of her eyes that she's gauging her opportunities, waiting for her moment.

"I'm her mother."

The big woman answers with a grunt of sound that conveys no meaning.

"I'm taking her with me. Do you think I won't use this on you if you try to stop me?"

"They told me about you," the nurse says with dogged bovine obscurity.

"It's important. You've got to understand I'm serious about this. She's my child." She hisses it vehemently: "She's *my child*."

The nurse looks at the revolver, looks at her face, looks her up and down. There is absolutely no clue to what she's thinking. "All right, miss. What do you want me to do?"

Carefully now. Aim the revolver at her. "Stand up."

The woman gets out of her chair and looms. Got to be at least five-eleven. Maybe six feet.

"What's your name?"

"Mrs. Strickland."

"First name?"

"Melinda."

"All right, Melinda. Go over there and face the wall. Put your hands on top of your head. I want your nose right against the wall."

The nurse obeys. "Now what?"

"You don't move until I tell you to move. You speak only if I tell you to speak. Not before. Understand? Say yes."

"Yes."

"Now don't move."

Testing it, she takes a pace back and a pace forward, making a few noises, cocking and uncocking the revolver, holding it ready, watching the nurse. The nurse doesn't move.

An actress on the television screen is emoting: shouting, striding back and forth, declaiming her lines, chewing up all the scenery on the set. The volume is turned very low; the shouting is barely audible. "You lied to me! You told me Steven was my natural brother! For twenty years you've been living this beastly horrible lie and you've made me part of it!"

All right. Got to take the chance.

She reaches down into the crib with both arms and sets the revolver down amid the plastic toys. While she checks the baby's diaper and wraps the thin sheet around Ellen (a blanket? no; the day is too hot for it) she keeps looking up at the nurse's broad back; and she keeps talking in a quiet steady voice:

"Listen to me now, Melinda. If you shout—if you do anything at all to draw their attention—I'll shoot you. Then I'll take the baby and run for it. They'll stop to examine your dead body and that'll give me time to get away."

Ellen hasn't awakened yet. If we're very lucky she won't wake up until we're out of the house. One hand under her spine now; the other under her head. Pick her up. Cradle her in the left arm, Ellen's head in the crook of your elbow. Make sure you've got her in a firm grasp.

Now pick up the revolver again with your free hand.

And keep talking all the way:

"You understand? Even if you're dead you'll still slow them down. You're just as useful to me dead as you are alive. If I have to kill you to save my baby then that's what I'll do. You think about that, Melinda. Think hard."

Straighten up now. Adjust the baby in your arm. *Don't drop the Goddamn gun—be careful, idiot!*

"You can turn around now. Go over to the door."

The nurse lowers her hands and looks around. If she's surprised by what she sees she gives no sign of it. There is menace in her uncomplaining cooperation. She walks on white rubber-soled shoes to the door and stands there, just waiting. Very calm. What does it take to upset the cow?

The television is peddling caffeine-free coffee. She comes past it and waggles the gun at the nurse. "Are you listening, Melinda?"

"Tell me what you want, miss."

"I want you to get down on the floor. Then you pull the door open—all the way open, right back to the doorstop—and then you crawl out onto the landing. You stay close to the wall and you crawl on your belly all the way into the master bedroom, so they can't see you from down below. I'm going to be right behind you with this gun. Do you know anything about guns?"

"Some."

"This is a twenty-two magnum. That mean anything to you?"

"High velocity, I guess."

"You're a nurse. Ever worked in an operating room?"

"No. I'm not an RN. I'm a practical nurse."

"But you've had some training in anatomy."

The nurse nods, acknowledging it.

She curls her thumb over the hammer of the revolver and levels it toward the nurse's wide face. "If I fire it right up your asshole—I'll let you picture what it'll do to your insides. It'll rip all the way through and probably tear the top of your skull off on its way out."

The nurse's expression never changes but her throat thickens when she swallows. It's reaction enough.

"All right, Melinda. Down on the floor and open the door. Let's go."

The baby yawns.

52 The baby's eyes pop open and she recognizes the familiar green flash of them. She smiles down and croons very softly to Ellen; cradles and cuddles her; wraps the sheet a little tighter around her.

The baby stretches—arms and legs thrusting out in all directions, shoving her hand, painfully poking a breast—she has to hold the kid in both arms to keep her secure but she's still got the gun in her hand and her eyes on the nurse; and the nurse clearly has made up her mind not to take stupid chances but to wait for a sensible opportunity.

Don't give her one.

"Go to sleep, Ellen. Go to sleep, little baby. When you wake up everything's going to be wonderful."

The baby's mouth works. But the eyes drift shut and after a few minutes she points toward the door with the revolver and the nurse gets down on hands and knees, pulls the door open wide, drops flat and worms her way out of the room.

Stay right behind her now. Don't let her go around any corners out of sight. Keep her in view at all times.

Below, Jack Sertic says, "It's not like there's a deadline or anything. We can fill the gap. I'll phone Montreal, the stuff can be airborne in two hours."

"Never mind," Bert says. "We've got enough to handle with the flight coming in tonight and the one coming in Saturday midnight. Talking about eight, ten million wholesale. What time's it?"

"Twelve thirty. Few minutes past."

The baseboard has dust webs and flecks of dried mud from hunting boots. Marjorie never was much good at keeping things clean.

"Got the firepots ready out on the field?"

Come on, Melinda, you can move faster than that.

"I hate these midnight pickups any more. Are these cards made? You get older, you start going to sleep earlier. I don't keep the kind of hours I used to. You want to cut the cards? When I was a kid I was a real night owl, never saw the sun before two, three in the afternoon sometimes. But I don't know. Now I'm lucky if I stay awake for the ten o'clock news on channel five. Queen, four, nine, big ace. Dealer control. Ace bets five. Come on, everybody fold, I'm not proud, I want the antes."

If the baby wakes up now and starts to cry . . .

Watching the heavy haunches roll from side to side she's thinking, Melinda—what an absurd name for this water buffalo. My God—from this angle this scene is pure farce.

"What's the bet?"

"Al bet five bucks on the ace."

"Without me."

"Fold."

"Hell with it. Take the antes."

"Shit. I got wired aces—back to back—and what happens? They chicken out on me. What a bunch of pinheads. How'm I gonna make my fortune off you pinheads?"

"Your deal, George."

In the bedroom she pushes the door nearly shut and stands up; she crosses to the bathroom door and looks through to the hall and then quickly turns and points the revolver at the nurse; but Melinda is still lying on the floor waiting for instructions.

Presumably Marjorie is still downstairs preparing sandwiches for the boys. If we time this right we can sneak out the back while she's serving lunch in the front room.

"Okay." She keeps her voice down. "Don't talk. Stand up. Face the wall there until I tell you to move."

She goes back to the door and stands with her ear by the open crack, listening to the clink of poker chips and the voices of the men below as they idle away time waiting for an airplane in the darkness.

Now the stillness ticks. She caresses the baby, hugs her close, listens to the sound of her breathing—reconstructing on the psychic bridge between them the lines of contact and understanding that are familiar but too long disused. We're going to have to learn each other all over again. . . .

Two things happen simultaneously: two voices. Melinda whispering, "I got to stand here all afternoon like a bump on a log or what?" and, down below in the front room, George Talmy's voice—"Hey, those look real good. I never get tired of good cured venison."

"Shut up," she hisses at the nurse. She hears Marjorie's voice below: "You want beer or what?"

Bert: "Beer's fine. Just bring us a six-pack, we'll sort it out. Thanks, Marjorie."

She comes past Melinda, moving swiftly now. "Come on. Keep quiet. *Move.*"

She opens the child gate. A bit of a squeak; nobody is

likely to question it—if they hear it and think about it at all they'll take it for the nurse going downstairs to get a bite of lunch.

She goes downstairs first, going down sideways one step at a time, keeping the gun and one eye on Melinda behind her while she negotiates the stairs. At the second step up from the bottom she stops. She warns Melinda with a gesture and the nurse stops three treads above.

Keeping the revolver leveled and cocked she watches the nurse unblinkingly while she listens to the sounds from the kitchen: the opening of the fridge, the scrape of something being removed from a fridge shelf, the chunk of the door closing, Marjorie's footsteps and voice: "You want glasses or just drink out of the cans?"

Bert's voice is faint: "Just the cans. Stays colder that way."

Marjorie's footsteps recede.

Down to the bottom of the steps now. Cradle the baby. Keep the gun on the nurse. Whisper: "That way. Out the back door. You go ahead of me now."

Then they're out the back door and elation washes over her. Ellen darling—we did it. That was the hardest part.

She wags the gun at the nurse. "Walk. That way."

Into the woods—and she sees it when the nurse hesitates, thinking about letting that long branch whip back into her face. "Don't do it, Melinda. I'm watching you. Keep going."

Down to the pioneer road. No sign of the dog. The baby burbling now, soft questionings, not yet fully awake. Melinda hiking along the center hump of the road, white shoes filthy.

It's hard to walk with the baby in her arm and the gun in her hand; she can't see her own feet and it's hard to watch the baby and the nurse and the uneven ground at the same time.

"Slow down. Stay closer in front of me."

"You know you ain't going to get away, miss. You know that, don't you?"

"I like it better when you don't talk."

They go on, an odd procession. She's beginning to listen for the sound of Charlie's airplane but all she can hear is their own footfalls and the cicadas and a conversation taking place in the trees among the birds.

It's turned into a beautiful day, my darling Ellen. In your honor I'm sure. Do you like airplanes? It'll be noisy of course but I imagine not as noisy as that helicopter you're used to. I hope you like Charlie. I hope he likes you. What are your views on moving to San Diego? I expect you're going to—oh!

Caught under something—root or rock—her foot won't come loose in time and she feels herself pitching forward; she flings out her right arm to break the fall and rolls on her right shoulder into a shallow puddle in the Goddamn rut but she's still got the gun and she has protected Ellen in her grasp and the baby just laughs, thinking it some sort of game, so there's no real harm done and let's just get to our feet and never mind a bruise or two—

She hears the fast thumping of footfalls and the snapping of branches and knows she's been hearing it for several seconds before realizing what it is: she searches frantically, getting a new grip on the revolver and whipping it up.

Bitch!

She sees the big white dress fleeing through the woods, weaving and dodging, flickering among the trees—arms batting about to fend off branches; feet scrabbling on the slick ground; an ungainly passage that makes a lot of noise but doesn't put distance behind the nurse very fast. She's still easily within range.

Bitch.

Aim the revolver—draw the hammer back to full cock—take a breath, let part of it out, hold it.

Hell. What's the point. They'd hear the shots.

Go ahead. Shoot. They'll have no idea which direction
the shooting is coming from . . .

She watches the nurse gallop out of sight back toward
the house.

Face it. You never would have shot her. It's just lucky
she didn't call your bluff sooner.

The baby is starting to cry.

"Okay Ellen. Okay. We're going."

Hurry now. Hurry.

Run . . .

53 Gasping for oxygen she fumbles for the handle and
gets the door open and tosses the revolver in and
climbs into the Jeep. The baby is caterwauling at full decibels,
flailing arms and legs.

I know. You feel exactly the same way I feel. Let me
out of here! Right? Okay—okay. We're going. Hang in there,
kiddo.

She fastens the shoulder belt down across baby and all;
snugs it tight; grips Ellen firmly and turns the key.

It starts right up. Thank heaven for small blessings. It's
still in dual drive low range where she left it so she doesn't
need to struggle with that.

She jams it into low gear and with one hand strong on
the wheel points it off the road and holds the baby tight while
the Jeep caroms off a stump and jounces toward the fence.

It would take an extra hand to shift gears. She leaves it
in low and gingerly depresses her foot on the accelerator;
braces her forearm across the steering wheel and clutches

Ellen tight and she's doing maybe ten or twelve miles an hour when the Jeep collides with the fence and stops short and damn near breaks her arm.

Jesus.

The engine has stalled. She can feel an ache in her neck. She lifts her arm off the wheel and works her fingers, makes a fist and then shakes the arm roughly with a wanton need to know.

Hurts like hell but everything works. Just bruised, evidently.

The baby wails. She strokes Ellen's face and peers out through the windshield. The Jeep has bounced back a couple of feet from the point of impact and she can see the outline of its hood against the mesh of the fence. There's the glitter of broken glass beyond the fence—pieces of headlight lenses.

Made a hell of a dent in that son of a bitch fence. One or two more and maybe it'll give way.

At first she doesn't recognize the sound; then because it's quite faint she's not sure whether she hears it or not. She opens the door and leans her head out into the open air and now she can hear it quite clearly: the drone of an airplane.

It grows steadily louder and she hears a change in its pitch. Descending now; throttling back.

Charlie. God bless him.

She shoves in the clutch and turns the key. The starter grinds.

Oh shit. Have I busted something in the engine?

Then it catches and roars. She backs her foot off the pedal and has a hard time ramming the gearshift into reverse. Backs up nearly to the road and that's when, looking back, she sees the Bronco back there, engine whining high, bearing straight down on her.

54 The Jeep gathers speed, rushing the fence. She's got her foot hard and flat on the gas and she's braced against the wheel again, heedless of the pain in that arm, tensing her left hand and arm around the baby in a grip an ape couldn't pry loose, lowering her head instinctively to protect her eyes if the windshield goes, hearing the thunder of the overstrained engine and the high whine of the gearboxes, feeling the seat pitch around as the tight shoulder and lap belts yank her around with it, aware of the Bronco speeding toward her from behind and everything it means.

She's not sure whether the screaming is Ellen's or her own.

Impact. Ellen is nearly torn from her grasp. A great rending racket all around her—compound of tearing metal and crunching glass and screeching friction. She knows only a desperate need to keep her foot jammed down on the throttle. She's got the fingers of her right hand locked around the wheel and for a moment the pressure of her own weight is so great that she's sure either the wheel will shatter or her arm must break. The seat is lurching, turning, tipping to the side. She blinks and tries to see through squinted eyes; images flash but she has no clear idea of what's happening; things jerk back and forth, there's still the cry of the engine, the right side of the Jeep is up in the air somehow and it's threatening to turn over and crush her but then it rights itself, slamming down, sliding off something, skidding sidewise before the wheels get purchase and the seat jerks forward violently

190

enough to slam her skull back against the padded headrest.

The wheels are bumping on things now, spinning; the Jeep is bucking around like a wild horse and her foot slips off the gas pedal. Instantly everything calms down.

A tree looms straight ahead. She pulls the wheel to the right and feels around with her foot for the pedal. The Jeep obeys: a slow turn to the right, a grinding climb past the big tree.

"Ellen—Ellen darling—we made it through!"

55 It wasn't the windshield that broke, thank goodness. The outside mirrors are gone—one empty of its glass, the other torn completely from the vehicle—nothing left but the jagged base of its mounting. There are horrendous scratches across the hood and the front of it is buckled up in an odd shape. The Jeep feels as if it has been twisted askew.

But the engine continues to pull well and she's gathering speed along the pioneer road, feeling as if the Jeep is crabbing sidewise. She manages to shift gears one-handed while the Jeep lurches back and forth within the guiding ruts of the road.

She reaches up to adjust the rear-view mirror and gets a glimpse of the Bronco back there beyond the gate: they've got the gate unlocked and a man is swinging it out of the way and the Bronco starts forward.

Beside the gate she flashes on the swirl of mangled metal that somehow she broke through. It looks utterly impenetrable.

The road curls amid the trees; she loses sight of things

in the mirror. How far to the airstrip now? Can't be more than a minute or two.

Has Charlie had time to find it?

"Take it easy, Ellen. It'll be all right soon. Calm down, that's a good girl. I know this is a hell of a trial for you. Hang in there, darling."

A bend up ahead; past it another. She doesn't remember any of this; she only came out here a couple of times and she wasn't driving and you never remember roads if you haven't driven them yourself.

Then without warning she's out of the trees and there it is—a long cleared strip running left to right, the late summer's grass gone yellow-green now.

High to her left she sees the airplane descending toward her on its approach run.

"Charlie." She whimpers his name.

He'll need most of the runway to stop it. She'd better be at the far end to meet him.

She puts the Jeep forward into the wide field until the wheels begin to hum and whine on the hidden steel mats under the grass; she accelerates up through the gears, not needing the four-wheel drive any longer but there's no time to take it out of dual range now so the gears keep whining and the engine keeps straining but she's up to forty-five and that's the end of the field coming up ahead.

She turns it around and stops.

Can't do anything but wait for him to bring the plane down. Then she'll drive right out to meet it and jump in with Ellen and they'll be out of this nightmare place for good.

The baby is silent. She looks down at her. Wide-eyed and contented. Sucking her thumb.

"You're all right. You'll do, kid."

She sits in an unaccustomed quiet, engine idling, stick in gear, clutch to the floor. The airplane drops closer. I love you, Charlie.

The airplane is on its invisible ramp now, lined up with

the opposite end of the field, coming in straight toward her. Half a minute to touchdown.

And then two things:

The Bronco comes slashing out of the trees up there alongside the far end of the runway—

And the helicopter swoops into view low across the treetops. It dips and sways out over the middle of the airstrip—hovering. Beneath the rotor she sees grass whipping flat against the steel mesh.

Her heart leaps to her throat.

They're going to block the runway . . .

No. Wait.

The helicopter is climbing—rising straight up as if on an elevator—and the Bronco has turned alongside the runway; it's coming down the side of the field toward her but the runway itself is clear.

God knows why but they've made room.

Maybe they're just stupid.

Who cares. You can make it, Charlie. Come straight in and pick me up and somehow we'll get out of here. I've still got the damn gun if we need it . . .

The thing went caroming all over the inside of the Jeep back there—a wonder it didn't go off—but now it's in plain sight on the floor in front of the passenger seat. She reaches down and picks it up.

When she looks up again she sees the airplane climbing away, steeply banking. *What?*

The helicopter is scooting around up there—its movements don't seem to make much sense. The Bronco has halved the distance to her Jeep and if she doesn't move now they'll have her but Jesus Christ, Charlie, what are you doing to me?

Running. Climbing. Turning back the way he came.

Receding into the sky.

The helicopter goes after him now, following him toward the clouds.

Oh Charlie you good-for-nothing bastard. You betraying son of a bitch.

She stomps the accelerator and pops the clutch and the baby cries out when the Jeep lurches into motion.

Hauling the wheel around one-handed she sends it off the field. Slams into the trees—downhill into raw wilderness smashing through brush, skidding past tree trunks, knocking down saplings, bursting into a daisy-flowered meadow, sliding half sideways down the steep slope.

God please help me.

56 In a frantic lunge against despair she rams the Jeep forward, seeking openings among the trees; the wheel chatters in her hand and she's clutching the baby protectively in her arm and both limbs are cramped but she can't let up. No telling how close they may be behind her and it won't be long before they catch up because she's breaking the trail for them. Got to find a way off this mountain . . .

The baby is yelling again.

She's trying desperately to think of a way out. Trying to remember the map but nothing comes to mind. Never been over here on the back side. Nothing here to see except woods all around.

She finds clearings and uses them—several times plunging into thick mud bogs before knowing they are there in the deep grass; only the low range four-wheel traction brings her through.

Smashing thickets she skirts a brown pond and fits between saplings as thick as her forearms; the side-mounted spare tire catches on one of them and begins to pull the Jeep around but she manhandles it through.

Ellen in panic tries to scramble out of her imprisoning grip. She has to let go of the wheel to confine the baby with both hands. A tire bangs against something and pulls to the side; she has to grab the wheel again; she tucks Ellen against her, lowers her chin, lifts the baby and pushes her mouth against Ellen's forehead. "Okay—okay—okay."

The tires jitter across a rocky patch, making a loud rataplan that jars all her bones; the frame of the windshield shakes so violently before her eyes that she feels caught up in a kaleidoscopic maelstrom.

"Hang on, baby girl. Yell all you want but just don't let go."

Then in a stand of pines she crosses a trail and nearly misses it but then it registers and she brakes to a slamming stop, fights the shift into reverse and backs up.

It's an overgrown track that looks like the sort of road forest rangers use—not much more than a hiking trail but wide enough to admit vehicular passage.

It goes uphill to the left, downhill to the right. That's south, more or less, and she goes that way even though she knows her best escape is northward; she goes that way because it's downhill and maybe it will lead her out of the mountains.

The track carries the Jeep out of the trees at the edge of a sloping meadow and the world opens before her. Worn green mountains all around; all the hillsides spill into a narrow valley that curves away to the northeast.

She can see cleared building sites down there—half a dozen scattered summer houses.

Where there are cabins there must be a road.

While she considers her options she hears a drone of distant engines and she sees them above the range quite some distance away to the north—a ballet of two tiny craft dark against the grey white clouds: airplane and helicopter weaving and bobbing and swaying as if performing some strange ritual dance.

The damn helicopter is still chasing Charlie.

To hell with him.

She continues down the track—hurrying, slithering on the weeds. Branches and thorns reach out to scrape and scratch the Jeep as it comes juddering by.

The ride is less brutal on this downslope. The baby's panic subsides; crying softly now. Keep talking to her. Keep reassuring her.

She's doing about twenty miles an hour—not very fast by normal standards but any faster and she wouldn't be able to stop in time to avoid the sudden rocks and holes that appear at intervals; she has to find a way around each of them— or bull right over it, mechanism gnashing.

Toward the bottom the slope grows steeper. The path begins to switchback. Hairpin turns—she has to back and fill. For a few hundred yards she runs back and forth along a descending Z-shaped series of terraces. Stopping and crushing the stick into reverse for the last turn she looks out the window up the long hill she's just descended—and sees the Bronco bouncing its way down from the top.

Bastards. Bastards.

They're not far behind—a couple of minutes, no more. She blasts out of the hairpin and goes lurching across the valley floor, following the faint track and hoping it will take her out to a road near those houses on the opposite slope.

"A kiss for my little one. Quiet now, Ellen. Stop blubbering, that's a good girl. I know you're scared and hungry and thirsty and exhausted—you've got a whole world of things to complain about—but Momma's got to think. You're just going to have to bear with me. I'll apologize later."

Thing is, as soon as we get out onto a decent road we're going to want all the speed we can get. That means shifting the controls on this beast—taking it out of four-wheel and low range. Converting it back to a road car. Now we've got to try and remember how to do that because they're not going to give us a whole lot of time to read the damn manual and work it out by trial and error. . . .

There's a hedgerow ahead, maples and oaks and birches—big trees masking whatever lies beyond. Directly above the trees, by some trick of random fate, she can see the distant game of tag that's still in progress between George Talmy's helicopter and Charlie's airplane.

They seem quite near the bank of clouds that hovers above the mountains and for a very brief moment she wonders why Charlie doesn't just fly into the clouds and disappear; then she's slowing down to drive into the hedgerow and she's got to concentrate on the trail. In the mirror the Bronco is nearly at the bottom of the switchbacks.

Out of the trees there's a tangle of thorn. A lot of bright color in here: it's dense and it feels tropical. The Jeep pries its way through thickets and without warning she finds herself poised at the edge of a stream looking at a white frothy flow of fast water and heaps of jumbled grey rocks everywhere. She barely stops in time.

The birling water makes a steady racket. It comes rushing around the bend in high-speed fury. A sizable broken sapling whips along the surface, smashing into rocks, caroming about, heaving and sliding past.

Christ. How deep is that river? Can the Jeep get across or has the rain swollen it too high? Is there a fording? Have any of those ugly boulders rolled into it?

Is this contraption waterproof? What happens if we get halfway across and the Jeep stalls?

Can I stand up and walk in that current with a baby in one arm?

If it's deeper than it looks can I possibly swim one-armed in that mess with the baby—and avoid smashing both of us up on those rocks?

Even if I could—where could we go to get away from them?

The Bronco will be on them any second now and there's no alternative, really.

I am endangering this kid's life and I'll do a term in purgatory for it but I honestly believe she'd be better off taking the risk of drowning than sentenced to a life with that verminous pig for a father.

"Here we go, darling. Hold tight."

She hammers it into low and puts it down the steep pitch into the water. Nothing to do but hope and pray.

57 Not too fast. Keep it slow and steady. Can't afford to lose footing in this treacherous water . . .

The flood buffets the side of the Jeep, rocking it. She fights the wheel, pulling back to the right, struggling against the Jeep's desire to slide away with the current. It feels as if the bottom is hard and flat—possibly a sunken paved bridge but certainly it was never intended for use at flood stage.

The baby is caterwauling herself hoarse; her face has gone red, splotchy around the nose.

Her hand on the steering wheel is numb. Her arm is giving out.

Sorry Ellen but I need this other hand; just lie here in my lap and please don't flail around so much.

Both hands on the wheel. Leaning her weight to the right—pulling the wheel—it's so *hard* . . .

Please give me the strength to hold it straight.

Her foot. Cold. Wet . . .

There's water coming up around her feet. Must be coming through holes in the floorboards.

The baby rolls off her lap onto the seat beside her and cries out. She can't take her hand off the wheel. "Don't move. Please, Ellen don't move."

The front wheels feel as if they're sliding toward the edge. There's something bearing down on the whitewater above her—a Goddamn tree limb or something. It looks big enough to slam us all the way around. Oh Christ . . .

The nose of the Jeep begins to rise. Lifting into shallower water it shakes free of the worst pressure of the current. The tree limb spins past behind her; she hears branches scrape across the back of the Jeep but she's climbing onto the bank now and she reaches down with her right hand to hold the baby in place on the seat.

The wheels slither on the slick mud bank; they're digging ruts in the earth but soon they've pawed the loose mud away and they're down to thick root systems. These give purchase and the Jeep heaves itself up onto solid ground.

The hiking trail curves away through another hedgerow. She drives right along, not even slowing down for a look back until she's into the trees. Then she stops the Jeep, picks up the baby and holds her in her arms while she looks in the mirror for the first time.

The Bronco is back there on the far side of the stream. Stopped. A man gets out of the passenger seat and walks forward to look at the crossing. He's wearing a checked shirt and jeans.

The shadows are tricky under those trees but it's Bert. He has a rifle.

Cradling the baby, crooning, caressing, she stares into the mirror and thinks about picking up the revolver and shooting the son of a bitch where he stands but in the end she just puts it in gear and drives on. Past the row of trees the trail meanders along the edge of a field and decants her onto a graded dirt road. She thrusts the clutch to the floor and pulls levers and hopes she's done it right; she starts up the road and is pleased not to hear any longer the meshing protesting whine of the low range. The Jeep goes properly up through the gears and she's doing a good clip by the time she passes the first house on the hill.

We could stop and go in there and ask for help but in the first place we might not get it and in the second place I'm committing a felony and I doubt we'd get a whole lot of sympathy from the police.

She's looking in the mirror. No sign of the Bronco yet. But Bert won't give up and go back. She has no doubt they're horsing it across the stream right now. If they don't capsize they'll be right after her.

And for certain they've put out a call on the CB radio. Wherever this road comes out into the world there's likely to be someone waiting for us.

Charlie, you son of a bitch, what a mess you've left us in!

58 Driving the graded dirt road at sixty miles an hour she is thinking:

I know this road. The Concord winery back there—Bert knows the man who owns it. The bald man with the strange accent—Hungarian, Polish, whatever he is. We had dinner with him and his wife at that place on Lake Champlain, remember? They invited us to two or three wine tastings.

Think, now. This road comes out to the paved highway a couple of miles ahead, just beyond the mouth of the valley up there.

The intersection's down at the foot of the hill. A Citgo

station on the corner. Nice clean restroom. That road goes on up to Plattsburgh. Going the other way I think it comes out onto one of the main highways you take to get down to Albany.

They'll probably have the intersection blocked.

Very matter of fact: All right, she thinks; then we'll just have to get rid of the Jeep and get around the intersection on foot. And let the bastards sit there all night waiting for us to show up.

59 At the crest of the last hilltop she stops and gathers the baby in both arms; thrusts the door open with her foot and gets out of the Jeep. Every bone and muscle is afire with pain.

North in the distance the two aircraft are still swooping in their odd Alphonse and Gaston dogfight.

Ellen reaches up with a finger and tugs at her lip. She gives the tiny finger a love bite and stares back down the road. In loops and whorls there are bits of it visible from here: several miles back is the steep hill she descended.

And there comes a dot that must be the fucking Bronco—hurrying down the switchbacks.

Not too far back; speeding to make up for it.

Son of a bitch.

She gets back in the Jeep and adjusts the baby in her throbbing left arm and drives down off the hill. Ahead in the distance above the trees she can see the V-shaped sign of the Citgo station.

Once in the woods she begins to search for turnings

and when she sees a mailbox ahead she eases her foot back on the gas.

No good; an old house trailer up on blocks with a huge TV antenna on top of it and a Volkswagen beetle parked nearby and a fat woman hanging the wash on a line.

No place to hide there. She drives on, anxiety climbing.

Two more driveways give access to small newish bungalows near the road. No hope there.

Another mailbox. The dirt driveway disappears into the trees to the left.

She takes it.

Not far in there's a small old barn beside the drive. It looks like a one-time carriage barn or a two-horse stable; not big enough for real farm work. The wood has gone pewter colored since its last coat of paint. There's a rusty plow beside it—the wheeled kind that's meant to be pulled by a tractor. The barn door hangs ajar—open a foot and badly warped, sagging on the ground and leaning.

Just behind it a stream cuts through, disappearing into tangled growth.

She stops the Jeep in the weeds and sets Ellen down on the seat. "Stay put ten seconds, my love. Be right back."

When she gets out of the Jeep the baby starts to wail again. "I'll be right back, damn it." She grasps the twisted edge of the barn door and bends it out far enough to make room for her head and shoulders.

Inside there are two splintered stalls on the right. The rest is an open floor—mud puddles and wet straw. It looks as if it's been in disuse for years but it still carries a horsey pungency compounded by damp earth and rotten wood.

There's room inside for the Jeep.

She tugs at the barn door but it's badly warped and jammed against the earth. It doesn't want to move. She kicks the damn thing and stands back yelling at it. Her curses blend with the baby's outcries.

She gets back in at the wheel and picks up the baby. "Shush now. You'll get all hoarse." She rocks the baby. Then with an abruptness that startles her an invention penetrates past the rage of frustration.

Of course.

She starts the engine and jockeys it back and forth until she's positioned the mangled wreckage of the front bumper beside the edge of the barn door. She locks the wheels sharp right and backs up, hooking the jagged ruin of the bumper against the door.

Use the horsepower of the Jeep to pull the damn door open.

It gives. But she hears something snap with a loud report.

She parks the Jeep inside. Grabs her handbag and the sack of baby things out of the back seat, collects the baby in her arms and climbs out.

When they emerge from the barn she sees that the noise she heard was the snapping of the rusty bottom hinge of the barn door. Opening it has scraped a raw fresh wound across the earth.

Damn.

Holding the baby she puts her back against the sagging door and leans into it, thrusting her heels into the earth. The door slides reluctantly shut. It's tilted against the building now, the bottom skirt bent out a foot or so away from the sill; but it'll do. You can't see the Jeep from out here.

No choice but to spend two valuable minutes kicking leaves and twigs across the tracks left by the Jeep.

Only when she's satisfied by the look of it does she hike away.

Hauling Ellen back through damp tangles under the trees she remembers the revolver but to hell with it. Not worth the bother to go back for it. There may not be time anyway.

That grinding noise. Is that the Bronco? Christ . . .

She swings around and peers back through the tangle, walking backward, feeling her way with one foot and then the other. She hears the Bronco slow down at the mailbox.

She can see a corner of the barn through there. Not the road, though.

It's stopping. The damn Bronco is stopping.

Easy now. If I can't see them, they can't see me.

It's starting up again. Going on along the road.

Thank God!

She soothes the baby, whispering to her, stroking her tiny forehead.

"Give them a couple minutes, darling," she murmurs. "Then we'll be on our way."

Oh Jesus. Oh Christ. *It's coming back!*

60 She hears it back up and change gears and come forward into the lane. She hears it stop somewhere just beyond the barn.

Bastards.

The sudden silence. Terrifying. She holds her hand near the baby's mouth, ready to clamp down if she must.

Does she hear voices or is it just her overstimulated imaginings?

That sagging corner of the barn—

If they come around there they'll be able to see her.

Come on, fool. Get out of here.

She pokes a toe back behind her and all of a sudden the wet earth gives way and she's sliding helplessly . . .

Oh!

Slithering. Out of control on this slick muck.

What—?

Don't panic it can't be far. . . .

Instinct brings the baby protectively against her chest, arms shielding Ellen from the twigs and stones. But it's a quick soft slide: a few feet of mud and her scrambling feet find purchase against polished stones.

She looks over her shoulder. The stream has parted around her boots. She's got her feet in the water. It's only six inches deep.

She hears, very loud, the snapping scrape of wood on earth and she knows instantly what it is: they're opening the barn door.

It'll take them five seconds to absorb what they're looking at—the Jeep in the barn—and a few more seconds to realize she's on foot and then they'll start looking for her footprints and in this God-forsaken mud it won't take them any time at all. . . .

She takes three paces upstream, turning rocks over with her boot toes, making a plainly visible swath. Then she turns, crouching, and moves downstream on careful feet, dislodging nothing, clutching the baby, murmuring in Ellen's ear: "Old Injun trick, kid, you betchum." Not for nothing did she sit through those awful Westerns with Daddy in the PX theaters.

She giggles. . . .

Hey. Calm down, Little Beaver, this ain't no time to go all hysterical on me.

She ducks under a fallen trunk that lies jammed across the gully; she eels past the clutching arms of a bushy thicket, letting it slide back into place behind her.

Careful you don't turn an ankle on these stones.

The stream bends around the exposed roots of a big maple. She picks her way over them, staying in the water, moving downstream as fast as she can, stopping at intervals to turn her head sideways so as to catch the breeze from behind her on the flat of her eardrum.

It's been a while now since she's heard their voices. Have they lost the track? Or are they right behind her, creeping up?

Don't speculate. Don't think at all. Just move. Keep going . . .

Ten minutes? Half an hour? There's no way to measure time. Her ankles are weakening; were it not for the support of the boots she'd have caved in by now. Can't walk on these Goddamn stones any longer. This is just going to have to be far enough.

She climbs out of the stream and leans against the bole of a tall tree, propped on one shoulder, looking back the way she just came.

"Do you think it fooled them, little girl? Think we've got a chance?"

Who knows. All we can do is play it out.

She finds a place deep in the woods—a fallen log to sit on. Changing the baby's diaper, feeding her unwarmed milk, she listens to the forest.

"Just stick with your momma, kid," she says drily, "and we'll see what other nifty kinds of trouble we can get you into. If you want a dull peaceful life you picked the wrong momma."

61 With the baby balanced on her shoulder she trudges across the back of somebody's cornfield.

Just make it to that far corner; then we can rest again. Everything hurts. Everything.

The baby lies across her shoulder like velvet. No complaints now; no stirrings. Poor kid's exhausted.

I understand, Ellen. I know how it is. It's always harder to be a passenger than to be a driver.

Feels like a blister coming up on the left heel. Damn. All we need. Well what did you expect, feet all soaking wet and everything?

One foot and then the other. That's it. Just put one foot down and then put the other foot down. One foot at a time. We'll get there.

How far do you suppose we've walked? Time's it? Takes too much energy to shift things around so I can look at the watch; take a guess by the sun shadows.

Probably somewhere between four and six. Split the difference. Say it's five. I don't believe less than nine hours ago Charlie and I were making love.

Charlie. I wonder what happened to the airplane and the helicopter. Haven't noticed them since God knows how long ago. No sign of them now.

Hell with them. Come on. Almost to the corner now.

Nasty rip in the sleeve of this blouse from those thorns back there. Cheek feels all scratched from the thickets. Burrs in my hair, what'll you bet. I must look a sight.

Well this ain't no beauty contest, honey.

This is the corner. We can sit down now. Jesus—it feels as if I've got drill bits in my joints. God, that hurts!

Now then. What's the plan?

Are they back there? Tracking?

Maybe. Maybe not. You can't do anything about it so quit thinking about it.

Can't be too far to the Interstate. Keep walking east you're bound to find it.

What then?

God knows. Worry about it when we get there. One thing at a time. Too tired to think.

Let's see what we've got in here, kid. You want Gerber's applesauce or Gerber's apricot? Where's the Goddamn plastic spoon?

Here, quit making such a mess all over your face. You handle the mouth, let me handle the spoon, all right? Try to get the food inside the mouth, right? *That's* the idea.

Now stop looking at me like that. Like I'm taking food out of the mouths of babes. In the first place the damn things are too heavy to go on carrying. And in the second place Momma needs nourishment too, you know. One jar of Gerber's apricot isn't going to make that much difference in your life, kid, take my word for it.

God, it tastes good. I think I'm going to start eating baby food for a regular diet. If we ever get out of this mess alive.

62 She finds a narrow blacktop road and walks east on the shoulder. Every time she hears the rumor of an approaching vehicle she takes cover off the road.

The baby is delivering herself of long closely reasoned monologues in a language known only to herself.

It probably isn't very far in miles but she hasn't been able to move at a very good pace. By the time the country road takes her across another hill from which she sights the superhighway below her, the sun is setting; by the time she stumbles to the overpass the last of the twilight has dimmed to dusk.

The blacktop road isn't important enough to rate an interchange. It crosses on an overpass above the Interstate. She goes down along the right side of the hump of landfill and parks herself and the baby on the sloping grass fifty feet above the highway, protected from view by the bulk of the overpass.

Cool here. Cool now and it'll get cold soon. Wish we had a blanket—although God knows how I'd have carried any more weight.

Cars go by at infrequent intervals, headlights stabbing the road, but by the time they come in sight they are broadside to her, heading away. No chance of being seen unless she steps out onto the shoulder.

She lies back—aching everywhere but it is good to stretch out. She holds Ellen close. Is there anything we can do other than take the chance of hitchhiking?

If only my brain weren't so fogged. Just reeling.

Got to protect the baby. That's number one. Got to

keep us both out of Bert's clutches; that's number two. Got to get out of this area; that's number three.

Might as well go down there and stick out a thumb. Can't think of anything else to do. Can't think period.

Rest here a few minutes. Gather a bit of strength. Then go down and thumb—and be ready to leap back out of sight if you see anything that looks like the square silhouette of the Bronco.

Remember too—they may have alerted every sheriff and local cop and highway patrolman; every big rig with a CB radio. Knowing Bert and his capacity for rage he's perfectly capable of turning this into something no less noisy than the Lindbergh kidnapping.

Funny image: show some flesh; stick out a leg—make like Claudette Colbert in *It Happened One Night*—imagine the shock on some lecher's face when you step into the light and he gets a good look at you like a critter out of some low-budget horror movie all scratched up with ripped clothes and matted hair and this little E.T. in your arms talking to herself earnestly in a language from another planet. . . .

She awakens having no idea how long she's slept. Stars glittering overhead.

Ellen!

She's fine. The baby's fine. Snuggled right here in my arms. Poor kid's nose is running. Find something to wipe it—here, this'll do.

So stiff. Can hardly move. I'd give anything for a drink and a couple of aspirin. Anything except my kid.

Haven't seen a single car go by since I woke up. It must be very late.

She holds the watch close before her eyes and tries to turn it to pick up reflections of starlight. Very hard to make out the dial. Can't be sure but it looks as if either it's ten after twelve or it's two o'clock.

Either way, kid, past your bedtime. Let's see if we can't commandeer you a nice car seat to sleep on.

Which way? North or south?

South, I expect. He'll certainly have people watching the border crossings into Canada. We'll have a better chance to get lost in the crowds if we try to make it down to Albany or maybe even the city.

Of course nothing comes with guarantees. If only Charlie hadn't deserted us. . . .

The short descent to the bottom of the slope seems more painful than the entire afternoon's walk. The baby seems to have gained a lot of weight. The blister is raw and burning; the knees keep wanting to buckle; the small of her back feels broken; there are aches in all her ribs; her arms are like weights; her neck is in agony; she can't stand the smell of herself.

Whiplash Willie, where are you now that I need you?

For a long time she stands by the side of the road. All she can hear is the baby's breathing and the occasional half-hearted whoo-whoo of an owl.

A single headlamp appears on the hill to the south and approaches soundlessly. Can't tell if it's a motorcycle or a one-eyed car. Anyway it's in the opposite lane heading in the wrong direction. Better hunker down anyway; don't take chances. Make the lowest possible silhouette.

There's a wide grass divider between the roadways here; not much chance of being seen from way over there. The headlight turns out to be a boxy old car with one lamp blown out. It thunders under the overpass, throwing back a raspy broken-muffler echo; it rushes away into the night, taillights glowing an angry red. The silence it leaves behind makes things lonelier than before.

63 High beam headlights bear down, blinding her, and she stands in the garish brightness with her arm raised, palm out, cradling the baby in the other arm and thinking: If this is Bert or some cop then we've had it but we can't stay here forever.

Aren't those lights very high off the ground?

When she hears the first hissing sigh of air brakes she knows it's not a car.

He's braking hard and gearing down but it takes more distance than that to stop such a huge object and the juggernaut goes rumbling past her at a pretty good clip, turn indicators flashing. Semitrailer rig. Eighteen wheeler. Big high square monster. It'll be a way down the road before it stops. What do we do now—climb out of sight? Run for it? Hide?

I can't. Too tired. The bones and muscles just won't do it any more. I just can't.

She looks back along the road. Anything else coming? No. No reprieves there. Not a light in view.

With the handbag appended to her forearm from its strap and the sack of baby things over her shoulder like a hobo's swag and Ellen's weight sweetly painful in her arm she walks forward to catch up to the truck and find out what fate awaits her.

64 She trudges into the light with a stoic readiness to accept whatever will be.

He jumps down from the passenger side of the truck—a tall narrow stick of a man. His back is to the light so she can't see his face. He's got shaggy hair like a hippie from the sixties; he's bony and angular in some sort of windbreaker.

She says, "Thanks for stopping. We could use a lift."

He's getting a look at her now. "What happened to you?" His voice is soft and pleasant; no special accent but he talks very slowly, measuring the words.

"We're all right. We just need a ride."

"I've got a first aid kit in the cab. You'd better paint those scratches. Here, let me give you a hand with the baby."

"I'd rather—can you take these things?"

He takes the sack from her. "You're holding the baby in the wrong hand."

"What?"

"For climbing into the truck. You need your left hand free."

"Oh."

He swarms up into the cab and for a moment he's out of sight. Then he reappears, head down near the seat cushion—he's leaning across from the far side and now he extends his arm down and points. "Grab that chrome rail with your left hand. Put your right foot on that step. Okay, that's good. Now hike on up and swing your left leg into the cab. Come on."

He's got a grip on her arm and it's a good thing because there's a moment's disequilibrium hanging in midair when she feels as if she's going to pivot right out and fall.

He pulls her in onto the seat. Under the dome light she peers at Ellen, whose face is screwed up into a comical squint against the brightness; she's pawing at the air with both tiny hands.

"Okay Sluggo," she says, "calm down a minute. Everything wet under there?"

She looks at the driver. "I didn't realize these things were so high. It's like climbing to the second floor. Where's that bag of things? I need a diaper."

"Right behind you." He reaches around and produces it.

It surprises her to see a rumpled bed—sheets and blanket and pillow—arranged crosswise behind the seats.

While she rummages for a diaper the driver is pulling a professional sort of first aid kit out from under the dash. "Any cuts on the baby?"

"I don't think so."

She removes the old diaper and wipes the baby with a tissue and rolls the baby over to examine her from all angles. Now ladies and gentlemen I want you to look very carefully and you'll see what is truly meant by the expression Mother Love. I think I broke my Goddamn arm and forty-'leven other bones but there isn't a single bruise on this kid's delicate skin and I want that to be entered into the books by whoever's keeping score up there when it comes to parceling out that term in purgatory.

The trucker says, "You look like you lost an argument with two miles of barbed wire."

She replies with the first thing that pops into her mind. "My husband had too much to drink. He beat me up and threw us out of the car. I hope he drove into a tree."

She fastens the clean diaper and settles Ellen in her lap. "Right, Sluggo. That better now?"

The driver takes a bottle of alcohol out of the first aid

kit and opens it to soak a cloth pad. He waits until she takes it from him and begins to dab her face; he points toward the huge outrigger mirror beyond her window and she's surprised to see that it's at an angle where she can see herself in it. She begins gingerly to wipe at the scratches.

He says in a soft dry voice, "Your husband must have about sixteen real long fingernails."

It makes her look at him—really take a look—for the first time. He's younger than she thought at first. No more than her own age; no more than early thirties; perhaps even younger. The long hair is coal black. He's got a narrow blade of a face but attractive in its way. All his bones seem unusually long; perhaps it's only because he's so thin. He has large hurt eyes.

She meets his gaze. "I got into a bramble patch."

"I can believe that, lady. My name's Doug. What's yours?"

"Jennifer Hartman. This is Wendy. Say thank you to Doug, Wendy. What's your last name?"

"Hershey. Douglas V. Hershey. Like the candy bar or the town in Pennsylvania. No relation to either. Where you from, Jennifer the Mauled?"

"Baltimore. We took a vacation in Canada. Some vacation. I don't know what I'm going to do about Frank's drinking, I really don't. There, I guess I've got the worst of them washed off. Nothing seems to be bleeding now—I guess I don't need bandages. You wouldn't happen to have some water and a couple aspirin, would you?"

"No, sorry. Coffee in that Thermos."

"Thanks."

She uncaps it and the rich aromatic steam hits her nostrils. She pours into the cap. "Want some?"

"You go ahead."

She knocks it back, not minding when it scalds her throat. "God that's good. I don't know how to begin to thank you for picking us up."

"You ready to go now?"

"Any time."

"Here we go then."

He switches off the interior dome light and his hands jab at various levers and buttons and the big steering wheel. It all looks more complicated than the controls of Charlie's airplane. The engine begins to growl and the steel floorplates begin to vibrate under her feet, reminding her of the blister on her heel. Doug Hershey checks his mirrors and eases out the clutch and the rig begins to gather speed down the shoulder of the highway.

He says, "There's an all-night truck stop about twenty-five minutes down the road. I was going to stop there anyway."

I don't want to show myself in any damn highway cafe around here, she thinks. But what am I going to do about it?

Well you've got twenty-five minutes to figure that out.

The noise increases. Pretty much up to speed now, the rig moves out into the traffic lane and the driver relaxes back in the seat, hanging one wrist on the near rim of the wheel, glancing down at the baby asleep in her lap. He says something she doesn't catch.

"What?"

He rolls up the window. The blast of wind diminishes. He says, "I said she's a cute baby."

"Yes. She's very special."

She feels lightheaded with exhaustion. Her eyes move fitfully around within the unfamiliar enclosure. It has a smell—old leather, metal, engine oil, tobacco—that infuses her with déjà vu.

Of course. It was the smell of her father's camper pickup.

The seat is high and firm; her feet barely reach the floor. The truck rides more gently than she thought it would but she keeps one hand protectively on the baby just in case.

She says, "If there's someplace that's not out of your way where we can catch a bus—"

"Albany be all right? I'm picking up the thruway there, heading on west."

"What are you carrying?"

"Syndicated Van Lines. I've got a couple households full of furniture. People moving out west. I've got a two-bedroom house to Salt Lake and a three-bedroom to Portland."

"That's a long way to drive by yourself."

"I pull over and sleep a few hours every now and then."

He's got both hands on the wheel now; he's scowling. Suddenly he says, "I hate getting shoved into a position where I have to play God, don't you? Where you have the power over somebody else's life that you didn't even ask for?"

The earnest plea in his voice surprises her. She only watches his face, illuminated by the faint green glow of the dashboard and the on-off-on-off reflection of headlights off the dotted white stripe in the highway.

He says: "I don't want this decision. I really don't."

She has a premonition and it makes her hold the baby tighter.

It's a feeling like ice on her spine.

He says, "I'm not a hundred percent sure you're the right woman because the CB said she was blond. But there's some guy in Plattsburgh offering twenty-five thousand dollars reward to anybody who turns you and that baby in."

65 Dazzled by the lights she squints crankily and mutters, "Where are we?"

"Truck stop."

The rig grinds to a halt with a hiss of air brakes. He switches everything off. The sudden lack of vibration becomes not merely a silence but a void.

The touch of his hand on her forearm. "You awake?"

"Yes." Barely.

"You'd better not show your face in there. Anyhow you're in no shape for it. I'll bring some stuff out. What do you want besides aspirin?"

"I don't know. Something to eat I guess. Maybe some warm milk for the baby." She feels around the cab. "Where's my handbag? I'll give you some money."

"Never mind. Pay me back later. Hamburger all right or are you a vegetarian?"

"A hamburger would be heaven right now. Make it two."

He opens his door and climbs down. She can see his head and shoulders in silhouette. She's trying to keep her eyes open; dazed, she tries to focus her attention on the very important thought that hovers just out of reach.

He says, "You're just going to have to trust me, you know."

Then the door closes with a soft click and he's gone.

Groggily she rubs her eyes and begins to shake her head to clear it but the movement makes her aware of the headache.

She shifts to one side and sets the sleeping baby down on the seat beside her. Then she opens the door and steps down, hanging onto things, but still she slips once and abrades her shin. When she's standing on solid ground she braces both arms against the truck and leans on them. Her head drops forward and she sucks in deep breaths.

Finally she reaches up and carefully lifts the baby down. Ellen's eyes flutter and there's a moment of recognition but then she drowses again.

"There must be a ladies' room around here."

Carrying the baby she wanders toward the station. Several trucks are parked beside it and there are a few cars out front, one of them getting filled up at the pumps. She sees the Men's and Ladies' signs hanging above unlit doors along the side of the station; she tries the knob of the Ladies' but it's locked and she scowls at it for a long time before she turns away and plods sturdily around into the office of the station.

The attendant is still out at the pumps serving his customer. From the wall she unhooks the restroom key with its huge wooden tag; she trudges back outside with the single-minded determination that comes with extreme exhaustion.

As she unlocks the door and goes inside she finally realizes what the thought was—the one that kept evading her in the truck.

Suppose he's in there making a phone call?

66 We've got choices. We could disappear back into the woods behind the place. We could just stay here in the bathroom and hope he thinks we've run off, and wait till he drives away and then try and hitch a ride with someone else.

We could call a cab.

She giggles.

Come on. Be serious now.

Lightheaded, I know. That's fatigue. But you can't afford to blank out your brain. Not now. For Ellen's sake . . .

She broods into the mirror. Holy Mother of God I look a fright.

I wish I had someone to pray to. I wish I believed.

She flashes on a long rainy high school afternoon: four girls earnestly reflecting why God, if he exists, should permit evil to prevail.

It all broke up over a rusty joke: "God isn't dead. God exists—and She's black."

She washes her face with cold water, scrubbing at her skin. Must think. Must use my head.

If he's called a cop or put in a call to Bert's house . . .

She dries her face on paper towels and gently begins to wash the baby. "It's not exactly the master bathroom, darling, but any port in a storm."

There's no more time for stalling. Got to make the decision. He'll be coming outside any minute now and if he finds us gone he's sure to raise the alarm.

What do you say, kid? Which way do we turn?

In a way it doesn't matter. No matter what direction we choose, it's a field mined with perils.

Listen: we've been taking ridiculous chances all day and all night. This is no time to stop.

Making the decision, she feels immediately lighter of foot. Ellen is no weight at all when she carries her out of the ladies' room.

There's a fat mustached cop just going into the men's room. He glances at her, then goes inside without any evident show of interest. Eyes wide with shock she retreats quickly

220

around behind the station and directly out across the dim asphalt to the rig.

By the time Doug Hershey returns to the truck with a take-out paper bag of hamburgers she's back in the seat with the baby. She gives him as bright a smile as she can muster.

He settles down behind the wheel and hands her the bag. "You really worth twenty-five thousand dollars?"

"I'm not. She is." The baby.

"You want to tell me about it?"

"Not now." She's found the warm milk. She's feeding it carefully to Ellen. "Can we go now?"

He says, "You're not heading for Baltimore, are you."

"Not really, no."

"Want to go west?"

"Salt Lake City? Portland?"

"Why not. I could use the company." He's switching things on, starting the engine. He hooks a thumb over his shoulder toward the bed behind him. "You get done eating, climb back there and get some sleep. Time you wake up we'll be past Cleveland. Oh—be careful with the shotgun up there. It's loaded. Once in a while we run into hijackers. You can pass it down to me if you want."

As he hauls the rig out across the apron she leans forward against the window to look back at the station and she sees the fat cop come out of the men's room. She's isn't sure whether he sees her in the cab but the brim of his trooper hat turns to indicate at least a casual interest in the departing truck and she pulls back away from the glass with a feeling of numb tired fear.

67 She wakes in strident alarm.

The baby is here—safe in the circle of her arm. But the truck isn't moving. Where's Doug?

When she sits up she bangs her head. She swears at the damn truck and ducks down to peer outside.

Turnpike service area. It's hot and steamy. The ratty remains of her clothes are sticking to her.

He's out there filling the tank, talking to another driver.

The baby wakes up and starts talking. Nobody else would be able to decipher it but she understands that Ellen is hungry. She finds the battered package and digs out one of the Gerber jars and feeds her.

She's just finished changing the baby when Doug climbs into the cab. "Hi."

"Where are we?"

"Near Rochester."

"What time is it?"

"Two-thirty, something like that. Here." He hands her the Thermos. "Fresh coffee."

When they're back on the road he says, "I'll show you mine if you'll show me yours."

"What?"

"I'm twenty-seven," he says. "I own a little piece of this rig. The bank owns the rest. I drive a truck because I'm restless and I like to be my own boss and also because I aim to be a country-western song writer and being alone on the road all day gives you plenty of time to write. I use that little

222

cassette recorder there. If I get to know you better I'll sing two or three of my songs for you. Born in Alabama and I've been married six years and we've got two boys, five and four, and considering I'm on the road half my life I think we've got a pretty good marriage but I guess I've been heartbroken enough times in my imagination and my memories to qualify me to write songs. I was a kid, I used to keep falling in love with women but then something'd happen. I'm working on a song now about how love is the bait they put in the trap at the beginning. It's really a poem, sort of. I'm going to send it to the *New Yorker,* I get it finished. You sure are a beautiful woman underneath all those bruises and scratches."

"Why are you doing all this? Why didn't you go for the twenty-five thousand dollars?"

"I don't know. Impulse? My romantic illusions, maybe."

But then he says, "That's not true. Not altogether. The way you looked standing on the side of the road with the baby in your arm—Madonna and child. But I'm not a teen-ager any more. I don't operate on sentiment. You know what it was? It was because you trusted me. I couldn't let you down."

"I was too tired not to."

"Well I don't care why you did it."

Later at 65 mph on the Interstate she climbs down into the passenger seat and has a long conversation with Ellen after which she puts the baby to sleep in the bed. Then she says to the truck driver: "Last night I was going to outbid the opposition. I was going to offer you thirty thousand dollars to save me and my daughter."

"Jesus. Why didn't you?"

"I just forgot."

"Maybe that's because you had an instinct that you didn't need to."

"You're coming on awfully strong as the good Samaritan."

A quick glance at her out of the side of his eye. "You

really don't want to trust anybody, do you. It's very hard for you."

"The last man I trusted—"

There's no need to finish it. She subsides and peers forward through the windshield: streams of cars on the highway; grey sky. He's got the air conditioning on and she feels chilled.

Her mind drifts. They run on into the afternoon. Occasionally she risks a glance toward him. The truck-driving dreamer in daylight; after a while she decides that he seems to have a deep understanding of silences.

68 "Where are we now?"

"Out of Chicago, headed for Minneapolis–St. Paul."

"What time is it?"

"Nine, maybe nine-thirty."

"What night is this?"

"Friday. I forget the date. It's the damn Labor Day weekend. Sunday drivers all over the place."

"Thanks for stopping to let me buy these clothes and all."

"Don't mention it."

"You expecting to stop again soon?"

"We could take a break next service area if you want. I'm already half a day behind—another few stops won't make much difference. We're taking a route a little farther north than they'd guess from my manifest. That's just in case somebody happens to be looking for this truck, I mean. I doubt they are but what the hell."

"I don't know how to begin to—"

"Don't. You hungry again or what?"

"I've got to make a phone call."

"Okay," he says. Then after a little while: "Want to talk about it?"

"It's something that came on me just a little while ago. You know how a fresh idea sometimes will pop into your mind when you're half asleep?"

"I get some of my songs that way."

"I've been running away for months. The baby and I are still running right now. I'm tired of it. Hell, I'm just tired period."

"You can talk about it if you like. I'm a good listener."

"You really are. And I probably owe you some truth. It's the least I can do. Who knows. Maybe you can turn it into a song."

"And sell it to Willie Nelson and make my fortune. You go right ahead. We've still got a couple thousand miles to go."

"How do you keep awake? Do you take pills?"

"I used to. Went to cocaine for a while too. Lucky I never freebased but once or twice—but even so spent three months in a rehab program getting off everything. Now I settle for coffee, a little No-Doz now and then. I get tired I go to sleep. I've got a funny metabolism though—I can go a long time without sleep sometimes."

"I tried cocaine once. Made my nose run for three days."

"You're lucky if that's all the contact you had. Stuff can turn you inside out. You get real paranoid."

"I know. I've seen it. I'm a prude about it." She hesitates. Then: "I left my husband when I found out he was dealing coke."

"This the guy that's after you now?"

"The same. I don't mean street-corner peddling—I'm talking airplane loads. He's in the importing business. The wholesale end, you might say."

"You married this man?"

"I married him. Had his child. This feels awkward but I like telling you about it. I've never talked to anybody about it."

"You just go right ahead. I'm starting to write that song already. Make up for that twenty-five thousand dollars I didn't collect."

"There's not so much to tell. I decided to take the baby away from him and raise her myself. I knew he'd try to find us. He's got a lot of money to spend on detectives and whatever it takes. It seemed obvious we wouldn't have much of a chance unless we had a lot of money to spend on keeping out of his reach."

"You mean it's not just the baby he's trying to get back. You took his money too."

"It was her money. He owed it to her. Not to me, but the baby."

"Well you've got her now. That's what counts."

"You're very trusting. You haven't even heard my husband's side of the story. I stole his money and I stole his child. I don't feel guilty and I have no sympathy for him. What does that make me?"

"I don't want to hear his side of it. I believe you."

"Why? I'm a total stranger."

"Look here: the only way you can find out whether you can trust somebody is to trust him."

"You mean trust someone and see what happens."

"You trusted me. See what happened? Got yourself a ride fit for a queen in this luxurious Cadillac limousine."

She's thinking of Bert with a smoking rifle in his hand and the flailing body of a deer whirling against a tree. She says, "I know how the drug business operates. It can't exist without people getting killed. I don't know if he's ever pointed a gun and shot someone dead. But he's capable of it . . . . I stole from him. I guess that doesn't make me the good guy. You have such a nice simple belief in things. I trusted someone else recently and it didn't work out so hot."

"What happened?"

"I'm not sure. I've been trying to replay it in my mind. Do you know anything about helicopters?"

"Happens I do. When I was nineteen I used to work on them in the navy. Engine mechanic. Why?"

"There's the service area coming up. Can we stop at a phone?"

"You bet."

She's looking at the shotgun. He's wedged it up into the foot-well on the passenger side where it's out of reach of the baby's curious proddings. With her eyes focused on the trigger she says, "You know I hate the son of a bitch. I want my revenge. It came to me a little while ago how I can fight back."

69 Trusting Doug to look after the baby, she changes five dollars into coins and gets the phone numbers from directory assistance for the New York State Police and the Clinton County sheriff's office and the appropriate branch of the federal Drug Enforcement Agency, which turns out to be in Burlington, Vermont.

It's best to call all three, she's decided, because knowing Bert's penchant for paying people off he may have bribed one or another of them and it only makes sense to cover all the bases. At least one of them is bound to take action.

She tells each of them more or less the same thing:

"Never mind who I am. Take this down. Got your pencil? Ready? There's an unregistered private landing field on federal land two miles east of Albert LaCasse's house on the Fort Keene road. An airplane will land there at midnight tomorrow to deliver several million dollars' worth of narcotics. Albert LaCasse and his men will be there to accept the delivery personally, and you can catch them red-handed. You're welcome and good night."

It's only when she's on her way back to the truck that she realizes how it can go wrong: if any of those law enforcement agencies is in Bert's pocket they'll warn him off in advance and he'll simply reschedule the delivery for another time and place. Her effort will have gone for nothing.

But it's worth the try.

70 Sunday night after nearly a full day's delay caused by the need to find a garage that was open and capable of replacing a bad front wheel bearing she kicks off her shoes and dances with Doug Hershey to the jukebox in a roadside joint in Wyoming. It's a bluegrass sort of record with a solid three-quarter beat by someone she's never heard of— John Starling—but she likes the music. The lyric is something about a hobo on a freight train to heaven.

She feels the steady pressure of his hand in the small of her back. They move unhurriedly to the three-quarter beat and he keeps a little polite distance between them so that she is reminded of the proprieties of the junior prom at the base school in Darmstadt.

She likes the gentility in him: he wants to be a friend—he doesn't seem to be on the make.

Calmed by the music she's thinking: I deserve a good break just now. I deserve a friend.

You trusted Charlie too. Remember that.

The unanticipated thought darkens her mood. She feels vaguely ashamed of it.

All of a sudden Doug says, "Takes two to tangle."

She rears back. "What?"

"I was just thinking. It takes two to tangle. Cute line for a song."

Past his arm she has one eye on the baby who sleeps in her new blanket on the vinyl seat of the booth. Ellen spent the whole day talking incessantly, commenting on everything in the truck and everything that went by outside. The baby has always been singularly curious about the world around her. Maybe she's going to grow up to be a scientist—or a poet. But first she's going to have to learn to speak in real words.

The record ends. Something else starts playing—too fast to dance to unless you're wired to a high-voltage generator—and they return to the booth and their iced teas. He says, "Tell me about your friend and his airplane again."

"I don't want to talk about it."

"Maybe you left out something."

She feels petulant. "He bugged out on me."

"Yes, but why? Maybe he had to."

"There was room. He could have landed."

"Where was the helicopter then?"

"It went climbing up out of the way."

"Strange thing to do, don't you think?"

She squirts lemon into the tea and fishes for seeds with her spoon. She's beginning to like the stuff.

"I thought so at the time. But whatever they had in mind, they left the runway wide open for Charlie. He could have picked us up. He didn't. That's the bottom line."

"Maybe so. Maybe not. I keep coming back to what you said about afterward. When you kept looking up and you'd see old Charlie up there dancing around the sky with the helicopter."

"It looked like some sort of dogfight."

"Sure. He was distracting the helicopter. How big's that helicopter?"

"You can get four people in it."

"That's pretty small. So it's not too fast. Your friend Charlie could have just put on the throttle and his airplane could've run right away from them. But he hung around and kept playing cat and mouse with the chopper. You think he did that for fun?"

"I have no idea." She fixes the baby's blanket.

"If I was inclined to give my friend the benefit of the doubt I'd have to guess maybe he was trying to make that chopper mad enough to keep chasing him around the sky—so it couldn't find you and the baby. You think you'd still been able to get away from those guys on the ground if the helicopter had been right up there keeping watch on you all the way?"

Her fingers pluck at the blanket. "I didn't—I never thought of that." She feels defensive. "It doesn't change the fact he ran away and left us there."

"Maybe he figured you had a better chance on the ground."

"But that's just not true. If you knew what we went through—"

"If I was that helicopter pilot and I saw this airplane coming in and I wanted to stop him, I'd let him go right ahead and land. I'd figure I had a lot better chance if he's on the ground than if he's in the air. In the air he's a lot faster than I am."

230

"We could have taken off. I've seen Charlie deal with obstacles on the runway. It's part of the students' emergency training. He could have bounced the plane right over their Bronco if they'd tried to get in the way."

"All the helicopter had to do was hover directly above Charlie's airplane. He'd have been pinned—might as well be nailed down. There's no Cessna in the world could take off against that downdraft."

Something in her eyes. She grabs a paper napkin out of the dispenser and presses it against her eyelid.

She hears him say: "I think Charlie must have seen what they were up to. Maybe he waved himself off and suckered the helicopter into that game of tag because he figured it was the best chance he could give you."

"You men stick together, don't you. How about the way he never came back to look for us."

"Sure—and lead them right to you."

"Damn it, you're on his side, you don't know. You weren't there. He ran out on me."

"You want to be mad at him, don't you. Makes things easier. Helps you prove you don't need anybody. You can get along by yourself. The hell with Charlie, he chickened out so you don't have to think about him any more. You want to look at me a minute?"

She looks up reluctantly.

His big eyes sorrow at her. "Look how he betrayed you. You're here. You've got what you came for. You got the baby and you're on your way home."

She wipes her eye again and examines the napkin closely as if to single out the offending particle. After a while she looks up. "You son of a bitch." Then she laughs.

They get in the truck. As she hands the sleeping baby to Doug for a moment and prepares to climb into the bunk her foot slips, dislodging the shotgun. It tips over with a bit of a clatter. "Oh dear. Sorry."

"Safety catch is on. It's okay, no danger. I'll put it back. Go ahead."

She gets settled. He puts the baby down beside her and picks up the capsized shotgun, wedging it back in place. "All set? Nighty-night."

When they drive out there's a highway patrol car at the curb and she sees a khaki-uniformed trooper in the phone booth. It isn't clear whether he's watching the truck depart.

She sleeps soundly in the bunk behind the seats, lying on her side with the baby in a gentle one-arm cradle. She's used to the growl and shudder of the truck now.

Somewhere around dawn they cross the border into Utah. The baby has decided to cry for a while, probably in general protest—going on strike as it were. The racket is piercing and she tries to quiet Ellen but the kid isn't having a bottle or a pacifier or any gentling at all. Her arms and legs keep windmilling petulantly.

Doug keeps looking in the big mirror outside his window.

The baby's caterwauling subsides at last. Grudgingly the little mouth agrees to pout around the pacifier.

"Is there something in the mirror?"

"Came out of an airport road back there. Been behind us half an hour."

She leans forward until she can see alongside the trailer through the mirror on her side. As they go into a bend it comes in sight back there—a big station wagon a little way behind, keeping pace.

"It looks like just one person in it—the driver."

"Probably using us for a pace car," Doug says. "Sometimes they do that. Keeps them awake or keeps them from speeding, I don't know. Maybe some people just get nervous blazing their own trail. Hell, if it was trouble he'd have caught up by now, I guess."

He doesn't sound confident.

232

The station wagon is still dogging them an hour later when they pull off the Interstate for fuel and breakfast. The station wagon doesn't take the same exit. It goes on down the freeway. From the angle of the truck's cab it's impossible to see the driver's face but that doesn't matter now.

She picks up the pad of waybill forms from the jumble of oddments in the open dashboard compartment and finds the stub of a pencil. "Doug—I want you to do me a favor."

"To wit?"

"Give me your address. I want to send you something when the baby and I get home. And I want us to keep in touch."

"Sure, you bet. To the latter. But no to the former. I'll make my profit from Willie Nelson. Don't send me anything. It'd just cheapen the satisfaction I get from being a good Samaritan."

"You're a silly son of a bitch."

"Yes ma'am."

Back on the road before eight o'clock they are barreling west with Salt Lake City another hour or two ahead of them when they come past an entrance ramp in light traffic and Doug, glancing in the mirror, stiffens.

He glances at her: his expression renders speech unnecessary.

She studies it in the mirror. It's three or four cars back. "That's either the same station wagon again or a twin for it."

"I'll slow down a little. See if it's the same license plate."

"I didn't think, before. . . ."

"I did."

He drops the speed and the other cars pull out and overtake the rig but the station wagon hangs back, keeping its distance. "I can't see the license plate. Too much vibration in the mirror. But then I don't need to," he says bleakly. "He's shadowing us all right."

"Could it be an unmarked police car?"

"Maybe. I doubt it. Whatever that is, it's not a Utah plate. Wrong color."

"Can we lose him?"

"In this freight train? Not a prayer. You want a wild guess, I'd say it's one of those shortwave jokers with a police band radio in his car, maybe picked up that twenty-five thousand dollar reward broadcast, saw you and the baby in the truck here and thinks maybe he can earn big money by playing amateur detective. Tell you what—I think I know a way to get rid of him."

"How?"

"Talk to him. Scare him off." He grins into the mirror. "I can look real mean when I set my mind to it. Here we go."

She hasn't time to protest: he's already swinging off the highway into the roadside rest area. Picnic tables and trash bins and the middle-high sun blasting all of it.

Sure enough. Back there the station wagon follows.

Doug sets the brake. "Man, you ain't never seen *mean* yet."

"Doug, for Pete's sake don't do anything foolish. He may be a trooper. Look—maybe we ought to . . ."

"You just leave everything to the iron duke here, lady."

Setting his jaw, he punches the door open and jumps down and trots around the nose of the rig and then pauses, hooks his thumbs in his belt, and swaggers toward the station wagon as it pulls in forty feet away. The sun throws reflective shafts painfully from its chrome and glass; she still can't see the driver.

There's one other vehicle in the parking area—a dark blue Mustang, one of the original ones. A very thin old man, having emerged from the restroom, slides into the car. She hears the door chunk shut.

She has the baby in her arms; she thrusts the door open with her foot, climbs down into the shade and peers toward the station wagon, curious to see what sort of creature would have followed them this many hours.

Doug marches toward the station wagon with the plunging no-nonsense stride of a man who's had enough and now intends for the guy to come out of the car and explain himself.

The Mustang backs up out of its slot and goes away up the ramp toward the Interstate.

Now the station wagon door opens, fanning a bright swath of sunlight across the pavement, and the driver comes straight out as if on wheels.

He doesn't even look at Doug. He's looking straight at her and the baby.

He has a rifle in his hand.

Doug begins to speak. The rifle lifts and turns and, with hardly an effort to take aim, barks once.

Doug spins around and falls.

The muzzle of the rifle turns toward her.

It's Bert.

71 With the baby in her arms she stares at him in utter disbelief. He's shot Doug. Just there. Like—like *that*. Like a paper target . . .

She wants to scream. Nothing comes from her throat but a hot gust of silent pain.

There is an onrushing blast of sound: an approaching bus on the Interstate.

She sees its reflection in the window of the station wagon's open door. The sound makes Bert hesitate and for a little while they both stand frozen as if in some crazy tableau.

Running through her mind is the most ridiculously un-important question:

How the hell did he find us?

God knows. What does it matter? Could have been anything.

That fat cop with the mustache, or maybe the trooper in khaki—phoning in a report, looking to collect $25,000; the report relayed to Bert; a fix on the truck, its license plate numbers, the highway it was traveling; a quick charter jet flight to that airport they passed early this morning—then just wait by the side of the road in the rented station wagon until the truck came along . . .

The bus slams by with a heavy whoosh. Bert is holding the rifle straight down alongside his leg so the people on the bus won't see it.

Now he lifts the weapon into sight and begins to walk forward. Not hurrying.

"All right now Madeleine. Give me the child. That's a good girl. Just take it easy and everything's going to be fine."

He talks to her the way you might talk to an insane person; he contrives to sound quietly confident and calm but the extra edge on the rasp of his voice betrays the throbbing depth of his rage.

She feels her eyelids flicker. Sensations carom through her flesh, contradicting one another. This is like one of those suffocating dreams in which you try to run but your muscles are imprisoned and nothing will move.

Walking toward her he holds his body twisted slightly to one side because he's using both hands on the rifle, one of them extended in front of him.

All we've been through—to come to *this*?

He says, "There were a million cops waiting for the plane." For a moment she doesn't know what he's talking about.

236

Involuntarily she steps back. Her rump strikes some part of the cab. She's trapped here against the truck.

He says, "Was it you that tipped them? I figured it probably was you. They got the shipment."

A truck goes by; the rifle drops out of sight again. In the wake of the noise Bert says, "They got the Jamaican pilot and Jack Sertic and Phil Quirini. Got George Talmy, too. They didn't get me. I had a friend in uniform who owed me an obligation. He got me out of there. They never identified me. I've always been a little too quick on my feet for those assholes."

His eyes seem a trifle too intense, too bright. Is he on something? Some of his own drugs, to hype him up?

Why doesn't a car appear? Why doesn't somebody come?

"Nobody's going to get hurt." He's still talking in that same tight little voice. "Everything's fine."

Behind him Doug is twitching on the ground, crawling around in a slow circle like a half-crushed beetle.

"Madeleine. You listening to me?"

She has no voice.

"Bitch—you're dead!"

Bert does something to the rifle. The metal clacks shut: the sound intensifies the pitch of her alarm and in her mind she's shrieking obscenities at him: *Get away you cocksucker— leave us alone—you fucking son of a bitch*—GET AWAY FROM MY CHILD!

He comes on, relentless, moving like a mechanism, oblivious to her rage.

Twenty feet between them now; no more. He's got no need even to aim the thing at this short a range.

With an awful dread she feels shuddering paroxysms of her own hatred; she feels hysteria cresting in her. It all erupts and a howl detonates from her as if from the throat of some wild rabid animal and it's as if she has nothing to do with it,

237

or with the terrible conflagration in her. She's lost control: she feels her lungs suck for air and she watches her enemy swim in the blood-red haze of her vision—and in one sudden bright abject moment of exhausted clarity she knows she has lost.

Come on then, you bastard. Kill me.

. . . Why doesn't he *shoot*?

Then she knows. Of course.

Of course!

"Wait!"

The force of her own explosive voice startles her. She holds the baby up in front of her.

He stops in his tracks: he scowls. "Jesus, Madeleine. Even you can't be that insane. You honestly think you can use your own child for a shield?"

Quickly she shifts Ellen's weight into one arm, freeing the other. She knows what she's doing now. God knows where the knowledge sprang from.

"Back up," she shouts. *I need just a little more space. Just another second's worth of time.*

She's holding Ellen almost at arm's length in one hand now and Ellen begins to wail.

She tightens her grip on the flailing baby's tiny jump suit.

"If you drop that child so help me . . ."

Oh Jesus. Bert isn't going to do it. He's calling her bluff.

He's starting toward her again.

There isn't enough time. Oh Goddamn you black-hearted bastard.

No more hysteria. Come on—come on . . .

She jabs the free left hand into the open cab behind her. Her fist closes around the stock, slides up to the trigger guard, hauls the shotgun out into view.

She brings it down across the baby's tummy and grips the forestock in that hand and, pinning the baby against the crook of her elbow with the shotgun itself, levels it at him.

"So help me God, Bert, I'll leave your brains all over this parking lot."

Bert gapes at her: at the shotgun, then at her face.

She's sweating as if in a steam bath. Doug's words from last night bat around in her head: "Safety catch is on. It's okay, no danger."

She has no idea on earth where the safety catch is. And she doesn't dare look down at the shotgun in an effort to find it. Any sign of hesitation or uncertainty and he'll be all over her in an instant.

The baby is yelling powerfully now; too much racket to make herself heard. She gestures with her chin and now she steps away from the truck, beginning to walk toward Bert.

He stands his ground, squinting, trying to think his way through this.

She makes soft shushing noises and the baby gradually stops shouting.

There's a lever right on top, just next to her thumb. She can feel it. It's bent to one side. Could that be the safety?

Try it.

She's watching Bert. His frown is a little puzzled. She feels the tab of the metal lever click slightly when it moves an inch to the other side.

"Get in the car," she says. "Drive away."

He crouches and sets the rifle on the ground and stands up again, holding his empty palms out to her. Now he smiles—she remembers the chill of that smile—and he resumes his calm approach as if it had never been interrupted.

"Should have shot me when I had the rifle," he says. "At least you could have rationalized that as self-defense. Now I'm unarmed. You won't do it."

The smile has settled on his face like a death's head rictus.

He's going to walk right up and take the shotgun away from her.

He believes she's bluffing.

He knows about her and guns.

He knows she's not going to shoot him.

She watches him come forward.

He's three paces away, nearly in jumping distance, when she says very quietly, "It's not me I'm protecting, you see. It's the baby."

She depresses the muzzle of the shotgun by leaning her whole torso forward and points the damn thing in the vicinity of his knees and pulls the trigger.

72 She picks up the discarded rifle and tosses it into the station wagon. She's still shaking. Her arm throbs from the blow of the shotgun's recoil and her ears are ringing and the baby is at it again, doing her loudest, and she can't think of anything sensible to say to the kid except this:

"You're right. Screaming is the only possible proper response to all this."

Doug looks up at her with dulled eyes. She says, "I can't lift you. You're going to have to help me."

He struggles to get his legs under him. There's blood high on the chest of his shirt. Maybe with luck it's high enough to have missed the lung. He says, as if apologizing, "Doesn't hurt too bad. Deep wounds usually don't."

"I'll get you some help."

Over there near the truck Bert is bellowing at her but she gives him no more than a glance, hiking the baby up firmly in one arm while she gives Doug the other and helps him to his feet and assists his stumbling progress toward the station wagon. She gets him into the back seat, tosses Bert's suitcase on the floor to make room, and helps Doug lie down on the seat.

Then she looks in the ignition. No keys.

Just like Bert. So methodical he put the keys in his pocket, even way out here—even with all that on his mind.

She gets out of the car, baby in one hand and shotgun in the other, and walks toward the truck. She detours wide around Bert, ignoring his pleas and threats, and reaches up into the cab to take the keys out. Then she closes the driver's door and goes around to close the passenger door and only then does she look down at the man she once lived with.

"Give me the car keys."

He broods up at her. The constriction of his voice betrays the effort with which he is attempting to keep pain at bay. "How about getting me an ambulance?"

"You'll live. Strip your shirt off. Use it for a tourniquet. Sooner or later somebody'll stop and give you a hand."

"CB radio—the truck."

"I don't know how to use it."

"Jesus God almighty you fucking bitch, get me some help. You've smashed my fucking kneecap, you know that? God knows if I'll ever walk straight again."

She's very calm. "Throw me the keys, Bert, or I'll shoot the other knee." She works the pump action of the shotgun, one-handed, tossing the empty paper cartridge out and seating the next one. Aren't you glad you taught the little woman how to shoot skeet, you great macho gun handler?

She points it at his knee. The one that isn't shredded. "The keys."

He bends his head back in an arching spasm of agony. Unmoved, chilled, she taps his knee—the good one—with the muzzle of the shotgun.

He cries out. She watches him dig clumsily in a trouser pocket. With a vestige of defiance he throws the keys away and then his head sags against the pavement.

She picks up the keys. He lies panting with his eyes

half shut and unfocused. She hesitates—but there's nothing left to say to him. She walks away.

"Madeleine . . ." A husky croak. "For the love of God . . ."

She settles the baby in the station wagon and shuts the door and starts the air conditioning. Then she twists around. "Doug?"

"Still here." Lying on his side, fetal, he tries to smile. "My fault. I used you. I'll try to make it up. . . ."

"You shoot the son of a bitch?"

"In the knee. He'll survive I'm sure. I just don't figure to make it easy for him."

"That's all right. Long as we whupped him."

"Where's the nearest hospital?"

"No idea. Don't worry about me. No real harm ever comes to the iron duke."

73 It's another hot one in Van Nuys and she's been sitting in this damn car altogether too long but on Ellen's account let's not take chances. It's wise to check everything out.

That limo's been sitting over there in front of the air freight depot for twenty minutes with the guy reading the magazine at the wheel and maybe his chauffeur's uniform is a fake.

There's nobody else hanging around looking like surveillance. But you can't afford to be lax. Bert may be in the jail ward, betrayed by the confessions of his former employees, but he may still have people looking for his kid. And this is a risky place to be, a risky thing to do: suppose they've traced the Cessna to the field where they rented it in Plattsburgh? Suppose they've found some connection between there and here? Suppose the pestilential Graeme Goldsmith has found some way to trace you in this direction?

They wheel a crate outside on a hand truck. The chauffeur gets out and opens the deck; the two workmen lift the crate into the trunk. The chauffeur talks briefly with them and gets back into the limousine; she watches him drive away while the workmen go back into the depot.

Now then. Any other possibilities? Somebody over there in the coffee shop watching through the window?

Come on. Caution's one thing. Paranoia's another. Like the man said, you've got to learn to trust. Trust people and trust your instincts.

Given the vagaries of the postal service I wonder when that $30,000 will arrive at Doug's house in Birmingham. I expect his wife will be a little surprised. She's already asked a thousand questions, you know. While he heals he'll tell her the truth and it'll sound outlandishly far-fetched.

Well Mrs. Hershey will just have to trust him, won't she.

She opens the window and switches off the engine and the air conditioner. Then she gathers up the baby.

"Christ, you're getting to weigh a ton, you know that?"

Ellen replies with a sequence of cryptic noises.

She carries the baby across the field and hesitates outside the door. The rumble of his voice penetrates through from inside; she can't make out the words but the timbre is as precisely identifiable as a telegrapher's fist. She pushes inside. He has his profile to her and his feet up against the wall; he's on the phone but he looks around to see who just came in and all the planes and angles of his face sort themselves into a whole new arrangement as if a kaleidoscope had been turned.

"I'll call you back." He hangs up. Drops his feet off

the wall and swivels to face her and thinks about getting up out of the chair.

For a long interval he sits that way, poised, staring at her, and it's hard to credit but there are tears welling in Charlie's eyes.

She says, "I want you to meet my daughter."